Enjoy!

BLOODY GRAND

Katie Gailey

Katie Gailey

authorHOUSE®

AuthorHouse™
1663 Liberty Drive, Suite 200
Bloomington, IN 47403
www.authorhouse.com
Phone: 1-800-839-8640

First published by AuthorHouse 2/5/2008

ISBN: 978-1-4343-3443-5 (sc)

Printed in the United States of America
Bloomington, Indiana

This book is printed on acid-free paper.

Other titles by Katie Gailey:

Spirit Lake

Dedication

This book is dedicated to Tess Riley, my biggest cheerleader, the one who kept me writing when my life was falling apart.

Thank you to all who wrote the history of Grand County; without you, this book wouldn't have had the meat it has. And thanks to Terry, my husband, for love I didn't think I was worth.

CHAPTER ONE
MAY, 1882

Annie was at an age when one feels indestructible. The past was thankfully behind her, and a new life was about to unfold...if only she managed to survive the last seventy miles!

For ten uncomfortable days, seventeen year old Annie Mitchell had been crossing the Great Plains of Missouri, Kansas, and eastern Colorado by train. Her destination was a small mining community called Grand Lake, located in the heart of the Rocky Mountains.

Annie had departed the train in Georgetown, Colorado, and had boarded a stagecoach which would take its passengers northwest through one of the roughest mountain routes called Berthoud Pass. It climbed to twelve thousand dizzying feet above sea level, and was completely impassable in the winter except by snowshoe. The driver had flogged the horses into a whiplash start, slamming Annie forward into the lap of an elderly man across from her.

"God's Teeth!" cried the girl. Then, remembering her manners, she pushed herself back to her own seat. "I beg your pardon, sir." The man just turned his head and sniffed.

Conversation was next to impossible due to the constant jostling. As the rickety vehicle barreled up the narrow switchbacks and over the Pass, Annie could've sworn they'd left the ground had not another impact jarred her teeth.

The young girl tried desperately not to lurch into the woman next to her. Annie wanted to brush away the stray coppery curl which had fallen into her blue eyes, but she didn't dare loosen the white knuckled grip on the wooden window of the coach door. She felt as if bones were being torn from their sockets, and her stomach roiled with each sickening jolt as the uneven wheels thudded over stones and ruts.

Annie was so travel worn and exhausted by the time the stage crossed the somewhat lower Cottonwood Pass and pulled into the stop at Hot Sulphur Springs that she wanted nothing more than to lay down in the dirt and sleep for a week.

While the other passengers entered the stage stop for a hot drink and a bite to eat, Annie climbed wearily out of the coach and limped about, stomping her feet to recirculate the blood into her numb backside and legs.

"God's Teeth and Nightgown!" Annie swore miserably.

"Excuse me, ma'am, are you all right?" drawled a deep voice behind her. Turning irritably, Annie found herself gazing up into pale green eyes. Though tall herself at five foot seven, this man was well over six feet, with broad shoulders barely contained in a black shirt. Loose brown hair hung to his shoulders, and a bushy mustache couldn't quite hide sensuous lips which were spread in a friendly grin. A long straight nose, winged eyebrows and strong chin were framed in a square, ruggedly handsome face.

Annie soon realized she had been staring too long for politeness sake and stuttered a bit breathlessly, "Y-yes, I'm fine; only a bit travel sore." She fought the need to rub her aching backside. She glanced around; no one else seemed to within hearing distance, but she blushed all the same.

"Where are you headed, ma'am, if you don't mind me asking?"

Regaining her composure quickly, Annie gave the stranger her brightest smile and replied, "A town called Grand Lake. I'm going to live with my uncle and aunt."

His green eyes lit up. "I'm heading for the Lake as well. I guess we'll be riding together from here. My name is Will, Will Redmond." He touched his wide brimmed hat, then looked askance at Annie.

Again she found herself gazing at the tall stranger, her stomach fluttering pleasantly. "It's very nice to meet you, Mr. Redmond," she replied, unexpectedly shy. Her past experience with men had left her a bit tentative of their motives. Suddenly Annie didn't know quite what to do with her hands.

Redmond's grin widened, and Annie caught a glint in his eyes which made her insides quiver. Then he asked, "Don't *you* have a name?"

"Oh, yes, I mean, uh," Annie sputtered, "m-my name is Annie Mitchell."

Will Redmond stuck out his hand as he said, "Nice to meet you, Miss Mitchell. It *is* Miss, ain't it?"

Annie studied his huge rough hand a moment, then put her own smaller one into it. As they touched, a jolt ran through her, and she looked up quickly to see if he had felt it, too. But his friendly expression had not changed, so she quickly tried to cover her confusion.

"Y-yes, it's 'Miss'. Do you also live in Grand Lake, Mr. Redmond?"

At that moment, the thundering retort of gunshots rang out. Redmond grabbed Annie around the waist and threw her to the ground, his body covering hers.

"Stay down," he ordered, then leaped to his feet and sped down the street in the direction of the shots.

Wide-eyed, Annie spat the dirt from her mouth and raised herself a bit to see what was going on. Already a crowd had formed in front of a saloon called the Antlers, only a few buildings away from where Annie lay.

A bandy-legged man sauntered out of the saloon, both of his side arms drawn as he strutted into the dusty street. He was clad in a bright red shirt, dirty trousers, and fancy snakehide boots with silver spurs that clanged with each step. A drooping, bushy mustache completely covered both sides of his mouth. The most noticeable feature, Annie saw, was a huge, wide-brimmed sombrero on his head.

"Texas Pete!" called a man wearing an apron who had followed the armed individual from the saloon. "We're all sick of you shooting up this town whenever you feel like it. You nearly crippled Hank Barton when you shot his bootstraps off just now. And there weren't no call for it neither."

The man called 'Texas Pete' turned slowly and faced the unarmed bartender who had confronted him. Immediately, Will Redmond moved to the front of the crowd and drew his pistol.

"That'll do, Pete," Redmond stated quietly. "I've got a bead on you, and you know damn well I hit where I aim."

4

Texas Pete turned his head slightly, eyeing the tall, steely man to his right. Trembling now, Annie felt the tension in the air as the two men sized each other up. In the meantime, the bartender had backed slowly through the wooden swinging doors of the Antlers Saloon. Apparently, he had surmised the situation was in better hands than his.

"I don't want no trouble with you, Redmond," stated Texas Pete loudly, as he turned to face the taller man with the Colt aimed at his heart.

"Then you should have thought about that before you started shooting up the saloon." drawled the tall man with the green eyes.

"I was just having a little diversion," wheedled Pete, his pistols still cocked. "Can't a man have any fun in this town anymore?"

"Your fun's over...here in Grand County, Pete," answered Redmond. "Drop those two pearl handles in the street real easy, and everything will be just fine."

Pete stiffened. "And what if I don't?"

"Then I'm gonna kill you where you stand," replied Will Redmond smoothly.

The crowd stepped back a few steps, and Annie froze at the calm but deadly tone of the stranger she had just met.

Long seconds passed as no one moved or said a word. Texas Pete stared hard at the tall man with the revolver, but Will Redmond's hat was so low over his brow that his eyes were in shadow.

Finally, Texas Pete carefully uncocked his guns and flipped them back into the side holsters. "All right, you win, Redmond, this time."

Will and a few of the other men escorted Texas Pete across the street to the jail.

Annie lay in the dirt another moment more before she realized the hair-raising incident was over. Slowly she pushed herself up and began wiping the dust from her gray traveling dress. When she glanced around, the occupants of the Antlers Saloon had already retired to their drinks, and the street was empty again.

Moments later, Will Redmond came striding toward Annie. "You aren't hurt, are you?" He began beating the fine brown dust from the front of her dress. "I apologize for throwing you down like I did, but stray bullets can be mighty unhealthy."

Annie, still shaking, asked, "What happened, Mr. Redmond? What was the shooting all about? And why did *you* get involved? That man might have killed you."

"Please, call me Will, Miss Mitchell. You see, it's my job, ma'am. I'm the Undersheriff of Grand County. Besides, I knew Pete wouldn't shoot me. We used to run together in the early days, before I became a lawman. He's pushed his luck around here one too many times, I'd say. There's folks who are mighty tired of his acting out.

"Couple of years back, ole Pete got into a fight with a man named Beatch. Instead of shooting him , Pete struck Beatch over the head with one of his guns. Beatch swore out a warrant for Pete's arrest. Later, Pete sees Beatch in the street with the warrant in his hands, so he snatches it away and tears it to bits right in front of Beatch.

"Pete left town after that for awhile. Maybe this time he'll leave for good after he gets out of jail. If he doesn't leave on his own accord, I fear somebody might take the law into their own hands one of these days. He's made too many enemies in the County."

"Is it always like this?" asked Annie incredulously. "Are there gunfights in the streets like this all the time?"

"No, no, Miss Mitchell, please don't get the wrong impression of Grand County. It's still young and rowdy sometimes, and sure, there's some scuffles every now and again, but it's basically a real safe place to live."

"I'll have to take your word for it, Undersheriff. How much farther is it to Grand Lake?"

"Only about twenty-five more miles along the Grand River, I mean, the Colorado River. The government changed the river's name when they named the Rio Grande River down in Texas, so now our Grand River is the Colorado River, but the town is still Grand Lake and the lake is still Grand Lake. Kinda confusing, ain't it? But it's a nice ride."

"But not too bumpy, I hope?" queried Annie as she gave in and actually rubbed her backside.

Will Redmond reddened to the tips of his ears. "It's a little rough, but you'll be safe with me along."

"Are you expecting trouble?" queried Annie.

"We've had some holdups along this route. When some of the miners don't strike it big, they tend to look for easier pickings from the passengers and payrolls. But don't worry; that's why *I'm* riding the stage."

Annie found she *did* feel safe with the tall handsome lawman.

The passengers boarded a short time later. With a slap of the reins and a quite colorful curse, the driver whipped the horses and they lurched away from Hot Sulphur Springs.

"Next stop is Coffey Divide," stated Redmond. He and Annie sat across from each other and continued to converse companionably as the miles were eaten up.

"So where are you from, ma'am?" Will asked.

Annie kept a stranglehold on the window as the coach tossed the occupants like popcorn. "My father has a little farm in Arkansas, north of Ft. Smith. I've been attending school at Miss Mary Flynn's Academy for Young Ladies in St. Louis for the last four years."

"Well, I'll be damned...excuse my language, ma'am. I'm from Missouri myself. My Pa had a farm outside of Sedalia."

Before Annie could stifle her natural curiosity, she asked, "How did you find your way into this wilderness then? Isn't it a bit out of the way for a Missouri farm boy?"

Redmond stared off into the distance as memories of his childhood flowed over him for the first time in years.

Annie blanched at the momentary silence. "I-I'm sorry, Mr. Redmond, it's none of my business. I didn't mean to be so personal."

Will shook his head, clearing the cobwebs of his past. "Don't apologize, ma'am, your words brought back a bit of homesickness for a moment or two, that's all.

"My Pa always had dreams of making a stake in silver until the Coinage Act of '73 drove silver coins out of circulation, and the whole country was put on the gold standard. He wasn't going to pull up stakes for gold, so we stayed on the farm.

"Then in '78, Congress made the Treasury Department buy between two million and four million dollars of silver per month at the market price and coin it into silver dollars."

"So your whole family came west to look for silver?" asked Annie.

"No, by then my parents were too old to pull up roots. Me and my two brothers heard about the lodes in Leadville and the Comstock in Nevada, so we headed west. We got this far, it seems, and stayed."

"Do you still mine, Mr. Redmond?"

"My brother and I sold our mine some time ago. Miss Mitchell, please call me Will. We'll probably be seeing a lot of each other. Grand Lake ain't that big."

Annie blushed. "All right, but you call me Annie then."

Will Redmond sat a little straighter on the seat and touched his hat brim. "My pleasure...Miss Annie. You said you were going to stay with some kin? Maybe I know them. What's the name?"

"My uncle is Benjamin Daily," she replied brightly.

His friendly demeanor dropped away immediately, and the pleasing grin became a cruel scowl. It was as if black, ominous clouds suddenly covered the sun, leaving the day gray and dangerously still. Veins strained just under the skin on the Undersheriff's forehead, and his face flushed as he struggled to bring himself under control.

Annie was bewildered and a bit frightened by the abrupt transformation. She couldn't think what had brought it on...except the mention of her Uncle's name. Her eyes widened as she realized Will Redmond knew her uncle and must dislike him intensely.

Redmond's expression seemed different now, edged with a new tenseness. He crossed his arms and replied coldly, "Why would anyone send a young innocent girl like you into the clutches of that polecat? Well, I guess it ain't none of my business. Nice meeting you, Miss Mitchell, but I don't think we'll be seeing much of each other after all."

Without another word, the Undersheriff stared stonily out the window. Annie gaped at him, bewilderment written openly in her wide blue eyes. She turned away quickly before anyone could see the stinging tears blurring her vision. She had lost a budding friendship before it had time to blossom, and for no reason but that she was Ben Daily's niece.

As the stage continued the final leg of the journey, even the beauty of the surrounding mountains couldn't keep the past from rearing its ugly head and unhappy memories washed over Annie. She wasn't about to share with anybody the *real* reason she had traveled a thousand miles from home, alone and unchaperoned.

Less than two weeks before, Annie had been studying for her final exams at Miss Mary Flynn's Academy in St. Louis when her father had arrived posthaste.

"Gather your possessions, girl; Miss Flynn has informed me of your recent conduct and you're leaving this place," stated Aaron Mitchell, evangelical justification written into every pore. "I always knew that red hair of yours was a sign of the devil. Nobody on either side of the family ever had hair like yours. I should've known when you were born; Satan must have sent your sainted mother and me a changeling. You've disgraced your family and yourself trifling with a pimply-faced boy who never had any intentions of marrying you."

Annie had thought she was in love, but the deceitful young St. Louis banking heir, Martin Blake, had played fast and loose with her heart and virtue, and the scandal that followed had been too much for the school proprietress, Miss Mary Flynn.

With few words, Aaron Mitchell had explained that her only living relative, Benjamin Daily, who was Annie's dead mother's half-brother, had agreed to take her in. Now Annie was being thrown away by her own father and sent headlong into the wilderness to live with strangers.

Stone-faced, Annie's father had driven the distraught girl straight to the depot to put her on the westbound train. Aaron Mitchell had pushed a wadded handkerchief into Annie's hands containing three dollars in coin. She had stared wretchedly at her father's back as he stalked away, without so much as another glance in her direction.

The train ride from St. Louis to Georgetown, Colorado, had been long and lonely, and Annie had spent the interminable days gazing miserably out the dirty window, tears streaming down her cheeks. With one youthful indiscretion, home was now forever dead to Annie; her father had made that painfully clear.

When Annie had first caught sight of the Rocky Mountains, rising majestically out of the flat plains of eastern Colorado, she had felt something akin to hope fill her resilient young heart once again. Maybe this new place, still a bit wild like herself, would be a new beginning. No one knew of her past, except her uncle. Somehow, Annie vowed, she'd make a new life for herself out in the West.

But Will Redmond's abrupt rejection was a bucket of cold water, dousing her hopes of a new friend or a better future. The Undersheriff was acutely silent on the last leg of the trip. He sat across from Annie, silently staring out the window, as if she wasn't even there.

At the Coffey Ranch, the stage stopped. Annie, Will, and the other passengers went inside the farmhouse for a hot drink. Annie sat with the others on a long wooden bench, sipping the bitter black brew as she glanced furtively at the tall Undersheriff, gulping his coffee while standing at the door.

After a change of horses, the stage lumbered up a steep moraine. At the top, Will Redmond's confusing rudeness was suddenly forgotten. Annie was unexpectedly awestruck by the panorama of snowcapped peaks and rolling green forests which seemed to soar into the fluffy clouds in the endlessly blue sky. The last part of the rough road paralleled the green mountain range as it curved, and Annie felt as if they were indeed heading straight into the heart of the Rockies.

As the stage rolled into Grand Lake, Annie was a bit shocked by the crudeness of the small town. The main street was muddy, full of ruts and gigantic boulders left from the age of glaciers, though at least one hundred feet wide.

Scattered buildings were made of rough unfinished boards and battens, mostly unpainted. Others were constructed from hand-hewn logs chinked with mud. The walks in front of the buildings were raised several feet above the mire and consisted of coarse planks nailed together. Rough-looking men in worn overalls and faded coats walked past, looking as defeated as the horses, tied to the hitching posts.

On the right, Annie could see a sparkling blue lake peeking between the buildings and trees. The stage passed a livery, an assay office, and a saloon called the 'Dandy'. At the end of the main street was a large building which looked like a hotel. None of the businesses looked particularly busy.

When the coach came to a halt in front of the General Store, Will unlatched the door and quickly jumped out. He turned and formally offered his hand to Annie, and she caught a look of some strong emotion on his unsmiling face before he masked it with a civil nod.

Again, as she put her hand into his, she felt something run between them, but he quickly let go as soon as her foot touched the ground. Tipping his hat, Redmond said quietly, "I'm sorry you're here, Miss Mitchell. I hope you don't get caught in the crossfire."

Before Annie had time to react to the startling statement, Will Redmond had turned and stalked away.

"Annie? Annie Mitchell?"

She whirled around and was immediately engulfed in an embrace by a large man with a big stomach and smelling of cigars and whiskey. She quickly surmised that this man must be her Uncle Benjamin Daily.

When he finally released her, Annie took a step back and studied him. She noticed at once that his round-face, slick black hair, and brown eyes looked nothing like her mother, his younger half-sister. Annie observed that the expensive-looking waistcoat barely covered Ben Daily's barreled chest and belly, and his boots seemed too shiny and out of place in the muddy street.

Annie had learned from her father that Benjamin Daily was a lawyer who had moved from Chicago some years back to take over the duties as superintendent of a mine called the Wolverine up the Bowen-Baker Gulch.

"Lookee here, little Annie," Ben Daily puffed, apparently quite winded from his walk across the street. As he eyed her up and down, Annie felt even more uncomfortable, as if he could see through her clothing.

"Here's Mary's little girl, all grown up and coming to live with her Uncle Ben. Well, Marian, that is Mrs. Daily, is pleased as pudding that you're coming. The good Lord didn't see fit to bless us with any children, so you'll be the daughter we never had."

Annie felt slightly repulsed by Ben Daily, though she was unsure whether it had anything to do with Will Redmond's violent reaction to his name or just Daily's own overbearing countenance. She found herself taking a few steps backward while her Uncle regaled on about her 'pretty blue eyes' and 'sunny red hair'. It was done so loudly that it seemed to Annie like a staged political address she had once heard on the bandstand at a park in St. Louis.

Annie glanced back at the building Will Redmond had entered, hoping to catch another glimpse of him. It was across the thoroughfare from the General Store, and she assumed it must be the jail. Though Redmond seemed completely ill-mannered and rude, Annie had found herself completely intrigued by the Undersheriff.

"Let's get your bags and go have ourselves a nice dinner at the Farview before we start for home. I want to show *you* off," Uncle Ben was saying as he threw his heavy arm around her shoulders.

The young girl glanced around and saw that the few people on the street were staring curiously at them. After tossing her carpetbags into a wagon tied to a post, Ben Daily escorted his niece down the boardwalk and around the glistening lake on a well-trodden path.

Ben talked the entire time on the path around the lake about himself and his business, but Annie tuned him out and enjoyed the scenery. The calm blue water surrounded by green pine trees, aspens, and surrounding mountains were the most beautiful things she had ever seen. She wanted to stop and take it all in in silence, but she knew that would never happen with Benjamin Daily around. She made a promise to herself to come back to this path alone and sit on one of the many big boulders and spend the whole day here…one day.

Ben and Annie crossed a footbridge and approached the Farview House, a two-story rectangular log building with a wide porch and ten or fifteen men lounging on the railings and steps. When the occupants noticed Annie, their raucous conversations stopped mid-sentence as they all gaped at her, again making her feel as though she indeed had nothing on but her chemise.

Though tall and willowy, with deep blue eyes and hair the color of copper, Annie was quite unaware of her ability to turn heads. Still feeling the sting of rejection from her lover in St. Louis, her own father, and now Will Redmond, she felt a bit disconcerted by all of the sudden male attention she seemed to be attracting.

"Well, boys," Uncle Ben bellowed as he pushed Annie out in front of him like a prize heifer, "this is my niece, Miss Annie Mitchell, from back east. She's come to stay with her aunt and me."

For a second, nothing happened. Then, as if an alarm bell had gone off, the men on the porch began flooding toward her, removing their hats and licking their hands to smooth down already flattened hair. Annie was soon engulfed by a swarm of males of all ages, sizes, and odors; all of them talking at once and trying to touch her arm or get her attention. Turning this way and that, Annie soon became frightened when she could no longer see her Uncle.

"Break it up! Break it up!"

She heard a deep familiar voice over the cacophony of noise around her. A few of the closer faces were unceremoniously jerked out of her view, and fresh mountain air began to cool Annie's flushed cheeks as Will Redmond continued to pull the men away by their shirt collars. The crowd gradually began to disperse, and Annie's tremulous smile was all she could muster as thanks.

Will stared at her for a moment, his thoughts hidden behind a wooden expression, then turned to the crowd which had become remarkably quiet.

"You fellers act like you've never seen a female before," Will snorted irritably. "Leave her be now. Make way and let her have some supper."

He put his hand firmly under Annie's elbow and half-lifted her up the stairs and into the Farview House. When the door was shut behind them, Annie turned to Will.

"Thank you, Mr. Redmond, that *was* rather scary. You seem to have to save me a lot since we've met," she said shakily, unable to look at him as she felt the blush run up her neck and into her hot face.

When the tall Undersheriff didn't reply, Annie glanced up into his hooded eyes. He was staring intently at her, a war of emotions seeming to wage battle within. Annie found herself gazing at his sensual lips, and, as if in a trance, they slowly swayed toward each other.

Annie lifted her face toward his...then the door behind them was pushed opened, and the strange attraction was broken. Will stepped away from her, looking as if he'd been scalded.

"Thanks, Redmond, for getting my niece out of that predicament," Annie heard her uncle say grudgingly as he pushed past them. Will seemed to tear his eyes away from her, then aimed a glare of sheer hatred at Ben Daily.

"If she's supposed to be *your* responsibility, Daily," Will growled, his jaw clenched, "then watch out for her! She could've been hurt or worse in that mob." Without another glance at Annie, Will stalked past them.

Ben saw Annie staring after Will and snorted, "He's an arrogant bastard, girl, and a dangerous one, with a hairpin temper and a penchant for violence. Watch him, though, because he's gotten by on his good looks for too many years now. He's not for a girl like you, though. He'd chew you up and spit you out as soon as he had his way with you.

"Lawman, indeed!" spat Ben Daily. "He and those rapscallion brothers of his should be locked up. And they will be, sooner than they think, if I have any say in it. As for those boys outside, I think they were quite taken with you. We'll have plenty to choose from when it's time to marry you off."

Before Annie could reply indignantly at his high-handed way of discussing her future, she was propelled into the dining area and introduced to Mrs. Lydia Elder, the proprietress.

Lydia Elder was a gaunt-faced woman who looked as if she had worked hard all her life. But when the older woman smiled, the warmth of her expression convinced Annie that she had made her first real friend.

"Welcome, Annie, I hope you like our little community. It's a bit of paradise, if I do say so myself."

Bobbing a curtsy, Annie replied, "It's nice to meet you, Mrs. Elder." Glancing around at the cozy parlor, Annie asked, "Is this a boarding house?"

Lydia Elder beamed, "Yes, Miss Annie, the Farview House has four sleeping rooms upstairs and several tents out back where miners and immigrants sleep. And please, call me Lydia."

While Annie and her uncle were being seated, Lydia Elder went out onto the porch and banged a spoon on the back of a metal pan, calling the men in to eat. They swarmed into the dining room as they had around Annie, leaving her breathless and a bit frightened once again.

But just as quickly, Mrs. Elder clapped her hands together and a hush fell over the room. "You boys be on your best behavior for Miss Mitchell here," she began in a stern, matronly voice. "We don't want to scare her out of town, now do we?"

Every head turned toward Annie. Having some space between herself and the crowd, she glanced around the huge log table at each man... the older weathered faces, the young eager ones, and all at once, she noticed the one face she was surprised to see again. The Undersheriff's eyes, though, were lowered to his plate.

"Well now, who's hungry?" asked Mrs. Elder, breaking the silence when she noticed the direction of Annie's interested look. She hadn't missed the interchange between Annie and Will at the front door.

The men dove into the hot steaming food on the table, piling their blue china plates with heaps of mashed potatoes, slabs of venison, lake trout, biscuits with honey dripping, and several berry pies for dessert. Mrs. Elder and her helper, a young girl in a white apron, made many trips back and forth to the kitchen, restocking serving bowls and filling cups with strong hot coffee.

Thankfully, Annie was saved from much conversation because her uncle monopolized the table with a running dialogue concerning the local political situation. Glancing through her lashes, she kept her eye on Will Redmond as he stared at his plate while shoveling food into his mouth. He never once looked up at her or at Ben Daily. Annie tried to listen to Ben Daily's tirade until she felt herself begin to sway from boredom and exhaustion.

After what seemed an eternity, Ben finally pushed himself away from the table and said with a flourish, "Annie, girl, it's time to go meet your Aunt Marian."

When Annie rose, the scrape of chair legs on the wooden floor was deafening as the men fumbled to their feet. Surprised by this unexpected show of gallantry, Annie smiled timorously at the many pairs of eyes which stared back at her.

"Thank you for a lovely meal, Mrs. Elder. Good evening, gentleman," she replied quietly.

One of the younger men, a boy with curly brown hair about Annie's age, clamored around the table and stood in front of her, kneading his hat in his hands.

"Miss Annie, my name's Charley Burn," he began shyly, his prominent Adam's apple bobbing up and down, "I...well...I...uh...I was wondering whether I could have a dance with you on Saturday night."

She glanced questioningly at her uncle, and Daily boomed jovially, "Well, of course you can, boy. We'll bring Annie to the dance, and you can *all* have a dance with her, can't they, girl?"

Annie found herself bristling at Uncle Ben's irritating propensity for making decisions for her. But realizing she was completely dependent on his good graces for a roof over her head, Annie decided it might be wise not to argue. She merely nodded her head demurely and turned to go.

As they walked down the Farview's wooden steps, Uncle Ben was chuckling to himself.

"What's so funny, Uncle Ben?" she asked, pulling her shawl around her shoulders against the crisp mountain air. The lake shone like glass in the setting sunlight as they made their way along the path back toward the main part of town. Annie likened the rounded mountain straight across from the Farview to a man's balding head, and smiled at the image.

"You, my girl, are the honey, and every man and boy in this county are the bees. It's amazing what a pretty young face can do to a bunch of ragtag miners."

Annie couldn't understand her uncle's meaning; the only man in Grand Lake with whom she might possibly be interested in hated her because she was of Ben Daily's blood.

They retrieved Uncle Ben's wagon. The temperature had dropped considerably from the warmth of the day. Almost dark now, Annie watched the colors of the forest fade to mellow gray, then to inky blackness. As they headed north out of town, the pungent smell of pine filled her nostrils, and she made a wish on a bright star that she be on the verge of a grand adventure.

"Where exactly do you live?" she asked while being jolted once again over uneven ground.

"I've got a spread between here and Gaskill. It's a good walk, but not far by wagon or horse. Of course, in the winter, only a sleigh or snowshoes gets through, and sometimes not even then."

He chortled to himself as he glanced in Annie's direction. "I probably should've taken you directly home, but when I saw how comely you are, I *had* to see the reaction you'd cause." He chuckled again, holding his round belly. "And you *did* stir up some reactions, didn't you, my girl? Even that bastard, Redmond, wasn't immune."

Annie started when Ben mentioned the Undersheriff. What did her uncle mean, 'wasn't immune'? She desperately wanted to ask more but didn't feel comfortable with Ben knowing she had any interest in the Undersheriff. She had been fooled once by a man she fancied, landing her here in the middle of nowhere with a relative she didn't know, and she surely didn't need another man to complicate her life.

"Pa might be right," Annie mused unhappily to herself, when she realized she had been thinking way too much about a stranger with green eyes who wanted nothing to do with her. "I might have the devil in me after all."

Ben and Annie arrived at his cabin less than an hour later. A rotund woman with brown hair liberally streaked with coarse gray emerged from the opened doorway of the large log home and drew Annie into a suffocating embrace against her ample bosom. When the woman, apparently Ben's wife, Marian, held the girl at arm's length to look her over, something about the woman's eyes chilled Annie.

"Oh my stars, what took you so long?" complained Marian Daily. She pulled Annie into the cabin, saying over her shoulder, "Oh, Benjamin, she's a little beauty, now isn't she?"

Annie wondered testily why everyone talked about her like she was not there. She glanced around the Daily home. It was large for a log structure, with stairs leading up to another floor where Ben and Marian apparently slept. The parlor was furnished with an expensive blue velvet settee and matching wing chairs on either side of a stone fireplace. A crystal chandelier hung from the beamed ceiling and illuminated the room with the warmth of many candles.

"You should have seen the ruckus she stirred up in town, Marian," Ben exclaimed as he pushed passed the two women. He went directly to a sideboard, poured himself a generous dollop of amber liquid from a crystal decanter, and downed it in one gulp. "She's going to guarantee me votes for the next election, or my name isn't Benjamin J. Daily."

Annie was confused once again by his statement.

"Oh, Annie, we are so glad you've come to stay with us. Benjamin and I had wished for children, but God just didn't see fit to bless us with any." Marian took out a handkerchief from her corseted bosom and dabbed her dry eyes...only for effect, Annie surmised.

"I'm terribly tired, Aunt Marian," Annie finally said, fatigue dragging her down, "may I go to bed now?"

Marian Daily threw up her hands and exclaimed, "You poor child, you're dead on your feet. Come with me; I've fixed up the sewing room for you."

Turning to her uncle who was working on killing the whiskey one glass at a time, Annie called out, "Good night, Uncle Ben. Thank you for taking me in. I'll try not to be any trouble."

Ben's words were a bit slurred as he replied, "Glad to have you, my girl, glad to have you. And don't you worry, *you'll* be worth every penny..."

Aunt Marian led Annie toward a closed door which led off the parlor. She lit a candle on a small table by the door and led the way into a tiny room. An iron bedstead covered by a calico quilt atop a feather mattress stood against one stark wall. The only other furniture was a washstand which held a pitcher and bowl on top and a covered chamber pot on the bottom shelf. Against the far wall was a plain wooden wardrobe made of pine. One darkened, curtainless window broke up the bareness of the room.

"This should do nicely," stated Marian as she set the candle on the edge of the washstand.

Marian Daily left to retrieve Annie's carpet bags, and the girl experienced a moment of panic as she suddenly realized this strange place was to be her home now. She stared around the spartan room and wondered what Aunt Marian had meant when she said she had 'fixed it up'. Annie took a deep breath as tears threatened to spill down her cheeks.

"There's water in the pitcher, so you can wash up. Tomorrow we'll drag in the big tub, and you can have a proper bath. There's nothing worse than the dirt of travel, I always say," finished Aunt Marian as she bustled back into the small room, dropping Annie's carpetbags on the floor.

Approaching Annie, whose legs were trembling with fatigue, Marian patted her head as she would a pet and left without another word, pulling the door firmly closed behind her. Annie half expected to hear the sound of a key turning in the lock.

The weary girl sank onto the bed, causing the springs to squeak loudly. The tears which had threatened now ran freely. Suddenly, she missed the only home she had ever known, the little dirt farm in northwest Arkansas from where her father had decided she could never return.

Annie lay back on the narrow bed and stared up at the bare pine timbers which supported the roof of the log structure. Completely drained, she thought about her wish for a grand adventure. She knew it was not to be.

Her life would be dictated by her aunt and uncle, then she would be married to someone of their choice. Her life had never been hers, after all. First, Martin Blake had deceived her, then her own father had abandoned her, and now here she was, dependent on another man, Ben Daily. After removing her dress and shoes, Annie sank deeply into sleep, dreaming of green eyes and gunshots.

The next morning when Annie awoke, she panicked, forgetting where she was for a moment. The bare walls were alien, and when she looked out the small window, she could see pine needles on the surrounding trees outside. The early morning air in the little room was frigid. How could that be? In northwest Arkansas or in St. Louis, the room should already be steaming by this time in May. So why was she shivering under the quilt?

Grand Lake, Colorado. Oh yes, now she remembered.

She arose groggily and donned a wrinkled blue dress from her unpacked bag. But at least this garment was cleaner than the travel-stained one she had left on the floor before she had collapsed the night before. Breaking the thin sheet of ice in the ceramic pitcher on the washstand, she poured the frigid water into the bowl and splashed some on her face.

Last night she had been so exhausted, she had literally fallen into bed and was asleep almost before her head hit the soft down pillow. Now her dark copper hair was in snarls, having come loose from the snood in which she had had it somewhat contained. Pulling the tangled wire from her hair, she carefully removed the pins and brushed the dusky, curling mass until the dust and grime from days of traveling were all but removed.

Annie hoped Aunt Marian had meant it when she mentioned a real bath because both her hair and and her body were beginning to smell like some of the unwashed men who had crowded around her the night before at the Farview.

Tying back her tresses with a blue ribbon which matched her simple blue-plaid dress, she opened the door and entered the larger room used as a parlor. No one seemed to be up and around yet, but she heard soft humming and followed the sound through another door which turned out to be a warm and inviting kitchen.

One wall was completely enveloped by a huge rock fireplace which held a large cast iron pot suspended over a roaring fire. The luscious smell emanating from the pot made Annie's mouth water. On the opposite side was a dry sink and preparation area beside a cupboard of Blue Willow crockery.

In the middle of the room was a large table laden with several bags of potatoes, two loaves of freshly baked bread, and two chunks of cheese. The hauntingly beautiful humming Annie had heard came from another smaller room off to the side which she assumed was the pantry. Suddenly, a girl entered the kitchen.

Taken aback, Annie realized the girl was an Indian, the first she'd ever seen. Long black braids tied with thin thongs made of animal hide fell to her waist across a tan doeskin dress which was decorated with animal teeth and bits of bone. Knee-high moccasins made a swishing noise as the strange girl moved across the plank floor. When the Indian girl caught a glimpse of Annie in the doorway, her intense black eyes peered curiously into Annie's blue ones.

"I-I'm sorry," Annie began uncomfortably, "I didn't mean to bother you. I'm Annie Mitchell, and I've come to stay with my uncle. I-I only arrived last night, then I heard a noise from this room and wondered what it was..."

The Indian girl's face didn't change expression. She stared as Annie continued to babble her apologies.

Suddenly the girl held up her hand and cocked her head to the side. Annie stopped talking and listened. She heard the sound of a wagon approaching outside the cabin. She and the Indian girl were startled as the back door was opened so hard that it slammed against the wall.

A heavily muscled man with a thick black beard and mustache gawked at the two girls who stared back at him. On his shoulder he carried two big sacks, which he slung off and let fall to the floor.

"*Wheech* one of you *eez* the boss' new niece?" the burly stranger asked in a strange accent, then broke into guffaws of loud laughter. His hoots brought another older man in behind him. The second man was tall and slender with feathery blonde hair thinning at the top.

"What's so funny, Jacques?" the older man asked as he glanced uncomfortably from one girl to the other.

The one called Jacques couldn't contain his laughter as he told the other man what he had asked the girls. The older man just snorted and turned to Annie. "Please forgive Jacques, miss; he thinks he's a pretty funny feller sometimes. He's from the north woods of Canada so he acts a little odd. Don't pay him no mind. He didn't mean no harm."

He removed his hat and bowed toward Annie. "I'm Jim Calter. I've been hearing about you from town. We work for your uncle over at the Wolverine Mine. Tell Miz Daily we brought the flour from town. And please don't tell your uncle about what Jacques said He didn't mean no harm."

Annie nodded her head dumbly, and as the men turned to go, suddenly pointed at the Indian girl and asked, "Excuse me, but does she speak English?"

"Why don't you ask me?" answered the girl in perfect English.

Annie had the good sense to look as embarrassed as she felt. Jacques broke into more hoots of laughter as Calter hurried him out and closed the door behind them.

"I'm so sorry," began Annie, but the girl held up her hand again, and Annie stopped at once, her cheeks aflame.

"My name is Soft Dove," replied the girl stiffly. "I work for Mr. Daily, and I am Ute. This used to be *my* People's land, and now I have to work for the Whites who stole it."

Annie's blue eyes widened at the venom in the strange girl's words. "I-I'm sorry for your land; I thought we...my people...I mean, the ones who took your land...I mean, I thought your people were *paid* for the land taken."

"Paid? Our *payment* has been the death of our freedom, the death of my People, the end of our way of life. Of course, a spoiled white girl like you could not even begin to understand what we have had to endure because of your kind."

Annie was shocked at the vehemence in the girl's voice. "Listen, I'm sorry for what my people have done to you in the past, Soft Dove. I don't quite know what I can do to make it up to you, but since we're here right now, can't we try to be friends at least? Believe me, I'm not here to take anything away from you. And you'd be surprised at just how much I can understand the loss of your home and freedom."

The solemn Ute stared hard at the tall white girl for a moment, then broke into a shy warm smile. "I'm sorry I was so harsh. That man, Jacques, was making fun of *me*, and it made me angry. I suppose I was taking it out on you."

Relieved, Annie smiled back. Then her hunger made itself known in a loud growl.

Soft Dove walked quickly to the cupboard and removed a bowl. She dipped stew from the pot over the fire and brought the steaming bowl to the table. Annie sat, broke off a piece of bread from a plate beside her, and began sopping up the stew, hunger overpowering her manners.

When she had cleaned the bowl, she glanced up at Soft Dove's amused expression. Realizing that she must look like some wild starved thing, Annie burst into laughter. Soft Dove giggled quietly, hiding her mouth behind her hand.

Marian Daily entered the kitchen while Annie and Soft Dove were laughing, and a nasty scowl crossed her face. "Annie Mitchell, you are *not* to fraternize with the help. Soft Dove, go get the big tub in here for Miss Annie to bathe."

Annie fumed at her aunt's overbearing attitude toward her newfound friend and was disappointed as Soft Dove's face closed down to the blankness of earlier. She glanced once at Annie then went quickly out the back door.

"Annie, my dear," Marian cooed, the annoyingly endearing tone of last night back in her voice, "stay away from that savage girl. Mr. Daily and I watch her very carefully, never sure if she or one of her kind will steal us blind or cut our throats in our sleep. It wasn't *my* idea to hire her, and I'd just as soon send her packing and hire a white woman, but Ben says it's the Christian thing to do."

Annie stared at the cabin door, the words 'cut our throats in our sleep' rolling around in her head. She very much doubted Soft Dove could do such a horrible thing, but wondered about the hatred and anger she had heard in the Indian girl's voice.

Soft Dove entered the back door, dragging a large oval metal tub. Without a word, she took two buckets from the corner and left again.

"She'll heat up the water over the fire, and you can bathe," Aunt Marian stated. "Bolt the back door and no one will bother you. When you unpack, give the Indian your clothes to wash and press. Oh, did Mr. Calter bring this flour?" She patted one of the large sacks as if it were a pet.

"Yes, ma'am, he did," replied Annie as she followed her Aunt into the parlor. "Aunt Marian, what do you want me to *do*? That is, after I bathe."

The older woman turned and gazed at Annie with a puzzled expression. "What in the world do you mean, child?"

"Well, what I mean is, do I help Soft Dove? Or work in the garden? Or what? What do I *do* here...everyday?"

Marian put her beefy hands on her stomach and laughed. "Annie, dear, you are the niece of one of the most important men in Grand County. You don't *do* anything. That's why we have a servant. Your job is to be a respectable Young lady and attract a man worthy of your Uncle's position. A husband, children, and a house of your own will soon be *your* job."

Before Annie could react, she heard Soft Dove at the back door, burdened with both pails of water. Annie immediately ran to relieve her of one of the buckets.

"Annie Mitchell, I told you not to do that! Your Uncle *pays* Soft Dove to work for us," the Young woman huffed. "She's able to handle the heavy lifting. Her kind was built to work."

Frustrated and embarrassed, Annie retorted, "Aunt Marian, I'm *not* helpless! I have never had idle hands, even at school, and I would go mad sitting around doing nothing. Please find something for me to do. If you don't, then I *will* help Soft Dove anytime I see she needs it."

Marian harrumphed rudely, "Don't you dare be disrespectful to me, young woman, or you could find yourself out on the streets! You're lucky your uncle has such a kind heart to take you in, after what you put your father through!" She turned haughtily and sailed out of the room.

Blushing hotly, Annie caught Soft Dove's slight smile as she emptied the water into a huge cauldron hanging on another iron hook over the fire.

Annie stomped back to her room and prepared for her bath. She was suddenly enraged by events which were completely out of her hands: her aunt and uncle's arrogant attitude, the circumstances which had forced her to leave school and be foisted upon them, and the prospect of endlessly boring days which would drag on until her uncle chose a husband for her. And to top it off, her new friend was off-limits to her.

"God's Teeth!" Annie swore angrily.

When she finally returned to the kitchen, Soft Dove was pouring steaming water into the tub. She had moved it to a corner by the fire and had hung a multicolored blanket as a cover.

Annie felt she owed Soft Dove an apology for her aunt's rudeness but was hesitant about how to say it. "Soft Dove, I-I'm sorry for what my au--," she began but was stopped by the dark-skinned girl.

"No need, Miss Annie," she said quietly. "I don't blame you for your aunt's uncivilized behavior. I appreciate what you said and did in my behalf. But please, don't make trouble for me. I need this job...my family needs me to work and send them money. They have so little on the Uintah Reservation."

"Your family is really on a Reservation?" asked Annie incredulously. "Then why aren't you there with them?"

"I was...but the Christian missionaries, who taught me English, helped me obtain permission to work here, and your uncle's money goes to the Reservation to buy food and warm clothing for my People. My brother, Bear Hawk, refuses to accept the truth of our situation, but I am more realistic."

More curious now, Annie asked, "Do you live here, too?"

"Yes, I live in the barn."

"In the barn!" Annie exclaimed. "That's inhuman!"

Soft Dove turned away and murmured softly, "It's better than on the Reservation."

Annie felt the pain in the girl's voice. "You said you have a brother? Does he also live on the Reservation?"

"No," replied the Soft Dove, her chin lifting in pride, "Bear Hawk refused to be taken to the Reservation. He lives in the mountains... free. Everyday I fear he will be caught. He says he would rather fight and die than go to the Reservation."

Annie ached inside for Soft Dove's proud heritage which had been wrenched so heartlessly from her. "Please don't call me Miss Annie, Soft Dove, I'm only Annie. And I promise I won't do anything to jeopardize your job. I am all alone in this strange place, and one can never have too many friends, don't you agree?"

Soft Dove's taut expression softened as she stared into Annie's sincere blue eyes. "In front of your aunt and uncle, I must call you Miss Annie, but when we are alone, you shall be just Annie. Now get into the tub; you are beginning to smell like a dirty white girl."

The two girls laughed companionably.

***

On Saturday, several boring days after Annie's arrival, Mrs. Daily made a welcome announcement after dinner. "Annie, go put on your dancing shoes. Mr. Daily is taking us into town tonight."

Annie stared back and forth at her aunt and uncle incredulously. Ben Daily was leaning back in his chair, patting his rotund belly, and smiling.

"That's right, girl. You're going to your first big shindig in Grand Lake. There's a dance every Saturday night, either up at Gaskill or Lulu City, or down in Grand Lake. It's about time I showed you off to my voting public. I think the gossip about you has whetted their appetites well enough by now."

"But, Uncle Ben, I don't know how to dance," Annie replied hesitantly.

"What? A marriageable Young girl who can't dance? That's terrible!" bellowed Aunt Marian. "Well, you'll just have to follow the man's lead. Do you think you can at least do that?"

"I...I don't know. My father said dancing was the devil's worship and forbade me taking lessons at Miss Mary Flynn's Academy."

"Sounds just like your father," snorted Ben. "Don't worry, Annie, those ignorant miners don't know anything about fine dancing anyway. They'll be just as happy to sling you around the floor. Just follow your partner's lead, watch your toes, and hang on."

Annie dashed to her room, her heart beating faster with excitement as she brushed her long burnished hair and tied it back with a fresh ribbon. She wondered if Will Redmond would be at the dance. And if he was, would he dance with her? No, probably not, after their last meeting.

When Annie and the Dailys arrived in Grand Lake, they drove to the Nickerson House, a large hotel across from the jail. Two stories tall, the whitewashed building had a large front porch with pillars and a hand-lettered sign over the door. As Annie climbed from the carriage, she glanced back over her shoulder at the darkened courthouse, wondering about the green-eyed Undersheriff.

Inside the Nickerson House, the diningroom has been cleared of tables, and the chairs were lined up against the walls. At one end of the room, there was a table with all sorts of delicious dishes spread over a white damask tablecloth.

The candlelit chandelier in the middle of the ceiling softened the faces of the crowd of people who were milling about the room, filling the room with loud conversation. At the other end of the diningroom, chairs were set up for the men who would provide the music. Several bearded gents were tuning up their fiddle, banjo, harmonica, jug, and washboard.

Annie gazed around at the crowds, suddenly shy, as she walked between her Marian and Ben. Within seconds of entering, she was swarmed by eager young men, all shouting out confirmation that they had a dance reserved with her.

While Uncle Ben and Aunt Marian herded her through the throng, she unexpectedly caught a glimpse of Redmond, a head higher than most of the other men with whom he was engrossed in conversation. For a long intense moment, Annie and Will's eyes locked. Then, to her disappointment, he looked away as if the encounter had meant nothing to him. She felt herself flushing uncomfortably.

Before Annie had time to contemplate the snub, she was introduced to more folk than she could remember names. She found herself smiling at strangers who started up conversations and acted like they had known her all her life. Annie tried to quell their avid curiosity about her arrival but deftly skirted the real reason she was living with the Dailys.

"So you're Ben Daily's niece," wheezed a raspy voice behind her.

Annie spun around to see a grizzled, sunken-cheek old man standing in front of her. Unhealthily thin and several inches shorter that she, the old-timer chewed on a wad of tobacco.

"Y-yes sir, I'm Annie Mitchell," she replied politely, bobbing a curtsey.

"I'm Judge Joseph Westcott, missy; have you heard about me?"

Annie looked puzzled. "No sir, I'm sorry, I haven't. Do you know my Uncle?"

The old man snorted and spat out of the side of his mouth onto the polished wooden floor. "I'm the very first settler to this here place. When I come up to these here mountains, there weren't a white man within a hundred miles. Only me and the Utes and Arapahoes. I built me a cabin in Grand Lake City which is over yonder across the lake. When folks started moving up here, they didn't like paying my price for land so they started up this here 'village' on this side of the lake.

"Do you know how to fish, girl?"

Annie stared at the odd, little man, thinking he didn't look much like a 'judge'. He had on a fur hat, a ratty hide shirt, and tan britches with fringe down the side. His dirty white beard hung nearly to the middle of his chest, and his eyebrows looked as it they might have something living in them.

"No sir, I don't know how to fish."

"Well, that's how I survived up here all alone. It's a good livin'. I almost died, you know. I was sick in my chest when I first come. Clean living cured me though."

Annie began to back away as the Judge continued to rant a bit incoherently about all the slights he'd endured by the local townspeople. She perked up, though, when he mentioned her Uncle.

"That damned Ben Daily should be horsewhipped, in my estimation," stated Judge Westcott. "He is lower than a mountain rattler's belly. That jackass sued me over some of my *own* land he claimed he'd staked. If you're of his blood, girl, you'd better watch yourself. Somebody's gonna kill that rat bastard one of these days."

"I-if you'll excuse me, please," Annie stuttered as she began to back away. Here was another person, besides Will Redmond, who claimed to hate Ben. She glanced across the room toward a crowd of men where her uncle was pontificating, wondering how he'd made so many enemies so fast.

When the music started, Annie was relieved to be swung onto the floor by the boy, Charley Burn, whose Adam's apple bobbed so uncontrollably. Sure enough, her inexperience at dancing was completely overshadowed by her myriad of partners' enthusiasm, and her toes were stomped on as many times as she stepped on theirs.

The hours flew by as Annie danced and danced. One of the more graceful dancers was a nice-looking young man named Jules Thermon. He was in his mid-twenties, with a bushy mustache, wispy goatee, and kind sky-blue eyes. He seemed rather shy and unsure of himself which was quite endearing.

"And what do you do, Mr. Thermon?" asked Annie after they were out on the dance floor.

"I'm the County Clerk of Grand County," Jules answered formally as he stared over her head. "Miss Mitchell, I'd just like to say how you've brightened up our dull little town. Your uncle has given me permission to call on you, i-if that's all right with you."

"Thank you, Mr. Thermon, and yes, I'd be happy to have you call on me," Annie answered, trying to be polite but plainly disconcerted at his inability to look at her while they danced. After a time, it began to annoy her, so she stomped rather heavily on his boot. She was rewarded with a soft curse by the stiff Mr. Thermon, then a quick apologetic glance down at Annie.

She smiled sweetly and said, "At least you've noticed that I was here."

He blushed to his roots and replied, "I'm sorry, Miss Mitchell, for swearing in front of you."

"I don't care if you curse, Mr. Thermon, as long you know with whom you are dancing!"

He looked at her in horror, apparently unused to such forthrightness in young women. After their dance, he made a slight bow and sped away to join his mother on the other side of the room. Annie could tell the woman was discussing her with him as they both kept watching her.

But Annie was quickly claimed for another dance and soon forgot the nice-looking young public servant.

Around midnight, she flounced into a chair and fanned herself with her hand. Laughing at something one of the men had said, her gaze wafted around the crowded room.

Again, her eyes locked onto Will Redmond's, who was boldly staring back at her. She met his stare coolly, then made a point of looking away first. Suddenly, left breathless by her own audacity and the closeness of the crowd, Annie felt as if her lungs would burst.

"Excuse me," she panted as she pushed through the group of men waiting for a dance, "I need some air...now!"

"Let me escort you outside," suggested Charley Burn, her most ardent admirer.

"No, Charley, I need to be alone for awhile," Annie replied, smiling at the dejected look on the boy's blushing face. She hoped he thought she was heading for the privy and would leave her in peace. He had kept trying to claim every dance and was beginning to become a nuisance.

Annie walked quickly outside, gulping in the cool mountain air. The porch was crowded with the overflow of people from inside. Men smoked and argued politics in small groups, so she made her way down the steps and around to the back of the building which overlooked the mountain lake.

In the moonlight, the dark water glistened, mirroring the night's many stars in its surface. Annie's feet hurt from the hours of dancing and the great many clumsy boots which had crushed her instep. After a quick glance back to see that no one was watching, she sat down on the sand at the water's edge and unbuttoned her shoes.

Peering around once more, she quickly rolled down her stockings. When she had removed both, she lifted her skirt and petticoats and waded up to her knees in the icy water, letting the muddy bottom seep sensuously between her toes. For a moment, Annie wished she could shed all of her binding garments and dive headlong into the reflecting surface.

"That's not very ladylike, you know," purred that voice which had haunted her dreams in the past days.

She spun around and saw Will Redmond squatting on the bank beside her sloughed shoes and stockings. With arms crossed over his knees, his brim low over his eyes, she could not tell if he was serious or not. Instinctively, she felt she had to defend herself.

"It feels good, so I don't care if it is ladylike or not," she retorted, lifting her chin.

In the dark, she heard him chuckle and thought she saw the whites of his teeth for a moment. Then he stood up. She realized again how tall he was...and how wide his shoulders were.

"I wanted to apologize for my behavior when we first met," he said quietly, the cadence of his deep smooth voice stroking her seductively.

Unsure how to respond, she stood in silence.

"I know you don't understand any of the politics here, but your uncle and I have a history. And it ain't a very pretty one. In fact, I hate the man, and if I had my way, I'd see him run out of this County, or better yet, dead."

Annie blanched at his words, spoken so softly, making them seem even more deadly. She found herself frightened, yet still attracted to the Undersheriff. Her palms were wet, and she felt her throat thicken. Annie realized, all at once, she didn't care a fig about Ben Daily right then; she knew only that she desperately wanted to go on being in Will Redmond's company.

"I'm *not* my uncle, Mr. Redmond. Whatever animosity there is between you two has nothing to do with me," Annie replied softly.

"I told you to call me Will, remember?"

He took his hat off, and she could see the pale gleam of his eyes and a half-grin under his mustache. He suddenly took a step toward her, and Annie instinctively stepped backward. Her bare foot slid in the slimy mud, and she waved her arms wildly trying to regain her balance. Just before she fell, Will took a few giant strides into the water and grabbed her around the waist.

At his touch, Annie felt a lightning bolt shoot through her. His strong arm still around her, she glanced up into his face and saw, for an instant, his own reaction to the jolt that she had experienced.

Annie found herself gazing into the depths of his eyes, then fixating on his lips. He tightened his grip on her waist and slowly drew her toward him. Then, as if shaking himself out of a trance, he pulled her roughly back onto dry land and released her.

"Don't you know it's dangerous to be out all alone at night?" he asked gruffly as he put his hat back on, smoothing the brim and situating it low over his brow. "There are all kinds of wild animals in the dark." Annie could no longer see his eyes. She trembled, still feeling his arms around her. "Do you need any help putting on your shoes? I used to help my w...ma do up her buttons."

Annie was half-mad at his sudden changes of mood. One moment she had been sure he was about to kiss her, then immediately he acted like he was angry with her again. Baffled, she sat down on the sandy bank and began to yank on her stockings.

"No, thank you, I can do it myself," she replied. "But I want to know one thing. Why do you stare at me, and why did you follow me? One minute you act like you hate me, and the next..." She stopped, embarrassed by her own boldness.

Will squatted beside her again but wouldn't look at her. Staring out over the lake, he answered soberly, "I-I like you, Annie Mitchell, very much, and I'd like to get to know you better, but I can't...because of who your uncle is...a-and other reasons. It just ain't gonna happen. I'm sorry. I hope you can understand."

"I told you, Will, I am *not* my uncle," she exclaimed, laying a hand on his arm.

Will turned to her then, his gaze sizzling as it roamed from her thick dark hair to her blue eyes which shined in the darkness, then down to her mouth as he fought the urge to kiss her.

Finally, he dragged his eyes away and spat gruffly, "It just *can't* be, Annie Mitchell. Find yourself a rich man and marry him. Get yourself out of Grand Lake and away from Daily before you get hurt through him."

He rose quickly and stomped back to the front of the building, leaving Annie feeling empty and alone. The magical mood of the glistening lake was broken, and big tears blurred the beauty of the moonlit, silent water.

After Annie replaced her shoes and stockings, she wiped off the back of her skirt and walked slowly up the hill toward the Nickerson House. When she entered the noisy crowded room, it had lost all of its former appeal. She marched over to her uncle, who was caught up in a debate with two other men, and interrupted. "Uncle Ben, can we go home now?"

"Go home? Go home?" he sputtered. "Of course we can't go home now. It's the shank of the evening, my girl. These dances last until sunrise. Now go find one of those Young men who've been hanging all over you and dance the night away. Enjoy yourself."

He spun Annie around and pushed her toward the dance floor...and right into the arms of Charley Burn, who had been waiting anxiously for her return. He swung her out into the melange of other dancers.

Annie felt numb as she danced the night away, knowing that none of the men here could match Will Redmond in her heart and mind. What a world! Annie thought to herself miserably. How many mistakes can I make when it comes to men?

She fixed a smile on her face and endured until daybreak when the party finally broke up. Even though she had kept a watchful eye out, she had never seen the Undersheriff again that evening.

At dinner the next night, Ben Daily's own admission enlightened Annie as to one of the reasons why Undersheriff Will Redmond and others might not care for him.

"I am a very powerful man in this county, Annie," Ben began while cutting the venison.

He had come in from the Wolverine Mine and gone straight to the liquor decanter, so he was talking more freely now that his tongue was oiled. "When your Aunt Marian and I came out to this Godforsaken region from Chicago, I realized right away how incompetent the men were who ran this area. You see, most of these yokels didn't even finish grammar school. So of course, it is only natural for a man of my intelligence and education to run this County."

Annie shifted in her chair, pushing uneaten food around the plate. She had never felt comfortable listening to anyone brag about themselves. If Ben acted so high and mighty around others, she thought, it was no wonder he wasn't liked. But why would Redmond hate Ben so venomously that he wanted him to leave the county...or die?

Marian intervened between loud smacking bites. "I met your uncle when he was in law school, Annie. He was so dashing and smart. When his associates from Chicago offered him this position as Superintendent of the biggest mine in Grand County, well, of course, he couldn't refuse. It meant giving up a lot of things, I can tell you, like the opera, grand parties, servants who knew their places..." Marian glared at Soft Dove as the girl picked up Ben's empty plate to refill.

Annie blanched at her aunt's rudeness and tried to change the subject. "Uncle Ben, tell me about my mother. I was so young when she died; I have a difficult time remembering what she was like."

"Your mother was only my half-sister, Annie, and we were never close," Ben began after a rather loud belch. "My mother died when I was about twelve, and my father married your grandmother. I was at boarding school when Mary was born."

"Was my mother born in Chicago? How did she end up with my father in Arkansas?"

Ben and Marian exchanged glances.

"Your mother was raised as a gentlewoman," answered Aunt Marian, disapproval in her voice, "Then she ran off with your father and was disowned by your uncle's family. It caused quite a scandal."

Annie blinked in amazement. "My father *eloped* with my mother?"

Marian sniffed derisively and continued, "Your uncle's family did not approve of Aaron Mitchell. He was an itinerant preacher who completely mesmerized your mother. Mary wouldn't hear any advice from Ben or his father, and she ran away with Aaron against the advice of everyone."

"I can't believe my father did anything as disgraceful! He has always seemed so righteous and unforgiving," exclaimed Annie, her eyes huge in astonishment.

"Yes, we were *that* surprised when we got his letter asking us to take you." replied Ben Daily.

Annie gazed solemnly from her uncle to her aunt. "Thank you, Uncle Ben and Aunt Marian, for not turning your back on me, too."

Aunt Marian suddenly became extremely agitated and left the table abruptly. Ben said nothing but sat back in his chair, his fingers steepled. He gazed at Annie as if she were a prize mare, and he was contemplating her worth.

She felt so uncomfortable by Marian's swift departure and Ben's silence, Annie quickly excused herself from the table and went to her room. There she contemplated her own father's actions. Maybe Aaron Mitchell's guilt of eloping with her mother and not just Annie's failings that weighted him down and spurred his religious zeal, she mused.

After that night, Annie's days at the Daily cabin were spent exploring the surrounding woods and talking with Soft Dove when Aunt Marian wasn't around. Even as their friendship blossomed, Annie never mentioned the confusing feelings she had for the Undersheriff. Evenings were spent in the company of the Daily's, listening to their boring conversations or playing the spinet which graced the corner of the parlor.

CHAPTER TWO

Whenever Marian took her daily afternoon nap, Annie made a beeline for the kitchen. She and Soft Dove had become fast friends.

"I learned English from Christian missionaries on the Reservation," Soft Dove explained one afternoon.

The girls had stolen away from the house and were sitting under a tree beside a small pond not far from the cabin. They had kicked off their shoes and were lazily plaiting plant fronds into small baskets as the bright sun filtered through the tall pines.

"My family was herded like cattle to the Uintah Reservation in Utah when I was very young, stated Soft Dove bitterly. "I am only allowed to live away from it because the missionaries arranged for me to work for your uncle."

"Don't you miss your family?" asked Annie, feeling a bit homesick herself.

"I miss my mother and father dearly. My brother, Bear Hawk, refuses to be ruled by the Whites and continues to live freely in the mountains." She gestured to the snowcapped peaks which rose above the green carpet of trees surrounding them. "He comes to see me sometimes; you'll meet him one day."

Annie was enthralled by the ancient tales Soft Dove related concerning her People and their reverence for the land. Annie's favorite legend, which always made her cry, was about the lake which surrounded the town...both called Grand.

Soft Dove let her hands rest in her lap as she stared off into a time before either girl had been born.

"Before the White Man came, a group of my People, the Mountain Utes, were camped on the edge of the lake. A war party of Arapaho suddenly descended on the tribe, and all of the women and children were put on a raft in the middle of the lake for safety.

"But a terrible storm came up and capsized the raft, drowning all. After a terrible battle with our sworn enemies, my People defeated the Arapaho. Sadly, though our warriors lived, all of their loved ones were gone. The water and the land around were considered a sacred place of sorrow. My People called it 'Spirit Lake' after that, until the White Man came. I don't quite understand why they called it 'Grand'."

"Will, I mean, someone told me the lake was named after the Grand River because it's origins are in these mountains. But I think 'Spirit Lake' is a much better name for the lake, if it wasn't so tragic."

Soft Dove continued, "There is another tale also. The lake holds mist, and some say they see a White Buffalo rise up in the middle of the lake. That is also why it is called Spirit Lake. My People always called it Red Lake because when the sun begin to set, the water turns red."

Suddenly, Annie felt an intense need to unburden herself of the reasons she had been sent to live with her aunt and uncle, and Soft Dove's quiet acceptance and friendship finally convinced her to open up.

"After my mother died, my father became consumed with his church work. I was all alone. When I was sent away to school, I suppose I was looking for love. All of our social activities were strictly chaperoned, and it wasn't until this last year that I discovered how to sneak out to meet a boy who said he *loved* me. I thought we were sure to be married, so one night, he said if I loved him I would let him... so I-I gave myself to him. He had said he loved me over and over, but it turned out that he had been secretly engaged to someone else all along.

"After he'd had his way with me, he refused to see me again. It caused quite a scandal at Miss Mary Flynn's Academy. I've never seen my father so angry before. As soon as he heard, he drove to St. Louis, took me out of school, and sent me here. It was so awful; I don't think I can ever go home again."

Soft Dove's black eyes filled with tears after Annie recalled the heartbreak she had endured from the deceitful young man and from her father's abandonment.

"Do you still love that boy, Annie?" asked Soft Dove.

Annie thought for a moment before she answered, "No, I don't know now if I ever really loved him. I think I was in love with the thought of love instead of the boy himself. I can hardly remember what I was attracted to in the first place. And I sometimes have a hard time recalling what he actually looked like. I can only see him that last time, with a smirk on his face that I wanted to slap off. I wish I had!"

"My People are also passionate," whispered Soft Dove, "but my People love their children more than life and would never send a daughter away for giving her heart unwisely. Again and again, I see evidence of how differently the White Man thinks, and it sickens me. Do your uncle and aunt know of this thing that happened to you?"

"Yes," Annie began, "you heard my aunt threaten to send me away that first day, remember? But they must not think that I am *too* soiled. I believe Uncle Ben and Aunt Marian are going to try and marry me off to someone. Oh, Soft Dove, I don't understand the White Man sometimes, either."

Soon after, Annie began to receive a parade of callers each evening. Miners of all shapes and sizes from the boomtowns of Gaskill, Teller, and Lulu City 'just happened' to stop by after supper. With their hair slicked flat and their boots spit-shined, the suitors were systematically barraged with nightly campaign speeches by Annie's Uncle Ben.

Sitting side by side on the settee, drinking lukewarm tea, Annie and the unlucky man of the hour were barely able to get in two words to each other. And not one of the miners left a lasting impression on Annie. All of their faces and stories seemed to be mixed into a jumble of sameness, and she couldn't quit comparing them all to her memory of the broad-shouldered Undersheriff with the flinty green eyes.

Thomas Booth was one of the more entertaining would-be suitors though. "Excuse me, Mr. Daily, but I come here to see Miss Annie," he said in his straight-forward way. "Couldn't we be alone?"

"Son, where are you from?" Ben exclaimed. "Nice girls are not left alone with young bucks. Miz Daily and I are my niece's chaperones."

"I'm from Gold Hill, Nevada, sir, and I've only been in Colorado a few months," began Thomas, meeting Ben eye-to-eye, as he kneaded his hat in his hands. "I don't know much about politics, but I know one thing for sure. Miss Annie is the prettiest girl in the County, and I'm dying for a kiss."

Annie spit her tea right onto Marian's Persian rug. Then she laughed so hard at Ben and Marian's outraged expressions she had to excuse herself to the privy.

There were enough lonely young men anxious to woo Annie to please her ambitious Uncle and his bid for a seat on the Board of Commissioners of Grand County. Few of them came more than a couple of times because of Ben's speechifying. As much as they admired Annie, they couldn't abide Daily's constant campaigning.

Charley Burn, whose shyness and sincerity were expressed in longing gazes but not much conversation, was the exception. He didn't care how long-winded Ben Daily became as long as he could sit beside the girl of his dreams. He'd fallen hard for Annie, and knew if he just persevered, she'd feel the same eventually.

One evening, Annie overheard a conversation between Aunt Marian and Uncle Ben. "Why do you let those derelict miners keep courting her, Benjamin? You aren't thinking she should marry one of that lot, are you?"

"Don't worry, Annie's not meant for any of that rabble. I just need her to draw them here until the election. If they think they have a chance with her, they'll do just about anything, even change political parties and vote for me as Commissioner.

"I've *got* to get on that Board; George Miller from Teller has too much power and influence already, what with the Sheriff and Undersheriff in his pocket. If he gets any of his other flunkies on the Board, this county might elect *him* to Congress instead of *me*. Wouldn't you like to live in a big city again, Marian? Denver? Washington, D.C.?"

Annie was relieved to realize that Ben wasn't in a hurry to marry her off, even though it made her quite uncomfortable to be used as a pawn for his political ambitions. She'd heard about the conflict between Ben and George Miller, an attorney from Teller. Miller was Ben's bitterest political rival, even though they had once been friends. Both men thought only one could 'run' the County, and the hostile acrimony between them affected everyone in the small mountain community.

The next day, as Annie wandered boredly around the parlor, idly touching a curtain here, a vase there, she heard raised voices in the kitchen. She glanced up, knowing Aunt Marian had not laid down for her afternoon nap yet. Annie's curiosity soon got the better of her caution, and she tiptoed to the doorway of the kitchen.

She heard Soft Dove and a strident male voice speaking to one another in an unfamiliar language. Peeking around the corner, Annie watched as Soft Dove argued with a tall Indian clad only in a breechclout cloth. Annie found herself gaping at his muscular half-naked body.

His glossy black hair was loose and cascaded to his waist. His thighs rippled as he shifted his weight from one moccasined foot to the other while deep in intense debate with Soft Dove. He reminded her of a jungle cat she'd seen in a book; lean and magnificent, but dangerous.

Annie must have made some small noise because all at once, both the Indian and Soft Dove turned as one. The Indian was the most fierce-looking individual Annie had ever seen. But something about him made her stomach flutter, and it wasn't fear.

"Come and meet my brother," Soft Dove said as she held out her hand.

Annie was embarrassed at being caught eavesdropping and felt her face redden as she moved into the kitchen. "I-I didn't mean to interrupt," she sputtered.

"This is Bear Hawk, and we were disagreeing..again, as if you couldn't tell," Soft Dove smiled ruefully at her brother.

Annie held out her hand to Soft Dove's brother, studying him as he studied her. He glanced derisively at her outstretched hand but made no overture to take it in his own. His black eyes were more intense than Soft Dove's, and they seemed to devour Annie with their intensity. His name was apt because he had a chiseled hawk-like nose which separated his high cheekbones. A slash of lips were narrowed as he scowled at her.

Bear Hawk uttered something in his own language to Soft Dove. By the way he tossed his head in Annie's direction, she knew he was talking about her. She watched as Soft Dove answered angrily in a long barrage of unintelligible words.

Soft Dove finally turned to Annie and said, "My brother has much contempt for the White Man's ways, and he hates that I work here. He is always trying to convince me to go with him into the mountains and live as our People did long ago. But he is always in hiding, not really free. The White Man has just not caught him yet."

Annie stared at the two as their apparent disagreement continued. Bear Hawk suddenly stopped yelling at his sister and moved as swiftly as a panther toward Annie. Her eyes widened in fear at the stormy countenance on the young man's attractive face, and she took several tentative steps backwards until the wall stopped her retreat. Bear Hawk's face came within inches of her own.

She could smell the leather from the pouch he wore around his neck and the male musk of his skin as they regarded one another in silence. He boldly scanned her eyes, hair, and womanly curves as his heated glance swept over her body. Annie could feel sweat forming in her armpits and on her brow. She tried to meet his eyes without wavering, but her insides were quaking with fear...and other feelings best left unexplored.

At school she had heard the spine-tingling tales about marauding bands of rebel Indians who had refused to go quietly to the Reservations. Those tales had been told in the dark, and Annie had had more than one nightmare of screaming savages overrunning Miss Mary Flynn's Academy and murdering everyone in their beds.

When she thought she might faint from his scrutiny, Annie found her voice and said shakily, "Mr. Hawk, please back away; you are frightening me."

Bear Hawk's eyes widened, then he turned toward his sister for a translation. After Soft Dove told him what Annie had said, he burst into laughter. He whirled around and was gone before Annie had time to catch her breath.

Soft Dove laid her hand on Annie's arm, "My brother likes to intimidate, but he wouldn't really hurt you." Shivering, Annie looked past her and wondered if that were really true.

During the next week, Bear Hawk made daily unexpected appearances at the back door of the cabin. Always he came in the afternoon, when Aunt Marian was resting and Annie was free to be with Soft Dove.

If the girls were outside, his intense black eyes followed Annie's every movement. His sizzling gaze upset Annie tremendously. She would often excuse herself and escape into the cabin. When she did, he'd jump on his horse and ride away.

If the girls were in the kitchen, he would hunker in the doorway and stare appraisingly. Annie knew he discussed her with his sister, and it frustrated Annie when Soft Dove refused to tell her what he had said. Annie would have liked to become friends with him as she had with his sister, but he acted as though she were beneath contempt. And the language barrier kept Annie from trying to break through his stiff facade.

One evening Uncle Ben came home early and announced he was taking Marian and Annie into Grand Lake to the Theater. Annie was very excited as she had not been to town in days. Although she loved Soft Dove, she longed to make some white friends, too. And she hoped, deep down, she might see Undersheriff Redmond once again.

When they arrived in town, Annie's stomach knotted as they passed the jail. She tried to glance surreptitiously to see if anyone might be in the lighted office but was unable to get a clear view unless she craned her neck, and that would have been too obvious.

The local Repertory Company performed in a building in the center of town which also served as the Town Meeting hall. The long log building had a raised stage and was illuminated by cupped candles along the floor. The people milled about and drank punch before the performance.

"Annie," gushed Marian as she gripped the girl's arm and turned her around, "I want you to meet a friend of your uncle's. This is Mr. J. C. Brashears, one of the owners of the Wolverine Mine. Mr. Brashears, this is Mr. Daily's niece, Miss Annie Mitchell."

J. C. Brashears was tall with a long nose and thin lips. His clothes were impeccably tailored, and he wore a tall black hat. Annie immediately understood he must be someone of importance whom her uncle felt could help his political aspirations by Marian's tone. But something about the haughty man disturbed Annie; and she had the urge to wipe off the back of her hand after Brashears had regally kissed it.

"I am honored to make your acquaintance, Miss Mitchell," Brashears said in a crisp English accent.

"Nice to meet you, too, sir," replied Annie as she scanned the room, searching for the one face she most hoped to see. Suddenly she spied Lydia Elder across the crowd.

"Annie," exclaimed Mrs. Elder as she approached. "How nice to see you! I've been waiting for you to come to town again. Your aunt must be keeping you quite busy."

Mrs. Elder gave her a welcoming hug, and Annie was grateful to be pulled away from the disquieting presence of J.C. Brashears.

Later, Annie was introduced to Emma McLeary, the school teacher, and she felt an instant bond with the small blond woman. Having hoped to become a teacher herself someday, Annie offered to assist with the school in any way.

"Don't say that unless you mean it, Miss Mitchell, because I would love the help. Trying to keep the little ones busy while teaching the older ones is almost too much for one woman. There aren't many students, but they are all jewels, every sweet one."

Miss McLeary was suddenly swept away by her beau, John Appleby, and Annie stared after them, happy that she had made another new friend, and slightly envious of the obvious affection they held for one another.

"Annie, dear," cooed Aunt Marian from behind, "I would like you to meet our sheriff, Tom Roberts."

Annie twirled around, but her heart fell when she saw only one man and realized the Undersheriff must be still on duty. Sheriff Roberts had kind eyes which crinkled at the corners when he smiled. His face was roughened by weather, and his easy-going nature had a hint of steel in it which made it easy to see why people trusted him with the safety of their County.

"It's a pleasure to meet you, Miss Mitchell," drawled the sheriff, not much older than Will Redmond. "You've made quite an impression on our small village, it seems. And now I can see why. I take it you've had a few callers?" His eyes twinkled, and Annie blushed.

"Quit flirting, Tom Roberts, or I'm going to be absolutely jealous," Aunt Marian giggled like a schoolgirl.

"Don't fret, Miz Daily, your niece is safe from an old geezer like me," he smiled mischievously.

Although many of the young miners (some with whom she had endured an evening of tea at the Daily's cabin, and some she had not met before) clamored to sit beside her, Annie actually worried at one point that her uncle was going to auction off the seat next to her to the highest bidder.

Ben Daily finally decided on Virgil Hogton, eldest son of the owner of the Livery. Virgil was a complete stranger to Annie. She politely tried to make conversation, but his painful shyness left him tongue-tied and sweaty.

Annie was grateful when the house lights finally went down and the play began. She recognized a few of the townspeople who played the characters but was soon lost in the fantasy of the story.

The play was a comedy, and Annie laughed harder than she had for years. When it was over and the cast was given three standing ovations, the audience moved down the street to the Nickerson House for refreshments and dancing. Annie danced all night, this time really enjoying herself since the disturbing Undersheriff did not make an appearance. At dawn, the Dailys headed for home.

When they arrived at the cabin soon after the sun had peeked over the mountain tops in the east, Annie was nearly asleep on her feet.

"Oh, I wish you could have come," murmured Annie sleepily as Soft Dove helped her undress. "It was the funniest play; I've never laughed so much. And then I danced every dance. Oohh, how my feet hurt!"

Soft Dove smiled sadly as she tucked Annie into bed. She remembered, before her People were forced on the Reservation, how they had feasted and danced after each hunt. She remembered how she also had danced all night until exhaustion had taken her. Soft Dove was glad for Annie's happiness but bitter for her own loss.

Aunt Marian presented Annie with a cedar Hope Chest. When Annie looked bewildered, Aunt Marian was appalled. "Every girl must have a Hope Chest, child, for when she gets married. You need linens, sheets, pillow slips, nighties, undergarments, and your wedding dress. Your uncle and I will provide silver and dishes, of course, since fine things are scarce around here and will need to be bought in Georgetown or Denver."

Annie looked at the chest and snorted. She certainly did not want to get married, and she would rather spend time with Soft Dove than sew. But Aunt Marian would hear no dissent and put Annie to work every morning on a new piece of hope for the chest.

During the days following the play, Annie soon grew quite restless. Her isolation at the cabin was becoming intolerable. She wanted to visit Emma McLeary and help in the school, and she secretly yearned for an excuse to see Will Redmond again.

One night after dinner, Annie gathered up her nerve and made an appeal. "Uncle Ben, would you let me ride one of your horses into town?"

Both Ben and Marian looked up from their plates.

"Why would you want to ride into town alone, girl?" Ben harrumphed. "We've taken you there a couple of times, now haven't we?"

"Yes, and I do appreciate it, Uncle Ben," continued Annie quickly, "but I want to go in the daytime. I want to visit some of the friends I've made there."

"Like who?" asked Marian, her eyes narrowing.

"Emma McLeary, for one," stated Annie. "She said I might help her in the school sometimes. I'm a good rider; I've been riding since I was small. And I'd be back before dark, I promise."

"You're not planning to sneak away to meet with any of those miners who have been fawning over you, are you?" asked Aunt Marian suspiciously.

Annie felt herself redden.

"No, Aunt Marian," she began steadily, her head high, "I made a terrible choice at school, but I don't intend to make another. I thought I was in love. And it cost me my father, my home, and my education. I'll not make that mistake again, I can promise you."

Ben and Marian exchanged glances, then Ben replied, "And that is why we want to see you married, girl, and settled. Of course you may use one of the horses. Just tell me which one and when, and I'll have it saddled and ready for you. One of the hands will ride with you."

"No, I don't need one of the hands. I can go alone; I promise to stay on the road and be very careful. Please, Uncle Ben, don't make one of the hands come along as if I were a baby."

Ben rubbed his chin thoughtfully as he glanced at Marian. She shook her head slightly, but Ben replied, "I suppose if you're old enough to marry, you're old enough to ride alone into town."

Marian started to protest, but Ben cut her off with a look. Marian, who still had a look of doubt on her face, said stonily, "Don't give anyone a chance to gossip about you, Annie Mitchell, and that's my final word."

Annie beamed with happiness. "Thank you, Uncle Ben, thank you. And I'll be careful, Aunt Marian, not to cause any gossip."

Annie rode into town the very next day. The horse Uncle Ben had given her was a roan mare with a sweet disposition. Annie had often gone to the field and fed the horses sugar, and this one seemed to remember her kindness. Annie named her Sugar.

The ride to Grand Lake was very enjoyable. The aspen leaves were a crisp green and shaped like coins, light on top and dark on the bottom. The fluttery snapping sound they made as the wind whipped them had a soothing effect on Annie.

As she gazed up the trunks of the towering jack pines and watched them gently sway back and forth against the blue of the sky, she thought how blessed the Indians had been once, living as one amid these forests. For all of this to be taken away, it was no wonder they felt so much anger toward the Whites.

When Annie arrived at the village, she stopped first at the Farview House to say hello to her friend, Lydia Elder.

"Annie, how wonderful to see you," Mrs. Elder chirped. "You sit down and have a piece of my chokecherry pie. It's fresh out of the oven, and I've got some clabbered cream to top it."

Before Annie could protest, she was sitting at the long polished table with a steaming cup of coffee and a huge piece of pie.

"Did you come alone?" asked the kind woman.

"Yes, Uncle Ben gave me a horse to ride so now I can come anytime I want," gushed Annie between bites. "I was getting so bored up there. Emma McLeary said I could help at the school, but I couldn't come to Grand Lake without stopping in to see you."

Annie told Mrs. Elder about her life at the Dailys and how she'd become friends with Soft Dove. For some reason, she didn't mention Bear Hawk because he still made her a bit nervous.

Curiosity getting the better of her good sense, Annie decided to ask Lydia why Will Redmond hated her Uncle so.

"It started some years ago, I expect," began Mrs. Elder as she smoothed out her apron several times. "Will and his brothers had just come here from back east somewhere...I think Missouri."

"Are his brothers still around? I haven't met them," said Annie.

"Oh yes, one works over at Teller for that lawyer fellow...oh what is his name?" mused Lydia. "Miller, that's right, George Miller. I haven't heard very nice things about him, but you know how lawyers are. I even heard he killed someone back east, but that might not be true.

"Will's other brother placer mines, I believe, down by Willow Creek. Well, the boys, especially Will, had become active in the Democratic Party, and most folks around here were Democrats until the War of Secession. Then afterwards, some began saying that to be a Democrat was the same as being a traitor. Everybody chose sides, some Republicans and some Democrats.

"Will was only twenty-two then, you know, young and kinda brash. He and your uncle got into an argument over at the Dandy Saloon, and Will hit Ben Daily...knocked him flat on his back. Ben filed charges on Will and had him arrested, but nothing ever come of it except hard feelings."

"But that's not enough to want someone dead, is it?" asked Annie.

"A couple years later, after Will became the Undersheriff, he and his brother, Bass, filed claim on a mine up by Lulu City called the 'Sedalia'. When the boys were going to sell it, Ben Daily spread it around that it was worthless and scared off the buyers. Then he bought it cheap himself through another party and sold it for a big profit. That really galled Will. It's just been one thing after another, Annie, and it's built up over the years."

Annie thought over what Lydia had said. She could understand more of Will's anger toward her Uncle. He'd been ill-used by Ben and couldn't seem to get over it. Hate is a very damaging passion, Annie mused.

After the two women had talked for awhile more, Annie left, though promising to return, and went directly to the schoolhouse. When she tiptoed into the back door, Emma McLeary was reading one of Annie's favorite stories, "The Legend of Sleepy Hollow".

Emma transported both Annie and the students into a fantasy-world of goblins with heads made of pumpkins. Every child in the room was totally engrossed in the tale. When it was over, Emma looked up and noticed Annie for the first time.

"Class, we have a visitor," Emma exclaimed. Twelve pairs of curious eyes turned in Annie's direction.

"I know her," said one of the boys, "she's the new gal all the fellers are goony over."

Everyone, including Annie, broke into peals of laughter.

Annie was quickly accepted into the warm hearts of the children, and Emma allowed her to tutor the little ones while she instructed the older students. When the dismissal bell rang and the children swarmed out of the small schoolroom, Annie asked Emma if she might help again sometime.

"I'm happy for the assistance, Annie, so of course you may come," laughed Emma, "anytime at all."

Annie's days were busy the next several weeks. She dutifully sewed for the Hope Chest in the morning, then either went into Grand Lake or explored the forests with Soft Dove in the afternoon while her aunt slept. She didn't understand how Bear Hawk knew which days she was around the cabin, but he always showed up and stared at her, making her extremely uncomfortable.

Because the population of Grand County was so spread out, dances were held every Saturday night either at Grand Lake, Lulu City, Gaskill, or Teller. Annie was only allowed to attend the ones at Grand Lake as the others were too far away and usually became too rowdy.

Though Will sometimes attended the dances, Annie never saw him dance. When she allowed her eyes to drift in his direction, he was always either deep in conversation or staring intently at her, which could stop her heart. But he never approached her or spoke to her.

During the days Annie spent with Soft Dove, the Indian girl introduced Annie to the wonders of the Earth. Soft Dove taught Annie to recognize medicinal herbs, healing flowers, and edible plants and roots. In their favorite pond, the two girls often shed their outer garments and romped like children in the clear cold water. Annie came to love and appreciate the majestic mountains in which she now lived, and she couldn't imagine returning to the muggy, chigger filled land of her birth.

On one outing to the creek, Bear Hawk and two Utes made a surprise appearance. The girls were sitting on the ground with their backs resting against a giant lodge pole pine. Annie was glad she had already dressed, even though her hair was still wet and she was barelegged. It was disconcerting, being stared at by the Indians. Especially Bear Hawk, who tended to make her feel vulnerable with his severe scrutiny.

Soft Dove said a few words in her language to the men, and Bear Hawk replied haughtily, still gazing at Annie. Annie could feel her face redden and stared at her hands in her lap.

Though Annie didn't understand what Soft Dove and Bear Hawk were saying, she knew they were discussing her. She kept hearing the word Bear Hawk used to refer to her which meant 'Hair of Blood'.

When Bear Hawk stalked over to Annie and lifted a handful of her copper tresses to show to his friends, she recoiled in terror. When he saw her fear, he laughed and said something which made the others laugh as well. Angrily Annie jerked her hair out of his hands.

"Don't do that, Bear Hawk," exclaimed Annie angrily.

Bear Hawk suddenly stopped smiling and pierced her with his intense gaze. Annie quickly gathered up her belongings and started back toward the cabin.

Soft Dove caught up with her. "He doesn't mean to be disrespectful, Annie."

"Why does he stare at me so?" asked Annie, glancing back to see if he were following.

"My brother is sometimes hard to understand," was Soft Dove's only reply.

When the two girls reached the cabin, Bear Hawk and his friends were already at the back door, waiting silently.

Soft Dove spoke to Bear Hawk, but he refused to look at her when he replied. She argued for a few moments, then turned in frustration.

"Pay no attention to him. He says he is going to wait here until your uncle comes home."

"Why would he do that? Isn't that dangerous?" asked Annie incredulously.

"He will not say."

Uneasy, Annie moved around the stoic Indians and entered the cabin with Soft Dove. She went to her room to change clothes while Soft Dove began preparing the evening meal.

Annie heard Ben Daily's horse approaching and ran to the window. Coming home to three half-naked Utes at his front door, Annie saw Ben automatically reach for his pistol.

She ran to the front door, flung it open, and yelled, "No, Uncle Ben, don't shoot them."

Soft Dove was at her side in an instant, followed by Aunt Marian, who had just come down from her nap and was looking a bit disheveled and confused.

"What is going on here?" Marian whined. "Why are all of these savages here? Soft Dove, explain the meaning of this!"

Bear Hawk began speaking Ute... in a very loud voice. Everyone took a step back in surprise, and after a moment, Soft Dove gasped. Annie turned to look at her friend, only to see Soft Dove staring wide-eyed back at her.

"What's the matter, Soft Dove?" Annie asked in alarm as she turned from Soft Dove's stricken face back to Bear Hawk's impassive one.

Soft Dove answered quietly, "My brother is offering for you, Annie."

"What? What does that mean?" Annie cried, fear crawling along her spine.

"It means that he wants you for his *wife*," Soft Dove answered. "I told him that it is impossible, Annie, but he is stubborn. He won't listen to me."

Annie was stunned beyond words. She stared at Bear Hawk and thought of their brief encounters. He had always treated her with disdain and even laughed at her derisively. Why would he want to marry her?

"It's a very high honor, Annie. My brother could have any woman he wants from the tribe, and with his hatred of the Whites, I am very shocked that he would choose to take *you* as wife."

"I've always thought he hated me, Soft Dove," responded Annie, confused.

"He is too proud, and he keeps his feelings inside. But he is a good and honorable man, Annie," stated Soft Dove, pride evident in her voice.

"I cannot marry him though, Soft Dove," replied Annie kindly. "My Uncle would never allow it, and I-I don't love him."

"I know, but you would come to love him if you saw the fierceness of his heart. He is a great hunter and would protect you with his life."

"No, Soft Dove, it could never be! Should I talk to him?" asked Annie tentatively.

"He is too headstrong," spat Soft Dove. "Once he makes up his mind about something, his head becomes as hard as stone."

Fearfully, Annie glanced from the braves to her uncle to Soft Dove, the tension so taut it was almost humming.

Soft Dove turned to Ben Daily as he climbed down from his horse. She began to translate to Ben in a formal voice. "This is Bear Hawk, son of Bear Claw, respected hunter. He offers two ponies for the one called 'Blood Hair'." She stopped speaking and looked back at Annie with worry shadowing her eyes.

"What? What?" blustered Ben, his hand going to the holster at his side. "What does he mean 'two ponies'?"

Bear Hawk pointed at the two horses standing behind him, then at Annie. He said something else in his language.

Soft Dove continued to translate to Ben, "He wants you to take those two horses as a bride price for your niece."

Ben finally understood Soft Dove's words. He broke into laughter, holding his belly as it shook. Annie glanced fearfully at Bear Hawk and saw his rugged features darken with rage.

Still laughing, Ben turned to Soft Dove and wheezed, "Tell the young man that we don't do it that way. Annie is worth far more than only two ponies." He broke into loud guffaws again, and Aunt Marian grabbed Annie and dragged her back into the cabin. She slammed the door and ran for the rifle over the mantle.

"No, Aunt Marian," cried Annie as she jerked the gun out of Marian's hands.

"That heathen is trying to steal you, Annie, don't you understand? I've heard tell of white women being stoned for less, after being taken by savages," purported Marian, her eyes a little wild.

"No, Aunt Marian, don't worry, he can't force me to go with him," Annie replied evenly, as she tried to calm the older woman. "Uncle Ben is a great talker. He'll simply talk Bear Hawk out of it. You've seen him do that before, now haven't you?"

Annie had returned the rifle to its resting place and was holding both of Marian's shaking hands. At that moment, the front door of the cabin opened; Ben and Soft Dove entered. Annie heard the sounds of retreating horses and let out a sigh of relief.

Soft Dove's face was blank, devoid of any emotion she might be feeling. Without looking at Annie, she disappeared into the kitchen. A few seconds later, Annie heard the back door open and then quietly close.

Annie stared at Uncle Ben who still had an amused look on his face. "What happened out there?"

"Nothing, my dear, don't you worry your pretty little head," Ben began as he moved toward the sideboard where his whiskey was kept. After pouring himself a good-sized slug and downing it, he turned to the two women and said calmly, "Bear Hawk has offered me two ponies for you, Annie, but I told him no. I think you are worth at least three." He burst into laughter again.

"And he just went away? But where did Soft Dove go?" Annie asked.

"I have no idea," was his flippant reply. "Now let's eat; I'm starved."

But Soft Dove was gone, forever, and Annie was sorely grieved by the loss of her friend.

A few weeks later, on the first of July, Annie stopped in to see Lydia Elder. She told her about the incident with Bear Hawk.

"Lord, child, what a ruckus you seem to cause!" Mrs. Elder smiled and put her hand over Annie's. "If the young miners sparring over you isn't enough, now you've got Indian boys after you, too. But I wouldn't worry about it; there hasn't been any trouble with the Utes in quite a few years. And it looks like you'll be off the market soon anyway. I hear there's going to be a wedding in the near future."

Annie looked confused. "Whose?"

"It's all over town, Annie. You and J. C. Brashears. I assumed you've been busy planning your trousseau, and that's why we haven't seen you in town lately."

Annie's eyes widened in shock. J. C. Brashears? That man who owns one of the mines? How could she be expected to marry someone who is nearly as old as her uncle?

"But it's not true," Annie exclaimed. "I only met Mr. Brashears once, and he's...he's OLD! Uncle Ben would never agree to it."

Mrs. Elder's smile faded. Pity replaced it. "Around here, Annie, there are about fifty men to every woman as you have seen. But most are miners or lumberjacks with little money and no future. I suppose your uncle wants you to be taken care of, and Mr. Brashears has a lot of money..."

"I don't care about money," Annie wailed. "I want love!"

"Now Annie," Lydia said kindly as she wrapped her arm around the girl's slumped shoulders, "what could a young girl like you know about love? Believe me, child, love fades. Then you'll be glad of his money and the security it will bring.

"When my husband died, God rest his soul, I didn't know what I'd do. Thank the Lord, some of the good men around here had a house-raising for me, and I have this house as security. Security is a good thing for a woman, especially out here in a land dominated by men. Your aunt and uncle are only thinking about your future."

"My uncle is only thinking of his own political future," Annie spat vehemently. Then she put her head in her arms, tears welling up. She knew a lot more about love than anyone could ever guess. And because of that forbidden knowledge, she knew how awful an alliance without passion might be. Just the thought of J. C. Brashears touching her made her cringe.

"Come, come, dry your eyes. I'm sorry to have been the one to tell you. I thought you already knew. I'm so sorry, honey. It won't be so bad. He's rich. You'll have everything you ever wanted. Please don't cry, Annie."

Annie wiped her eyes with a napkin and rose. "I-I have to go."

Lydia watched the unhappy girl ride away. Anne didn't feel much like going to the school now, so she turned toward the lake and rode around to the uninhabited side.

She stopped at a clearing beside the crystal water and let Sugar graze. Annie walked down to the edge of the blue lake and gazed across to the village on the other side. Cocooned by the surrounding shadowy mountains, Annie's heart lifted for a moment as it always did by the land's timeless beauty.

Hopelessness quickly overwhelmed her again because Annie knew that if her uncle and aunt had decided she would marry, then there was nothing she could do about it. She was at their mercy, and the thought brought new tears to her already reddened eyes. She sat in the grass at the water's edge and sobbed miserably.

A few moments later, she heard the approach of a horse. When she looked up through tearstained eyes, she was surprised to see Will Redmond dismounting. Clad in a brown shirt which barely contained his wide shoulders and trousers which fit like a second skin on his long lean legs, Annie felt a little breathless as he approached. His hat was at a rakish angle, not pulled low on his forehead as he usually wore it.

She quickly wiped her tears with the hem of her dress and sat up straight.

"We keep meeting at the edge of this lake, don't we?" he said with a hint of humor in his voice which went directly against his otherwise unsmiling face.

"Did you follow me again?" Annie asked, feeling awkward.

"Yes, I have to admit that I did. I was heading for the Farview, and I saw you leave. I-I wanted to talk to you," he said, still standing stiffly at her side.

She craned her neck up to see into his shadowed face but could read nothing. She stared back across the lake until he finally sat down beside her.

"Well, at least you still have on your shoes," he mentioned sarcastically.

Still close to tears, Annie brought up her knees, wrapped her arms around them, and laid her head down. Will instinctively raised his arm and almost put it around her shoulders, but stopped himself.

"Are you all right?" he asked tentatively.

"Yes," she muttered into her arms.

"Do you want to be left alone?"

She looked up quickly. "No."

They gazed at each other, both wanting to say something but lacking the confidence.

Finally, Will broke the silence. "If there is ever anything I can do for you, would you tell me?"

"My uncle has decided that I'm to marry J.C. Brashears," Annie stated, frustration turning to anger. "But that should make *you* happy. Didn't you once tell me to marry someone rich who would take care of me? Well, now you're going to get your wish."

Will wasn't expecting her tone, and her vehemence surprised him. He had heard that a marriage had been arranged for her by that snake of an uncle with one of the owners of the Wolverine. Will hadn't even met the man in question, but he hated Brashears already for the pictures which appeared in his mind's eye of the wedding night.

He forced himself to say, "Maybe Brashears ain't all that bad, Annie. At least he's rich and he *can* take good care of you. At least he'll get you away from Ben Daily."

"I don't even know him, Will! I'm going to be forced to marry someone I don't know and don't love. And he's my uncle's best friend apparently. And he's so OLD!" she wailed.

This time Will did put his arm around her shoulders, and she turned her face to cry into his shirt. He hated Ben Daily for making her so miserable. Ever since the dance at the Nickerson House, Will had had feelings for Annie he couldn't control or understand. How he ached to grab her up and kiss her properly!

Will hated the emotions she evoked in him. Why couldn't he get her off his mind? No woman had ever had such an effect on him. Marcy, from the Antlers Saloon at the Springs, had been enough to take care of his physical needs since he had arrived in Grand County eight years ago. But lately, Annie's face seemed to get in the way...even with Marcy. He'd stopped going to the prostitute as often, and he always seemed to leave wanting more of something of which he couldn't even put a name.

And here he was, with his arm around this girl that he desperately wanted to take care of... and love.

"Whoa there," Will breathed, then realized he'd said it out loud, causing Annie to sit up and stare at him with those big blue eyes which made him weak in the knees.

Again Will had jerked away from her as if he'd been bitten.

Annie had felt so protected and safe in the crook of his arm, breathing in the male and soap smell of his shirt pressed to her nose. When he pulled away suddenly, she felt bereft of something she only knew she wanted more.

"The best thing you could do, Annie, is to marry that bastard and get the hell out of Grand Lake," Will growled with more feeling that he meant to show.

Wretchedly, Annie watched him leap onto his horse and gallop away.

At dinner that night, Annie pushed her food around on the plate, waiting for her aunt or uncle to break the bad news to her, which was already known by everyone in Grand Lake.

Finally, when she thought she might start screaming, Ben Daily pushed his chair back. He propped his hands on his big belly which looked as if it would pop the buttons of his waistcoat.

"Annie, my girl," he began in his 'speechifying' voice she was coming to hate, "your aunt and I have recently been in touch with someone who has asked for your hand in marriage. For awhile now we have debated the issue, you see, because we only want what is best for you."

The young girl wanted to snort rudely at the selfish man but merely stared at her hands clutched tightly in her lap.

"This man has very high connections, some all the way up to the White House, I'm told," broke in Marian Daily. "He's from a good family in England, and he's quite well-off. You would want for nothing. He'll build you a huge mansion, and you will be the toast of Georgetown society. Well now, he sounds so good, you're lucky I'm already a married woman!" she cackled.

"Have you already said yes for me?" asked Annie quietly.

"Well, he *did* offer more than two ponies," Ben chuckled, then became serious when he saw her stricken face. "You could do worse, my girl, and yes, I have already given my permission."

"Do I have anything to say in the matter?" asked Annie.

"No, you don't," replied Marian sternly.

"Well, I suppose it is settled then. May I please be excused?" asked Annie quietly.

"Sure, my girl, sure. Go give it some thought, and you'll soon realize how lucky you are."

Annie went into her room and cried herself to sleep.

The next afternoon after luncheon was served by the middle Threckald girl Marian had hired in Soft Dove's place, Annie was relieved when her Aunt went upstairs to nap. Annie had been informed that her 'fiancé' would be coming for dinner that night to make the engagement official, and she needed to get away by herself for awhile.

Climbing onto Sugar's broad back, Annie galloped north on the road which led away from Grand Lake. She had never been this way which led to Gaskill and Lulu City, the two mining towns closest to Grand Lake.

"I'll run away," she fumed miserably, but she knew she had nowhere to go. Her father didn't want her, so there'd be no help there. Soon, she would be tied down to a stranger whom she didn't know and didn't love. What a bleak future! Miserably, she took the left fork toward Gaskill which lay at the base of the Bowen-Baker Gulch.

The rutted road encompassed by primeval forest abruptly opened up into barren, stump-filled fields surrounding the ugly mining town. Smaller than Grand Lake, Gaskill had fewer buildings and nearly all were of rough logs. No plank sidewalks protected the walkers from the muddy main street, and though there were a few businesses, the biggest buildings were the Horgraine Hotel and the Robertson Boarding House where most of the miners who worked at the Wolverine Mine resided.

The Wolverine, the largest and most pretentious mine in the area, was located on the south slope of Bowen Mountain, nine miles northwest of Grand Lake. Since the boom had started to wane in 1880, though, many miners had found that the metals were not very forthcoming and were of such low grade that it took a lot to make only a little money.

Annie passed the Mercantile, saloon, and survey office. She headed for the Horgraine which sat up on a hill overlooking the town. She yearned for a cup of hot coffee. She dismounted and tied Sugar loosely to the hitching post. Annie lifted her skirt and made her way up the steep stairs and entered the double doors of the Horgraine Hotel.

The bell counter on the left was deserted. To her right the lobby was impressively decorated with tasseled red velvet curtains and matching chair coverings. A huge ornate fireplace built of porphyry - a fine shiny stone of iridescent colors - decorated the wall opposite the bell table. Gleaming in the light from the large floor to ceiling windows on either side, Annie wondered if the fireplace was only decorative or if it was truly serviceable in the deadly cold winters of which she had been warned would come. On the walls were mounted heads of deer, elk, mountain sheep, and bear stuffed to give the impression of still being alive.

Annie slowly dragged herself toward the arched doorway of the dining hall located at the far end of the building. Before she reached it, she heard the uproar of male voices, raised in heated debate, coming from the dining room. When she surveyed the room, she saw the entire area was filled to brimming with men, some in fancy-dressed suits and others in dirty denim workshirts worn by miners, lumberjacks, and ranchers.

As she scanned the room for an empty table, away from the cigar smoke and loud voices, it suddenly went deadly silent. To her dismay, she found that all eyes were upon her. Reddening, she turned to leave then felt a strong hand grip her elbow in a painful vise.

"I don't know how you got here, or why you're here alone," hissed a tense-sounding voice in her ear, "but this is definitely not the place for you to be right now."

Annie looked up into the stern face of Will Redmond. She allowed him to usher her out of the hotel and down the stairs to her waiting horse. Once there, though, she jerked her arm out of his grasp and turned on him rabidly.

"God's Teeth! Who do you think you are, Mr. Redmond, to be pushing me around?" she began as pent-up frustration and anger loosened her tongue. "I have just as much right in that hotel as any of those men do. I rode up here alone, and I intend to have a cup of coffee...alone, so get out of my way."

She tried to push past him, but he stood like granite in front of her.

"Settle down, wildcat, and listen to me," he said gruffly as he watched her fury double itself. "In there is a political meeting going on, and it's no place for a lone female."

Annie tried once again to get around him, but he grabbed both of her arms. In her rage, she swiftly brought up her knee to his groin. He doubled over, holding himself and groaning.

Annie's anger dissolved instantly when she saw his face go white as he writhed in pain.

"Oh Lordy, what have I done?" she paled. Will tried to breathe deeply and not pass out. "Will, I'm sorry, I just reacted without thinking."

A few moments later, when Will could stand straight again and his pale face regained some color, he grasped Annie's arm even harder than before, and with a furious look, dragged her across the muddy street toward a large clapboard building. Will slung open the double doors and pushed her into the darkened livery. With a quick backward glance, he pulled the two doors together, banging them so hard that some of the horses began to neigh in fright.

Annie went rigid with fear, unsure of what this man, whom her uncle had said had a hairpin temper and a violent nature, would do to her in retaliation. She watched his wide back as he took several deep breaths and let them out slowly. Then he turned toward her.

"I-I'm sorry, Will, I really am," she said in a little voice. "I didn't mean to hurt you, but you made me so mad, holding me like that and telling me what to do. I'm so tired of everyone telling me what to do."

"I guess I can stop worrying about you," Will said as he removed his hat and wiped the beads of sweat from his brow with his shirt sleeve. "You could pretty much destroy a man with that knee of yours. I pity any man who tries to take advantage of Annie Mitchell."

Annie saw the glint of his teeth in the dark and knew he was teasing her. She visibly relaxed and moved toward him. As she looked up into his shadowed face, she asked meekly, "So you're not angry with me?"

Will paused a second then suddenly reached for her, and she found herself in his arms, kissing him. Her feet no longer touched the ground, and it was preferable because her knees would have given way beneath her.

Nothing had ever come close to the breadth of sensations flashing through her system. The intense softness of his lips upon hers, his tongue snaking into her parted mouth, teasing her own tongue into response.

Nothing existed in the world but the two of them, clinging to each other in the darkness of the stable. Annie felt that pull deep inside her which 'nice' girls weren't supposed to know about, and she realized that she wanted Will Redmond, more than she had ever wanted anyone or anything in her life.

When he gently released her mouth, Annie wanted to cry out for more. He saw her half-closed eyes and swollen lips and knew the hay behind them was all too tempting. Slowly he lowered her to the ground.

Dizzy, Annie swayed as the warmth of him left her breathless. She opened her eyes and looked up into his face... only to see regret and something else she couldn't decipher stamped upon it. Suddenly embarrassed at being so wanton, she believed the regret she saw in his eyes was for kissing her, so she quickly backed away, straightening her mussed hair and wrinkled clothing.

"I don't know what came over me, Annie," Will said sheepishly. "I'm sorry."

"Don't be, Undersheriff Redmond," Annie retorted haughtily, trying to cover the searing ache which nearly overwhelmed her, "I've been kissed before."

She turned on her heel and tried to pull open the livery doors, but they were too heavy to budge. Almost in tears, she turned back to Will but found she couldn't meet his eyes.

"Before you go, Annie, I want to tell you why I dragged you out of there," Will began unsteadily. "No decent woman goes to a place like a hotel alone unless she's looking...looking... for a...companion... for the night, do you understand? I was trying to save your reputation."

"Oh, I see," Annie's eyes flashed in anger, "you didn't want any of those men to think me a whore, so you dragged me in here to treat me like one yourself."

"What are you talking about?" cried Will, frustration turning to anger at her stubborn willfulness. "I merely kissed you; I didn't treat you like a whore. If I had wanted to treat you like a whore, you'd be on your back in the hay right now with your petticoats over your pretty head."

Annie reached up to slap him, but he automatically reared back, so she missed. Frustrated, she balled both fists and hit him on his chest. Then she twirled and faced the door.

"Would you please open these doors?" She hissed through her teeth.

"Gladly," was his dry reply.

Annie ran across the street to Sugar and tried to mount. But since there was no mounting stone, she put one foot in the stirrup and was dancing around on the other foot as Sugar backed away. All at once, she felt two strong hands on her backside which boosted her into the saddle. Without a glance back, she reined her horse and bounded out of town at full gallop.

Annie's lips burned as she remembered the searing kiss and her own capricious behavior. Overcome by embarrassment, she thought how she had explored his mouth with her own as she had caressed his neck and run her fingers through his thick hair. How she had intimately fitted her body to his and wished for it never to end. And worst of all, how she still quivered with excitement at the thought of being on her back under him in the hay.

CHAPTER THREE

When Annie arrived back at the Daily's cabin, her face was flushed, both from the cool alpine air and from total humiliation. She had ridden Sugar hard down the mountain so she spent extra time rubbing the pony's lathered body.

Annie leaned against Sugar's sweaty coat. As she inhaled the sweet tang of the animal mixed with the odor of fresh hay, memories resurfaced of the forbidden deliciousness she had felt in Redmond's arms.

Tears filled her eyes when she recalled how unabashedly she had kissed him back, and if he'd made the slightest move to go further, Annie knew she would not have had the will to stop him.

"I must be a bad person like Pa said," Annie choked as she buried her face in Sugar's warmth. "It's probably best that I marry that horrible Englishman before I shame Uncle Ben and Aunt Marian with my disgraceful yearnings."

After seeing to Sugar's needs, Annie dragged herself into the house and went directly to her room. J. C. Brashears was coming in a few hours, and she must make herself presentable. Annie's movements as she washed in the little basin were leaden as an abysmal despair pressed down upon her.

She chose a subdued navy dress which buttoned to her chin and down her wrists. She had always hated the garment, but for tonight's event, it was the perfect frock, mirroring the bleakness of her mood.

Annie sat on the edge of the bed, staring at nothing, as the sinking sun's rays filtered across the floor of her room. When the shadows deepened and darkness began to turn her world as gray as her hope for the future, she heard Uncle Ben enter the parlor speaking in a loud voice. A quick rap on the bedroom door made Annie jump.

"Annie," rasped Aunt Marian, "Mr. Brashears is here."

She forced her shoulders back and raised her head, trying for a dignified demeanor. After taking a deep breath, she opened the door.

J. C. Brashears was standing beside the fireplace, casually leaning one arm on the mantel while the other held a glass of whiskey. He was listening to Ben complain about the faction in Grand Lake who had succeeded in moving the County Seat there from Hot Sulphur Springs.

"The Board of Canvassers even disallowed the ballots during the election of '80 because sixty-two voters from Grand Lake hadn't even lived in the County for the six month requirement. It was all legal and aboveboard," Ben expounded.

"Then why, pray tell, sir," began Brashears in his clipped British accent, "is the Seat still in Grand Lake?"

"Because the Board of Commissioners, headed by one George E. Miller, overturned it with the help of a judge he had in his pocket," finished Ben angrily. "But it's not going to remain so, I can promise you that. I have friends at the Springs who will back me in anything I propose so long as they get the Seat back there again." He threw back his whiskey in one gulp.

Suddenly he became aware of Marian and Annie standing quietly in the doorway. "Well, here is our little Annie, J. C.," Ben gushed as he drew Annie into the room.

She kept her eyes lowered, afraid that both men would see the feelings written openly on her face.

J. C. Brashears found one of her hands which she'd had clasped tightly in front of her and raised it to his lips. She glanced up as he pressed his lips to it while raking her with cold steely eyes. Annie shivered.

"I am most pleased to see you again, Miss Mitchell," he replied haughtily after releasing her hand.

Annie curtsied, using the movement to wipe off the clammy wetness she still felt on her hand. Brashears was as tall as Redmond, but not as broad of shoulder. The well-cut make of his suit of white linen over a light blue silk vest and matching cravat was complimented with a diamond stick pin.

His boots were of the finest kid leather, and Annie wondered how he kept them from being ruined by the muddy streets. His hair was clipped short around his ears making his austere face seem more prominent, and a brief image of those thin lips pressed against hers left her repulsed. Her expressive face showed her horror, and she found that she could utter no reply. Silence hung heavily in the air.

"Let's eat," Aunt Marian exclaimed suddenly, relieving the tension.

Annie felt as a bird might when a snake has it hypnotized and was about to strike. Wide-eyed, she numbly allowed Brashears to tuck her cold hand into the crook of his arm and be led to the dining table.

She answered the few questions J. C. aimed at her, but the conversation at the table was mostly dominated by Ben Daily. She felt Brashears' eyes on her occasionally but was determined not to meet those disturbingly dead eyes again.

While she pushed her food around on her plate, she contemplated the years ahead having to sit across a dinner table from this man who was so much older and now a bit frightening, too. Annie's tears were very near the surface, and Marian noticed Annie's lack of appetite.

"It's no wonder Annie keeps her figure, Mr. Brashears. See the way she eats like a bird?"

Annie stared at her aunt, alarmed at how close the comparison matched her earlier one. She glanced at Brashears, sure he must be hiding sharpened fangs and a forked tongue behind his well-mannered appearance.

After dinner, Ben patted his bulging belly and said, "J.C., why don't you take my niece out onto the porch for a breath of fresh air?"

Annie shot her uncle a pleading look.

Brashears declared, "Tis a fine night for just that."

He slipped a shawl from the hook over the front door around Annie's shaking shoulders as he pulled her to her feet.

"I don't think that is wise," she sputtered. "I might be coming down with a cold, Aunt Marian, and the night air wouldn't be good for me. Would it?" She thought Marian might see the desperate look on her face, but her hopes were dashed when Marian gave them both a push out the door.

"You two go get to know each other," she sang gaily. "A little mountain air will be good for you, child. Especially in the company of a nice gentleman like Mr. Brashears."

After the door closed and Annie was left in the darkness with the disturbing man, she immediately moved away from him to the other end of the porch. He followed.

"Miss Mitchell, your shyness with me is unwarranted," his oily voice came from close behind her. Annie drew the shawl more closely around her, thinking the knitted wool might somehow protect her from J. C. Brashears.

When he laid his hands on her shoulders, she shrank at his touch. He turned her around until she faced him. She stared at the diamond stick pin holding his cravat until he tipped her chin up.

"I won't bite you, Miss Mitchell, not yet anyway," he pulled his lips back from his teeth in what Annie supposed was a smile, though she realized she had never seen him do it before. It was slightly appalling. "I assume you know that I have asked your uncle for your hand in marriage, my dear."

"Y-yes, I know," Annie managed to squeak while dragging her eyes away from his unsettling silver ones.

"I have already received your uncle and aunt's blessing, but I wanted to formally ask yours now." He bent down on one knee, still holding her hand.

"Miss Mitchell, I would be honored if you would be my wife," he stated formally.

Her life had never been her own, Annie realized, to make her own choices. A man had always been there to make them for her, and she suddenly experienced a piercing resentment.

"I do not love you, Mr. Brashears," she stated honestly.

"Don't be ridiculous; love has nothing whatsoever to do with it, Miss Mitchell," J. C. Brashears replied bluntly as he released her hand and rose smoothly to his feet. "I am a businessman and have certain needs which must be met. I need an attractive wife to hostess social affairs, to stand by my side as I further my political career, and to give me heirs.

"I have never needed nor desired the conversation or company of women except in my bed; your breed is infinitely too silly and empty-headed. I will probably have many mistresses through the years which will be none of your concern. So if you expect 'love' from me, you will be sorely disappointed. This is purely a satisfactory business arrangement."

Annie was appalled at the cold-blooded future he described. She was to be nothing more than a breed mare, quietly doing his bidding and providing him with long-faced children. The chill of his manner and the loneliness which he promised would soon freeze the bloom from her cheek.

But maybe that coldness would be better than the gnawing, hungry feeling she got every time her thoughts turned to Will Redmond. She knew she could never hope to have Will Redmond on his knees in front of her. And she knew Ben and Marian Daily would just as soon abandon her if she disobeyed them. She felt friendless and hopeless.

"I feel I have no choice; so, yes, Mr. Brashears, I will marry you," she heard herself answer.

"So it is settled then," he stated briskly as he again kissed her hand. "We will discuss the date at another time. The evening grows late, and I must be on my way. Give your Uncle and Aunt my regards and thanks for dinner. Good night, my dear."

He left her staring after him as he mounted his horse and cantered off into the darkness.

"What have I done?" were Annie's only thoughts.

On the morning of July Fourth, Annie, along with Marian and Ben, rode into Grand Lake early. The town, decorated with banners across the main street, had planned many festivities, including a spectacular fireworks show over the lake, a play by the Repertory Group, and another all night dance at the Nickerson House.

As she and the Dailys arrived in town, Annie could see that many of the miners were already well into their cups for the celebrations. After witnessing several of them staggering down the main street, shooting into the air occasionally, Annie realized that the Sheriff and the Undersheriff would soon be busy handling all of the drunken revelers. Her heart sank, knowing that she would probably not see Will Redmond on this day.

Earlier that morning, she'd been relieved to hear that J. C. Brashears had removed himself to Georgetown on business so she wouldn't have to suffer his imperious presence.

One last time before she was forced to marry, she could dance the night away. By next Fourth of July, she'd be required to sit dismally on the sidelines with the other matrons and watch the young girls have fun.

The Farview House was their first stop, for Mrs. Elder and her minions were serving a hearty breakfast and then would be busily preparing a feast for the afternoon meal. After eating, Annie and Marian went into the parlor with the other ladies while the men sat out on the porch, smoking and talking of mining and politics.

Aunt Marian made a point of telling everyone that Annie was newly engaged to J. C. Brashears, magnate of the Wolverine Mine and other holdings in Georgetown.

"My guess is that he has gone to pick out an engagement ring for our Annie," gushed Marian. The women of the County, though few, stuck together even when their men argued over different political views. The ladies were most enthusiastic in their congratulations to Annie.

"Will you live in Georgetown after you're married?" asked Mrs. Raymond, the wife of the owner of the Assay Office. She was dark-eyed and pretty, even after five children, each only a year apart, and still another on the way.

"I..I...don't know," stammered Annie, uncomfortably.

"Annie," squealed Emma McLeary as she gave her a big hug, "you might beat *me* to the altar. Who will take my place at the school now? I was counting on you."

Annie smiled wanly at her friend, realizing that her dream of teaching was also being dashed by the future union.

Mrs. Elder entered the parlor, stating that she intended to 'rest a spell', and she caught the last exchange. She eyed Annie's reaction and saw the tears start to form.

"Annie, dear," she cooed, "would you come into my room? I'd like to show you something." Annie arose with Marian right behind her. "No, Marian, this is for Annie's eyes only. You wait out here with the others."

Marian harrumphed, "Well, I never. I *am* her nearest relative, after all." But since it was Lydia Elder's rooms to which she led the wan girl, Marian flounced into a chair for more gossip.

When Lydia and Annie had entered her private quarters, she sat the unhappy girl down on the bed and put an arm around her. "You must stop acting like you're discussing a funeral instead of your marriage, child."

"Is it that obvious?" asked Annie plaintively, tears spilling down her pale cheeks.

"It's obvious that you have less than strong feelings for Mr. J. C. Brashears. So my dear, when are you going to tell me the *real* reason you were sent to live with your aunt and uncle, and what's Ben Daily holding over your head to make you marry a man like Brashears?"

Annie had been carefully evasive about the reason for her arrival in Grand County. Folks might have speculated, but she had been determined that none would ever know, except Soft Dove, about the scandal.

Suddenly Annie wanted to tell Lydia. "I disgraced myself back at school in St. Louis. I thought I was in love with Martin Blake, a boy whom I believed loved me, too. Since we were going to get married, or so I thought, I-I gave myself to him.

"He wouldn't have anything to do with me afterward, and I found out that all along he'd been engaged to someone else." She turned to her friend and wailed, "I know it was wrong, and now I suppose I'm going to be punished the rest of my life for it by having to marry the odious J.C. Brashears. Oh, Lydia, he said he didn't love me and never would, it was just a 'business arrangement' to get 'heirs' and a 'hostess', and he'd have mistresses. How can I bear it?"

Lydia took a deep breath before she answered. "Young girls sometimes make bad choices, Annie, and that's what it was you made back in school...just a bad choice. You shouldn't be punished your whole life for one indiscretion. So forget about Brashears right now. Tell me what are you planning to do about Will Redmond?"

Annie's head shot up, her eyes riveted on the woman beside her.

"What do you mean?" asked Annie.

"A person would have to be blind not to see how you feel about him," Lydia scoffed, "and I am not blind."

"God's Teeth!" whispered Annie. "Is it that obvious?"

"So what are you going to do about it? Marry a man you don't love and be miserable? Or make that big ox of an Undersheriff realize that he loves you, too."

Annie lifted hopeful eyes. "You think he loves me?"

"There sure is something there," Mrs. Elder declared. "He's never acted this way over any other female as long as I have known him. I've watched how he stares at you whenever you are within eyeshot. Many a pining heart have wept over that handsome face of his, I can tell you."

"He told me to marry J. C. Brashears and leave the County," said Annie forlornly. "Then he kissed me like I've never been kissed before, not even by Martin."

"He actually kissed you?" Lydia asked in wonder. "Then it's a lot more serious than I first thought."

"I don't understand," replied Annie, a small sliver of hope trying to find its way through her wall of despair.

"I don't know, Annie. I just think you have to settle whatever is going on between you two before you marry anyone else."

"But how?"

Mrs. Elder squeezed Annie's shoulders. "I don't know, child, I just don't know."

Later that afternoon, the Glee Club performed a concert at the water's edge behind the Nickerson House. Crowds of folk from as far away as Lulu, Gaskill, and Teller attended. A celebratory atmosphere livened up everyone's mood, except Annie's.

Annie mulled over Lydia's words while keeping a sharp eye out for the Undersheriff.

"There *is* something between us," she reluctantly admitted to herself. "But what can I do about it?"

After a huge dinner at the Farview, everyone walked back to the theater for a dramatic performance of 'Romeo and Juliet' which left Annie in a paroxysm of tears as she compared the doomed love affair with her own life.

In a flash of insight, Annie decided she *must* tell Will Redmond how she felt about him before something prevented her from ever saying the words. She knew she had to see his reaction before she was forced into marriage with Brashears.

If, after hearing what she had to say, Will wanted nothing to do with her, then she'd obey her uncle and marry the horrible J. C. Brashears. But she had to try for some sort of happiness.

At the dance, Annie scoured the faces for the one she sought. Single, and still not formerly engaged, though everyone knew about the agreement, Annie was not without a variety of dance partners.

All was not as festive as it seemed. The lovesick Charley Burn, having heard that Annie was to marry the uppity owner of the mine for whom he worked, had drunk more than he ought. He clumsily swung Annie around the floor, becoming more angry when each dance ended and she was swept away by another. He stood on the sidelines, wretchedly watching Annie swing past on arm after arm.

Another equally smoldering face appeared around midnight. Will Redmond watched from the crowd as Annie smiled up into the faces of the men who held her. Redmond and Sheriff Tom had hauled in over twenty drunks during the day, some pliant and others who wanted to fight the lawmen or anyone else who stood nearby.

Barely suppressed frustration and anger had caused Will to erupt several times and bloody a nose or loosen a tooth with his huge fist. With every physical release of a punch, however, pent-up emotions had only increased in intensity instead of dissipating.

Finally, his good friend, Sheriff Tom Roberts, had urged him to go off-duty and take a dip in the cold waters of Grand Lake to cool off. Instead, Will headed straight for the Nickerson House. Since the searing kiss in the livery, Will Redmond had been haunted by big blue eyes, coppery hair, and the remembrance of Annie Mitchell's body's instant response to his own.

When he thought he couldn't stand it any longer, he pushed through the crowded dance floor, oblivious to everyone and everything in the hot stuffy room, and stomped toward Annie and the young miner in whose arms she was being held.

Rapping the young man on the shoulder with more power than he intended, the boy turned angrily until he saw the look of barely contained violence on the tall Undersheriff's face. Annie's partner stepped away, and Will Redmond took his place. He swung Annie around the room, though barely looking at her.

Annie was so surprised by his actions she was speechless. She gazed up into his unsmiling face as they flew across the floor to the beat of the music. She saw women talking behind their hands as she glanced around the room, and she knew they were discussing this unexpected behavior.

Undersheriff Will Redmond had never danced at any of the parties since he and his brothers had arrived in Grand Lake in 1875, or so she had been told. Never! And here he was, as smooth and light on his big feet as any of the best dancers.

When the music ended, Will leaned down and whispered in her ear, "Come outside, I need to talk to you."

When she didn't move but only continued to gaze at him in bewilderment, he grabbed her hand and pulled her out the front door. Moving her through the crowd on the porch, Annie's legs felt like pudding, and she feared they might collapse under her.

Redmond steered her across the street and around to the back of the courthouse.

When he reached the shield of darkness in the shadows of the alley, he swung her around until her back was against the wood of the building. Then he backed away from her and paced back and forth a few times.

Finally he turned to her, "I'm not sure why I did that...dragging you out in front of everyone, I mean. I'm not thinking straight, I guess, what with you being engaged to another man."

Suddenly it was time to say how she felt. "I don't care what everyone thinks, Will," Annie began, her voice as soft as the night air, "and you know as well as I that I do *not* want to be engaged to J. C. Brashears."

Will moved toward her, then slammed his hand into the wall over her head, making her jump in fright.

"Damn it to hell!" he exploded. "Why can't I quit thinking about you? Why do you haunt me so?" He searched her face for answers but only saw her parted lips and dusky eyes shining up at him in the dark. As they swayed toward each other, Will knew he was lost.

He put his arms around her, gathering her slim body to his large frame and lowered his head in a gentle kiss. This kiss was different from the heated one in the livery stable, slower, but no less intense. He parted her lips and let his tongue explore the inside of her mouth.

Her arms reached up and around him, and she used them to bring him closer. He pulled away for a moment, but she drew him back again and experimented with her own tongue against his.

His grasp grew tighter as he pressed her against the outside wall of the courthouse. She felt the hardness of his response, and she reveled in the aching sweetness of her own body's reactions. While one arm held her against him, the other roamed over her body, mashing the

fullness of her breasts then following her curves down to the roundness
of her hips.

Will gripped her buttocks tightly and pushed himself against her
until her legs spread slightly to allow him access between her thighs. Lost
in fiery sensations, she raised one leg and coiled it around one of his.

They both were breathing heavily now. As he began to inch up her skirts,
Annie suddenly realized what was about to happen. She pushed against
him, breaking the spell which was about to overwhelm them both.

"No, Will, not here,"she panted into his hungry mouth.

He raised his head, and she saw into the murky depths of the green
eyes which had darkened with passion. Using what was left of her
strength, she finally broke through to him and watched as he reluctantly
tore himself away. Both of them fought to catch their breath as they
stared at each other, only a hair's width apart.

"Jesus, I nearly took you right here," gasped Will, turning his back
so she couldn't see the bulge in his pants which threatened to rip open
the seams.

"Yes, and I almost let you," was her reply as she realized how close
they had come...and how desperately she had wanted it...still wanted it.

"I don't know what's happening to me," he groaned miserably as he
turned toward her again. "I have no right to do this everytime we're
alone. But I can't help it." He gazed at her, wanting some kind of
explanation.

"You must love me, Will Redmond, as I do you," she replied
seductively. "Why don't you just accept it and marry me?" In the long
silence that followed, Annie was suddenly appalled at her unmitigated
gall. She blushed hotly and turned toward the wall to hide her face.

"I can't," she heard him say quietly. "I'm already married."

Before she could react to the devastating statement, Ben Daily came charging around the corner, along with several of his cronies and Sheriff Roberts.

"Get the hell away from my niece, Redmond," barked Annie's uncle. "Sheriff, this man accosted an innocent girl, and in front of witnesses, forcibly dragged her out into the dark against her will. She is engaged to Mr. J. C. Brashears who won't take this insult too lightly. Arrest him, I say."

Sheriff Tom Roberts looked exceedingly uncomfortable. Daily had had Will arrested a couple of years ago when they had gotten into a heated argument, and Will had knocked Daily to the ground. Roberts had released Will due to lack of evidence; it had been only Daily's word against his friend, Redmond's.

But now, there were witnesses to Redmond's actions, so what could he do? Will *did* look mighty guilty and was saying nothing in his own defense.

"All right, Will," Tom said reluctantly, "come with me."

Annie quickly stepped forward. "Wait, what is he supposed to have done to me?"

Sheriff looked down at her upturned face, noticing even in the moonless night, the scrape of whisker-burn on her ashen cheeks. "According to your uncle, Miss, Will forced you into this alleyway to take advantage of you."

"That's preposterous, Sheriff Roberts," Annie said evenly, her head held high. "Mr. Redmond did not force me. I came quite willingly."

"Don't, Annie, think of your reputation," hissed Will, silent until now.

"My reputation be damned, Will Redmond," she blazed. "I'm not going to have you arrested when I wanted to be here as much as you did. I'm just sorry it had such an unhappy conclusion."

Will gazed back at her, clearly miserable.

Turning toward Ben Daily and the others who were staring at her with their mouths agape, Annie stated, "Uncle Ben, you cannot arrest a man for kissing me, not when I gladly returned that kiss. So call off your pack of bloodhounds and escort me back to the dance."

She pushed through the throng of onlookers, the ruckus having drawn more than half of the merrymakers who had witnessed their unusual departure from the dance. Her heart beat so rapidly in her chest that she thought everyone could hear it as she used all of her strength not to scream out her anger, hurt, and humiliation.

HE IS MARRIED!!

Due to her disgraceful admission, Redmond was not arrested. Ben was furious with the Sheriff for not doing his obvious duty and with Annie for consorting with the bastard, Redmond. None too gently, Ben all but pushed Annie back across the street to the Nickerson House.

Marian was mortified at Annie's apparent immodest behavior to which everyone in town was now privy. She grabbed Annie's arm, none to gently either, and left the dance, livid with anger. Both Marian and Ben fervently feared that J. C. Brashears would get wind of the scandal. On the way home, they railed against Annie's unseemly actions.

"How could you allow that brute to drag you out of a crowded place and into an alley? Don't you know how that appears to decent people?

It makes you look no better than one of those girls down at the Dandy," ranted Marian. "If Mr. Brashears should hear, and I can guarantee you the gossips won't be able to hold their tongues about this, you had better say that you *were* accosted by Redmond, if you know what is good for you, missy."

Later, Ben confided to Marian, "I hope Brashears *does* hear about it. Maybe he'll look at it as a breach of his honor and challenge Redmond. Brashears is a crack shot, it is well-known, and that would eliminate not only Redmond himself but also one of George E. Miller's right-hand men."

Annie was dead inside, and Marian's words and threats had rolled off her as water on down. She was too miserable over the news that Will Redmond was married to be worried about how her behavior might affect J. C. Brashears. It was now painfully obvious Will cared deeply for her, but Annie knew she could never be truly his...not when he already had a wife somewhere else.

And, if J. C. Brashears still wanted to marry her, she would soon be taken away from Redmond's town, though she knew she would remember the smoldering fire of his touch all of her life.

A long and miserable week later, Brashears did indeed return to Grand Lake. He was summarily informed of the scandalous incident between Annie and the Undersheriff, then had ridden directly to Ben Daily's cabin without commenting on it.

Annie was in the parlor playing mournfully on the spinet. Her heart, which she had thought could never be broken again after Martin Blake's deception, ached even worse as she recalled the moments she had spent with Undersheriff Redmond.

He had had many opportunities to tell her he was married, but he hadn't. He had kissed her twice, too, knowing that he was already wed to another. She felt deceived by him worse than what Martin had done to her. And yet, she yearned for him still.

Annie heard a rap on the front door, and Becky Threckald came in from the kitchen to answer it. Aunt Marian had gone into town to a Ladies Auxiliary for the Republican Party meeting. Annie had been confined to the house, and Sugar was off-limits to her.

J. C. Brashears marched into the cabin and removed his tall hat which he imperiously handed to the Threckald girl. When he spied Annie sitting at the spinet, he waved a hand at Becky, summarily dismissing her, and strode across the room.

Annie glanced up at him as he approached and saw the storm in his silver eyes. Her melancholy allowed her only a passing moment of care.

"Miss Mitchell, is it true what they are saying in town about you and the Undersheriff?" he demanded, all show of civility gone.

Annie stared down at the keys on the spinet and answered quietly, "Yes, Mr. Brashears, it is. I wantonly threw myself at the Undersheriff."

Before she knew what was happening, she was wrenched from the spinet bench and lifted to her feet by one arm, Brashears' flushed and furious face only inches from her own.

"I will not allow any impropriety, my girl," he seethed at her. "If you think you can cuckold me with a minor law official and get away with it, you are more stupid than you look. In the coming years, I will most certainly have many mistresses, but you, chit, will be the model of decorum. I have killed for less insult than this, and I will think nothing of killing you and your paramour if it ever happens again. Do I make myself clear?"

He had squeezed Annie's arm until it was bruised. She had been right in being frightened of this man, after all. The violence she saw in his eyes made her wince even more than the painful constriction of her arm.

She nodded her understanding, and he released her suddenly. Pulling down his unwrinkled waistcoat and straightening his cravat, he changed expressions faster than a rattler strikes...and with more deadly force, Annie thought.

"Now call the girl and order some tea, Miss Mitchell, as I have had a long dusty ride."

Annie was forced to sit with the despicable man during the rest of the afternoon, drinking tea and listening to his desultory conversation. More than once she wanted to rub her aching arm but was afraid to show him any sign of weakness.

When Marian arrived less than five minutes ahead of Ben, Annie was almost hysterical in her relief at their familiarity, so fearful had she been in the presence of J.C.. Brashears. Both Ben and Marian watched Brashears closely, trying to gauge his reaction to the recent scandal.

Brashears had been waiting for the couple to arrive because as soon as they settled themselves in the parlor, he stood up and began to speak.

"My absence from this humble burg has not been without consequence, I hear," he pointedly looked in Annie's direction. "But Miss Mitchell and I have talked it through to a satisfactory conclusion, haven't we, my dear?"

Annie, white-faced, could only nod.

"And so it is now time to make our engagement known to the world and set a date for the nuptials."

Ben and Marian exchanged satisfied glances.

Brashears turned to Annie and presented to her a small box wrapped in silver paper which Annie thought matched his cold dead eyes. With shaking hands, she opened it slowly and beheld a silver ring with a large diamond in the center. Brashears placed the ring on the third finger of her left hand. It snugged her skin as he slipped it into place, and she suddenly felt strangled by it.

"Oh, isn't this just wonderful, Mr. Brashears," glowed Marian, breaking the uncomfortable silence after waiting for Annie to speak. "When do you want the vows to be exchanged?"

"Two weeks from Sunday, Mrs. Daily, if you please," he replied easily as he watched Annie's wild-eyed reaction.

TWO WEEKS? ONLY TWO WEEKS?

Dizzily, Annie felt she might sink to the floor in a faint knowing that she had only two more weeks of freedom from this horrible man. Then she would forever be tied to a husband who had made it painfully obvious that he would think nothing of killing her, or worse, if she ever crossed him.

Annie desperately needed a friend and wished that Soft Dove was still here, or that she could go into town and speak with Lydia Elder or Emma McLeary.

The next day, after Aunt Marian retired for her afternoon nap, Annie quietly slipped out the front door and sneaked off into the woods, careful that Becky Threckald hadn't seen her from the kitchen window.

Annie hurried down the overgrown path which she and Soft Dove had made earlier in the summer.

Annie soon reached the place she sought, the pool where she and Soft Dove had so often swum together. The warm summer sun beat down on Annie's head, and she was perspiring from her brisk walk. She wrenched off the ring with the vulgar diamond and placed it in a knothole of a tree. After a cursory glance around, she quickly stripped off her shoes, stockings, and dress, clad only in chemise and pantalets.

Tossing her shed clothing over branches on a bush, she stepped into the cool water. Though she felt odd being here without Soft Dove, the gentle water and whisper of wind in the trees soon relieved some of the tension and anxiety in which she had been engulfed.

Stroking through the deeper water, Annie dove like a beaver several times, her head emerging from the cool wetness into the warmth of the clean mountain air. When her feet could touch bottom again, she lay back and floated, lazily watching the fluffy clouds skid across the blue sky overhead.

Annie's thoughts turned to Will Redmond, as they did often these days, of how his hands had felt as they ravished her body.

Suddenly, Annie felt something touch her leg. She doubled up and brought her feet down until they touched the muddy bottom. She stood waist-deep and searched the silty water all around her. Seeing nothing, she laughed at herself for being such a scaredy-cat.

"It was probably a pond trout," she said aloud. As she turned toward shore, a great whooshing noise behind her caused her to spin around.

Bear Hawk stood not two inches away, water slicking back his long black hair, and his brown chest glistened as the beads of moisture sluiced down the furrows of muscles.

Annie crossed her arms to cover her breasts as she lashed out. "Bear Hawk, you scared me to death. Now go away, this is a private bath."

She became immediately uncomfortable at the lascivious glance on his face as he raked her upper torso with smoldering black eyes. As she backed away, he moved forward, staying no more than inches away. She could feel the heat from his body although no part of him touched her. When she realized that as she reached shallower water, he was seeing more of her, she stopped.

"Bear Hawk, I'll scream if you don't leave this instant," Annie cried, hoping her voice did not sound as shaky as her insides felt.

Suddenly he reached for her, grasping her tightly, his arms like iron bands holding her trapped against him. He glided through the shallow water, hauling Annie with him.

"Let me go, Bear Hawk, and I promise I won't tell anyone," she pleaded.

Bear Hawk made no sound as he kept a steely grip on her and walked calmly out of the water onto dry land. He let her down so that she could walk but pushed her ahead of him toward her clothing. Annie tried to cover herself, blushing at the thought of how much more he might have done than merely look at her.

The tall Indian, clothed in nothing but a breechclout, pulled her cotton dress from off the bush where it lay and threw it to her. Annie backed up a bit, tossing her dress quickly over her head. Bear Hawk's piercing gaze followed her every movement as he had watched her when she was with Soft Dove.

Trying a change of tact, Annie took a deep breath and made her voice sound calm, "Have you seen Soft Dove lately? I'd love to see her again; I miss her." As she spoke, she began walking backwards toward the trail which led to the cabin.

When Bear Hawk flipped his head and issued a whistle, Annie turned and ran as fast as her bare feet would take her over the open ground. Glancing back once, she saw that she was not being pursued which gave her a renewed burst of speed as she darted over logs and under branches. Then she heard the sound of horse's hooves pounding through the woods in her direction.

Turning her head slightly, she saw Bear Hawk bearing down on her atop a black stallion with wild eyes. Before she could scream, she was grabbed around the waist and pulled atop the great beast's back. She was held tightly in front of Bear Hawk which forced her back against his wet body. With one hand holding her and one hand over her mouth, he guided the horse with his knees.

Bear Hawk turned the stallion in the opposite direction of the cabin and galloped through the forest, keeping well away from any known path. Annie's fear overwhelmed her as she realized he was taking her away from her world. Away from Uncle Ben and Aunt Marian, away from her friends in town, and away from Will Redmond.

She had heard stories of white women taken by Indians, never to be seen or heard from again. A cry rose up inside her, and a howl of anguish erupted from her which was lost in the wind of the tall pine trees whose branches whipped past her. The Ute took his hand away from her mouth, and Annie knew it would do no good to scream anymore. No one would hear her. And it would do no good to beg; Bear Hawk couldn't understand her words.

Bear Hawk rode hard until dark. Annie tried to remember trail marks, as Soft Dove had taught her, but as they sped on, the forest melded into sameness. Shock and fatigue overtook her as darkness approached, and she found herself sagging against Bear Hawk, the welcome warmth of his body heat overshadowing some of her fear.

Into the night they rode, stopping only to rest or water the big horse. Annie couldn't tell in which direction they were heading, but she knew they were continually moving upward into the mountains.

The air became much colder as they ascended the mountain, and Annie began to shiver in her thin dress and bare feet. Bear Hawk did not seem to feel the change in temperature but pulled her closer. When her teeth began to chatter, he reined in the horse and removed the multicolored blanket on which they had been sitting. As they remounted, he wrapped the blanket around Annie, tucking it in between them. Though he had not spoken more than an occasional grunt, she said 'thank you' quietly and snuggled into the welcoming cover from the freezing night.

Around dawn, Annie awoke with a start, still held tightly against Bear Hawk. She saw before her a new land. They must have crossed the Divide sometime in the night as Bear Hawk was carefully guiding the horse down a steep rocky slope. This side of the mountain was different from the west side, Annie noticed, although her mind remained a bit fuzzy.

The terrain was rockier, by far, and had fewer trees. Hardly any aspens could be seen, and other trees Annie didn't recognize graced the rugged landscape. Twisted, scraggly, stunted trees were evident in the barren soil as if the wind were harsher on this side.

In the distance, Annie saw bare moraines of dirt and rock left by glaciers as they had receded. In between the moraines, broad treeless meadows were in abundance, reminding Annie of the flat expanses of Kansas she had seen from the windows of the train on her journey from St. Louis only a few months ago. She thought of all that had happened since that train ride...she had been so hopeful of a new beginning for her life. Was this her destiny? Terror filled her heart with dread.

When Bear Hawk reined in the lathered horse at a rushing mountain stream, Annie leaned over the bank and drank deeply of the fresh water. She used her hand to splash water on her face, trying to revive herself. All of her muscles were sore, her hair in wild coppery tangles, and she wanted to lie down on the hard ground and sleep for an eternity.

When she turned, she saw Bear Hawk squatting beside the big horse, watching her intently. He was chewing on some dried meat, tearing away big hunks with his white even teeth. The big stallion grazed on tufts of green grass, and the glaring summer sun illuminated the duo of man and beast.

Suddenly Bear Hawk stood and sauntered toward her; she scuttled backwards like a crab, but he only reached down and handed her the rest of the dried meat. Gratefully, she gnawed on the stiff jerky, softening it with saliva until she could tear off a piece. It appeased her hunger as they continued to study each other in silence.

"You can't force me to stay with you," Annie said quietly. "My uncle will send someone after us. You can't go around kidnapping white women."

Bear Hawk rose as if she hadn't said a word and stalked toward her. He lifted her by her arm and boosted her atop the horse again. Grabbing the sinew reins, he flipped them over the stallion's head and leaped over the wide back in one fluid motion. He pulled Annie back against him and urged the horse on with a nudge of his knees.

Annie's tears coursed down her cheeks as the sun moved across the sky. Farther and farther they rode away from Grand Lake and the one she loved but couldn't have. She glanced back over Bear Hawk's shoulder once to the towering peaks which they had crossed and hope of rescue seemed impossible.

"By now, they should have started looking for me," Annie thought to herself. Bear Hawk knew these mountains, though, and she realized the circuitous trail which he had made would be hard to follow.

When they began their ascent of yet another impossible peak, Annie recalled how she had wished for a grand adventure. "Be careful what you wish for," Annie remembered her mother whispering to her when she was young, "for you just may get it".

CHAPTER FOUR

When Marian awakened from her afternoon nap, she soon discovered that Annie was nowhere to be found. After brusquely interrogating Becky Threckald until she made the girl cry, it became apparent that Annie must have slipped out sometime during the afternoon.

"Go to the paddock and see if her horse is still there, Becky," ordered Marian, furious at Annie's impertinence to disobey. "I knew it was a bad idea to take the girl in, but Mr. Daily insisted," Marian muttered to herself. "If a girl is no good, then it makes itself known sooner or later. I only wish her true nature had appeared *after* she was wed to Mr. Brashears. Then, at least, it would be *his* problem instead of mine."

Becky ran back into the cabin, out of breath. "The little pony she always rides is still there, Miz Daily."

"Go back into the kitchen and finish cooking dinner, Becky," Marian commanded as she dismissed the girl.

Becky had heard the gossip about Annie Mitchell and the Undersheriff on the Fourth of July, and she had seen firsthand the odious J. C. Brashears to whom Annie was engaged. And now Annie Mitchell was missing. She couldn't wait to tell her friends.

When Ben arrived, he was met at the door by a distraught and angry wife.

"It's all your fault, Benjamin Daily," Marian railed before he'd even had his whiskey.

He ignored her and bee-lined to the decanter. After his usual five shots, he calmly turned toward Marian.

"Now settle down, woman, and tell me what has you in such a state."

"Annie is gone," screeched Marian. She stalked to the table which held the decanter, poured herself a big swig, and downed it in one gulp.

"Mrs. Daily, you're drinking whiskey!" exclaimed her husband.

"I am quite aware of what I am drinking, Mr. Daily, now find your niece before Mr. J. C. Brashears withdraws his proposal of marriage and ruins you."

Ben rode into Grand Lake and discreetly asked around. No one had seen Annie since the Fourth of July. He rode to Gaskill and enlisted some of the miners. Paying them well to insure their silence, Ben divided them into groups of five to search for Annie.

The men rendezvoused back at the Daily cabin a day later. No one had found even a trace of her.

"What are we going to do about Mr. Brashears?" wailed Marian. "She has run away from him, and he is not going to be happy about it. Our good name will be ruined because of that ungrateful little trollop."

"Yes," mused Ben as he rubbed his numerous chins, "and J. C. just might take it as more than a personal insult. My political career could be over! That little minx has turned out to be more trouble than her mother. We should never have accepted her father's money to take her in."

"Do you think she could be heading back east?" asked Marian, dabbing away tears with a silk handkerchief.

"The stage and train schedules have been checked. No, she must either be on foot or is being aided by person or persons unknown," replied Ben.

"We had better inform the sheriff, or they might think we did away with her ourselves," huffed Marian. "I don't want any more impropriety attached to our name than what the ungrateful slut has already brought upon us."

"Yes, I suppose so," Ben said thoughtfully. "But if *my* men couldn't find a trace of her, then neither will the lawmen. They'll be the ones people will blame when they can't find her. Then Brashears can censure Roberts and Redmond, instead of me. This business might turn out all right after all, Mother. I want my supper now; there's no hurry. I'll ride into town tomorrow."

The next morning, Ben rode into Grand Lake and straight to the jail. Both the Sheriff and Undersheriff were sitting at their respective desks filling out paperwork.

"My niece is missing," stated Ben, haughtily. "It's your job to find her." Ben rather enjoyed the stricken look on Redmond's face.

"What do you mean...missing?" Tom Roberts asked.

"My wife woke up from her afternoon nap, and the girl was gone." Ben glared at Will. "And I wouldn't be surprised if you had something to do with this, Redmond."

Will Redmond rose from his chair and bore down on him. Ben backed up until his back was against the door. The expression on Redmond's face was so threatening Ben felt his bowels loosen.

"Exactly when did she come up missing?" Redmond growled, his angry face not two inches from the sweating shorter man's.

Tom stepped around his desk quickly and stood between the two men.

"Wednesday," Ben sputtered.

"TWO DAYS AGO?" Will's temper exploded. "And you're just NOW informing us?"

"All right, Daily, sit down and answer some questions," Tom said as he steeled himself for a physical confrontation between Will and Ben.

"If anything has happened to her, Daily, you'll be answering to me," hissed Redmond through his teeth.

"Is that a threat?" sputtered Ben, still uneasy at the sight of the younger man's big fists clenching and unclenching at his sides. "Sheriff, this man is threatening me. I will not have it. Arrest him."

"Calm down, you two," said Tom. "You can fight it out later. Now we need to find a young girl. Ben, did she take a horse?"

Ben related everything he knew and everywhere his men had checked. Will Redmond put on his hat, hooked his gun belt around his waist, and started to walk out.

"Wait, Will," called Tom, "where are you going?"

"I can't just sit here. She's been out there for two nights. You know how cold it can get when the sun goes down. If we don't find her soon, she'll die." Will's face was pale with worry.

"Where are you going to start, Will?" asked the sheriff.

"At Daily's," answered Will as he strode out the door.

"I'm right behind you," said Tom as he began to load a rifle.

Will rode hell-bent to the Daily cabin. There he began a meticulous search of the grounds around the cabin. In an ever-increasing circle, he carefully scanned every blade of grass, every broken twig, every mark in the dirt. When he came upon the pond and saw her stockings and shoes, the implications doubled him over.

The pain was quickly replaced with smoldering anger as he realized someone had dragged her out of the water, against her will. As he studied the footprints, he wasn't sure if the barefoot pattern was White or Indian.

But somehow he got the feeling it wasn't White. He searched the area, his stomach knotted in fear of finding her body. When he caught the glitter of something in a tree, he found the ring Brashears had given her lying in a knothole.

He continued to search and found tracks as she had tried to escape toward the cabin. Then he saw the horse's hoof marks which followed and the abrupt end of her small prints. The horse was unshod...Indian. With his heart in his throat, Will remembered the rumor of the Indian who had offered two ponies for her.

Will dashed back to the cabin to retrieve his horse. Tom and Ben Daily had just arrived.

"Did you find anything, Will?" asked Tom as he climbed off his horse.

"Yeah, an Indian stole her while she was swimming in a pond down that way," Will said, tossing his head back in the direction he had just come.

Turning on Ben, Will grabbed the jowly man's lapels and brought his face within inches of his own. "This is *your* fault, Daily, and if she's hurt in any way, I'm coming back and I'm gonna kill you. Understand?"

Ben's fat cheeks shook in terror.

"Stop it, Will," Tom shouted as he tried to break Redmond's iron grip.

Will Redmond released Ben with so much force that Daily fell backwards...hard. As he hauled himself to his feet, he accused, "Now you can add assault to the charges against him, Tom Roberts."

Tom gave Ben a hand up, trying to soothe the sputtering man. Will threw the ring in Ben's face and snarled, "Give this back to that pompous ass you sold her to."

"Will, wait until I can form a posse," Tom called.

"I can't, Tom. You can catch up to me." He turned to Ben Daily and spat, "Do you know who has her? It's that renegade Bear Hawk."

"I-I didn't think he was serious," sputtered Ben.

Tom looked confused. "What do you mean, Ben? Who is Bear Hawk, Will?"

"Back in '78, my brothers and I had some dealings with that damn Indian," began Will. "We had just arrived in Middle Park from Missouri, in search of gold. We'd camped on the banks of the Grand River by Hot Sulphur Springs, rowdy and itching to fight. Spending what little cash we earned from placer mining at the Antlers Bar across from the Post Office, we were raring to help the locals with the Indian trouble which had been brewing between the Whites at the Springs and the Utes camped downstream from the settlement.

"We joined a posse in the late summer by Junction Ranch. The Indians had been whooping it up, shooting toward the white settlers, burning grassland, and killing stock. When we entered their camp, only the women and children were there. The men were racing ponies over the hill. So we gathered up all the firearms into a pile while the squaws used smoke to signal the men.

"When the Indian braves came barreling into camp, we realized we were outnumbered. One of the Indians tried to grab a gun from the pile, and a hotheaded fellow, Frank Addison, shot him. He claimed the Indian had been one who had killed his father and brother six years back while the two were trapping furs on Grizzly Fork in North Park."

"What's that got to do with the one called Bear Hawk?" asked Tom.

Will continued, "Bear Hawk was young and hotheaded, and he tried to use his knife on Frank, but I stopped him. I remember thinking what a feisty young pup he was but didn't give him much thought again until later. The older Indians, Ute Jack and Washington, had been talked into giving up and going to the Reservation on the Uintah River in Utah.

"Me and my brothers left and went back to the Springs to gamble. Apparently so did the men who were supposed to be guarding the Indians. When they returned, a splinter group, led by young Bear Hawk, had sneaked away into the night. They went south over the mountains to Beaver Creek and followed the Grand River. Constantly on the move, the small group of renegades escaped without a trace. The rest, the old and the young, were herded to the Reservation. I never heard anymore about Bear Hawk until recently.

"Tom, I got to go find her. If that animal has her, there's no telling what he'll do. He hates Whites!"

Will jumped on his horse and rode off before Tom could stop him. Redmond doubled back to Grand Lake and packed provisions and his bedroll. He loaded a rifle and got extra ammunition for the Colt strapped to his hip.

Then he retraced his steps back to the Daily's and found the trail. He followed its meandering and convoluting path until dark, experiencing both respect and rage at Annie's abductor for his worthy attempt to hide their route. Knowing that he could do no more until daylight, he made camp.

At sunrise, Will again found the trail, stopping where they stopped and searching for some sign of Annie. Halfway up the mountain, he came across a tear from her dress, fluttering in the wind from the twig which had snagged it. Will brought the material to his nose, wanting to inhale her scent. He carefully tucked the tiny shred into his hat band and rode on.

"Damn it, why does that girl mean so much to me? Why does the thought of her leave me weak? No woman has ever had that kind of hold on me. What if I never find her?" He couldn't bear to think of it.

Will knew he should have waited for Tom and some reinforcements, but knowing that she was out there...somewhere with that Indian buck... left him enraged, restless, and most eager to continue the search. Will could finally admit that he loved her and knew that he damn well better find her soon.

Bear Hawk and Annie rode on, stopping only long enough to rest and water the horse. In the late afternoon of the second day, they stopped beside a small creek. Bear Hawk pulled Annie from the horse, and when her legs gave way, she sank to the ground in exhaustion. He lifted her in his arms and carried her to the bank of the creek.

Bear Hawk unwound a braided rope made of rawhide which had been snaked around the band of his breech cloth, and he tied it tightly around her ankle. Speaking in his language which Annie didn't understand, he suddenly grabbed her around the waist and dipped her foot in the icy water. She screamed and tried to fight him, but he kept a tight grip on her as he tied the other end of the rope around a nearby cottonwood trunk.

"*Pai-quey*," Bear Hawk muttered as he gestured with his hand. He surveyed the area for a moment before he leaped upon the stallion's back and rode away.

"Wait, Bear Hawk, don't go!" Annie screamed as panic overwhelmed her. He was abandoning her... tied to a tree with no food or weapons. "Come back, Bear Hawk, don't leave me! Please, I beg you, don't leave me alone!"

Annie used all her strength to pull at the sinew, trying to break it loose. As the sun dried the loop on her ankle, it shrank and became even tighter. She twisted and tugged until droplets of blood seeped from the wounds she was inflicting upon herself in her efforts to escape.

Annie scanned her surroundings. She had enough line to reach the creek, so thirst wasn't a concern. But how long would it be until some wild animal smelled her blood? Annie pictured her own grisly death as she imagined being torn apart by gnashing teeth and claws.

She laid her head in her hands and sobbed piteously. She thought about Will Redmond. "I'll never see him again. I'll never feel his arms around me. My bones will be forever lost on the side of this mountain. I DON'T WANT TO DIE!"

Fatigue and hopelessness overtook Annie, and she fell into restless slumber.

***

Will hardly slept a wink during the darkness. His mind conjured up horrible images of Annie in the hands of the savage who took her and he left powerless to help her. If it *was* Bear Hawk who had kidnapped Annie, Will definitely intended to kill him this time when he caught him.

When the sky began to lighten, Will saddled his horse and continued to track, praying that no sudden summer storms would pop up and wash the trail away. Even though he lost precious time backtracking when the rocky ground hid the sign, he carried on for the next couple of days.

After crossing the Divide and starting down the other side, Will removed a pair of worn field glasses from a buckskin bag. Will fingered the glasses lovingly as he remembered his father's words when he had given him the gift on the day Will and his brothers had left home and headed west.

"These will let you see far, boy, so that you can go far in life. Take care of your brothers, and if gold is what you're seeking, don't forget to look for it in the little things of everyday life."

Will's parents were both dead now, and he couldn't touch the field glasses without a tear blurring his vision. Blinking rapidly to remove the unmanly wetness, he brought the glasses to his eyes and scanned the surrounding valley.

Annie awoke slowly, like being pulled through thick mud. After she sat up and rubbed her gritty eyes, she explored her surroundings. The blood on her ankle had dried so she used her hand to cup some creek water over the soreness where the rawhide had cut into her skin.

She couldn't tell how long she'd slept, but the sun was beginning to sink behind the mountaintops of the west. Her stomach reminded her of the hollow feeling inside which needed filling, if she was to have enough energy to escape. She scanned the area for edibles but found none within her reach. So she drank as much water as she could swallow.

Next Annie searched for anything to use as a blade to cut the rawhide rope. The rocks were all rounded from the rushing of water over thousands of years, but she picked up two thin ones and tried to use one to chip the other. If she could only flake off a sharp piece, she could cut the sinew from the tree to which she was tied.

"And what will I do if I get loose?" she asked herself. "I don't know how to get back to Grand Lake, and even if I tried, these mountains are full of bears and wild cats."

She choked, close to hopeless tears once again.

"I won't give up! I can't! I have to keep trying as long as there is breath in my body," she shouted to the quiet glen.

She tried several different stones, striking them together over and over until her arm muscles were sore and her fingers bled. When she was almost ready to give up, she heard distant hoof beats approaching.

"Thank God," she breathed, her heart beating rapidly in happiness. She strained her eyes in the dusky twilight, trying to see who it was that neared.

She stood up and began to yell and wave her arms, "Help, I'm here, over here! Please help me! Over here! Please hel..."

Her voice broke when she recognized the big black stallion.

Annie desperately began pulling at the sinew holding her to the tree. Blood began to ooze down her ankle again as she tugged until her hands also bled. Fooled for a moment into thinking it might have been Will or someone else sent to save her, tears of frustration glistened in her eyes that it was her kidnapper...not a real rescue at all.

Bear Hawk leaped from the horse's back even before it came to a halt. In his hands was something, but the grayness of sundown made it look like a dark lump. He threw the bundle at Annie's feet, making her jump back, nearly falling into the creek.

Bear Hawk drew his knife and stalked slowly toward Annie, his eyes boring into her very soul. Petrified, she froze. She squeezed her eyes tight, waiting for the slash of the blade across her throat. When nothing happened, she peeked through her lashes and saw that Bear Hawk had disappeared from view.

Just when she began to think he might have been a figment of her imagination, she felt a tug on her ankle and pain swept up her leg. Bear Hawk was kneeling at her feet, sawing through the tough hide which held her captive. When it was severed, he carefully unwound the sinew from her ankle and rubbed the broken skin gently for a moment. When he raised his eyes to hers, Annie was amazed at the regret she saw there.

Bear Hawk rose smoothly to his feet until he stood close, peering into her face. He softly spoke a few words in his language. Annie was more confused than ever...at his return and at his change of attitude toward her. What he was thinking, she couldn't tell, but there was no longer that look of contempt in his eyes.

He gathered twigs and started a fire by striking two of the stones Annie had been trying to chip earlier. As the flames grew brighter, Annie warmed herself against the cold night air. The bundles which he had thrown at her feet were now visible in the glow from the fire. One was a dead rabbit and the other was the horse blanket.

He used a green stick to skewer the skinned rabbit and began turning it over the heat. With one hand, he flipped the blanket at Annie without looking up. She wrapped up in the blanket, still shivering from her former terror.

After they shared the succulent meat, licking the grease from their fingers, Bear Hawk lay in front of the fire propped on his side. He motioned for Annie to join him, and she bit her lip in indecision. She knew she should share the warmth of the blanket with him against the frigid night air, but she was terrified to be so near him.

Seeing her hesitate, Bear Hawk rose fluidly and reached for the blanket. He jerked it from around Annie, and she was flipped on her side. He spread the blanket on the ground and motioned for her again to join him.

"I'd rather freeze than lay with you," Annie stated indignantly as she wrapped her arms around herself and moved closer to the fire.

The thin cotton dress she wore as well as her bare feet were not much cover for the rapidly falling temperatures of the alpine night. Her teeth began to chatter uncontrollably.

Bear Hawk shrugged, pulled the blanket around himself, and lay down. Annie stared at the Indian, weighing the choices before her. As the temperature plummeted, she finally crept over to where Bear Hawk lay.

"I-I'm freezing," she whispered. "I need part of the blanket."

Bear Hawk's eyes opened immediately and he stared up at her for a moment. Slowly he pulled back the blanket and Annie lay down on her side with her back to him, trying not to touch him. But he put his arm around her and pulled her tightly to him, covering her with the blanket and molding his lean hard body to her back.

Annie stiffened, but soon she recognized the even breathing of sleep. Relaxed and warmed by his body heat, she soon drifted off.

Before dawn the next morning, Bear Hawk roused Annie with a grunt. As he walked away to relieve himself, Annie went to the creek to make her morning ablutions. When she caught a glimpse of herself in the still water, she gasped. Her face was streaked with dirt and her hair was a tangled nest with twigs and bits of grass sticking out at different angles. Though the water was icy, she dunked her entire head, face and all. As she swung her heavy wet hair back over her head, she glanced back.

Bear Hawk was staring at her, a look she recognized all too clearly written in his sensuous black eyes. She turned away quickly and began pulling her fingers through the tangles. Suddenly a green twig which had been peeled of bark was stuck into her line of vision by a brown hand. She looked up questioningly at Bear Hawk until he used another stick to pull out the tangles of his own straight ebony hair.

Annie got the idea and did what she could with the stick on her wild tresses. As she worked on the snarls, Bear Hawk squatted nearby, watching her every movement. When her hair was almost dry and hung more smoothly down her back, Bear Hawk lifted her effortlessly onto the back of the horse. Jumping up behind her, they rode off.

Although Annie tried to study the countryside in case she was able to escape, she soon lost all bearings, shaking her head at her own confusion when she thought they were heading west toward the peaks which they had already crossed.

Several days passed, each night Bear Hawk pulled her close to him while they slept. But, to Annie's relief, he never attempted to molest her, and he never tied her up again.

They began following an actual trail. Annie's hopes rose when she thought that this must be a well-known trail, and that even now, there would be rescuers closing in. Annie desperately hoped that one of them would be Will Redmond.

As dusk again turned another day to gray, Bear Hawk made camp. After he had started a fire, he walked into the forest. He returned a bit later with two ground squirrels. He handed one to Annie and began cooking the other over the flames. They had been having only one meal at the end of each day, chewing on jerky as they rode.

Annie was so hungry she wanted to eat the squirrel raw, but she made herself wait as the hair was singed off and the meat underneath began to smell delicious. When at last Bear Hawk began to eat his,

Annie tore into the little animal ravenously. She would have eaten the claws, tail, and head if Bear Hawk hadn't forcibly taken the carcass from her. Still hungry, she went to the creek and drank more water, thinking that she would never have enough to eat again.

As the fire died down, Bear Hawk pulled her close. Fearfully, she could feel his arousal through her thin dress, but he made no overture to take her. Grateful for his warmth, she allowed him to hold her close as they slept.

Will continued to track, day after day, until he lost the trail altogether. Almost in tears, he searched and searched for any clue or sign. When he finally was forced to give up, his chest felt like it was caving in.

"ANNIE, WHERE ARE YOU?" he yelled into the echoing mountains. Up until this moment, he had had every confidence of finding her and killing that damn Indian with his bare hands. Now, as his hopes waned, he doubted he'd ever see her again. And he knew he couldn't live with that. He had to find her, and after he made himself a free man, he'd marry her and never let her out of his sight again.

He put one foot in the stirrup ready to mount when he caught a glimpse of something toward the top of the mountain he'd just crossed... Smoke.

"It might be Tom or some mountain trapper," he thought, though his heart was thumping loudly in his ears. "But it's the only lead I've got." He mounted his horse and rode toward the smoke, fixing its location with landmarks.

Annie was jerked out of a sound sleep by Bear Hawk. He threw her onto the horse, mounted himself, and raced off into the darkness at breakneck speed. When Annie opened her mouth to complain, his hand covered it quickly. Terrified at this turn of events, Annie gripped the horse's heaving flanks with her legs and closed her mouth. When Bear Hawk was sure she wouldn't cry out, he removed his hand and held her tightly as they sped up the mountain.

As the slope increased, Annie and Bear Hawk leaned forward, the horse's mane flying into their faces. Annie felt, rather than saw, Bear Hawk's frequent glances back as if they were being followed. A rush of hope filled her when she realized it might be her rescuers.

When she tried to look back, Bear Hawk used his shoulder to bump her, nearly sending her flying from the horse. She gripped the mane tightly as Bear Hawk leaned into her and forced her face against the back of the animal. Almost lying prone on the horse with Bear Hawk on her back, she was prevented from a backwards view and from calling out.

On and on they rode in the pitch blackness of the moonless night. The horse seemed to know its way as Bear Hawk urged it off the trail. They entered a treed area and Bear Hawk brought the exhausted animal to a halt. As he dragged Annie from the back of the horse, she decided to make her discomfort known.

"Bear Ha..." was all she was able to utter before his iron hand came across her mouth again. This time Annie used her teeth and bit into the soft part of his palm. With a grunt of displeasure, he pushed her, sending her sprawling onto the ground.

He cut a piece of her already shredding dress, rolled the material into a ball, and stuffed it into her mouth. Then he removed the leather band across his forehead and tied it securely over her mouth, making any loud noise impossible. Annie could only grunt her anger.

All at once, Bear Hawk gripped her arms and brought her close to him, their faces only inches apart. Annie expected to see anger in his eyes but was surprised by the despair and desperation there. He fingered her hair, bringing it to his nose as he rubbed his face in the silky locks.

When he released her, it was to set her upon the rested horse and begin their journey again, this time going at an angle around the mountain instead of straight up.

Several hours later, just as Annie had begun to nod off, she heard something ahead. It sounded like human voices, and her spirits lifted once again. But when they rode into the camp, Annie realized at once that this was not a white man's settlement.

Dark-skinned braves, milling around the horse, stared up at Annie but spoke to Bear Hawk. Annie saw a few women staring resentfully at her from in front of the teepees they passed. She counted a total of twelve lodges and guessed there to be over twenty-five people in the camp. Though the night was dark, fires had been lit as if to welcome them.

Bear Hawk reined in the big stallion in front of a lodge and pulled Annie to the ground. He untied her mouth restraint just as the flap from the teepee was pushed aside. To Annie's great delight and relief, Soft Dove walked toward them. Spitting the wad of material to the ground, Annie broke free of Bear Hawk's grip and ran to her friend.

Embracing each other, Annie felt the tears spill down her cheeks.

"I'm so glad to see you," Annie cried. "Bear Hawk kidnapped me from the swimming pond, Soft Dove, and we've been traveling for days. I've been so scared."

"Hush, Annie, quit crying," Soft Dove spoke quietly. "You are being judged by my People. Show them your strength." The Indian girl pushed Annie away from her and turned her to face the gathering crowd which stood silently watching.

Annie wiped her eyes and raised her head high as she trembled inside. She stared at the unsmiling dark faces, meeting each eye boldly. When she thought her knees might give way, Bear Hawk suddenly was at her side, speaking in a loud voice to the crowd. Again Annie recognized the words 'Blood Hair' but nothing more. She looked at Soft Dove for an explanation.

When Bear Hawk quit speaking, the crowd looked at each other with astonishment written on their faces. Then they began to murmur among themselves. Soft Dove turned toward Annie and her brother, her face a blank.

"Come with me, Annie," Soft Dove said as she linked her arm in the white girl's.

Annie was escorted to the lodge from which she had seen Soft Dove emerge. Pushing back the hide flap, the two girls entered the darkened interior. Once Annie's eyes adjusted to the gloom, she studied her surroundings.

A small fire pit of dying coals glowed in the middle of the rounded room. Fur skins were laid out on two sides for beds, and parfleche containers of different sizes were pushed against the walls of the hide teepee covering. Spears, bows and arrows, and knives were against the wall closest to the door flap. Annie even recognized a Winchester rifle leaning over a pile of furs.

Above, hanging from the pine poles used as supports, Annie recognized the scent of some of the herbs Soft Dove had shown her. Hung to dry, their pungent aromas wafted throughout the small enclosure, intermingling with the leather and human smells.

Soft Dove led Annie to a soft cushioned skin and bid her to sit. Gratefully, Annie collapsed. "Soft Dove, I'm so glad he brought me to you. Now you can talk some sense into that brother of yours and make him take me back."

Soft Dove, unsmiling and formal, stared back at Annie.

`"You can't go back, Annie, not ever," the Indian girl said softly.

"What do you mean 'not ever', Soft Dove?" Annie asked, a streak of fear creasing her brow. "M-my uncle will send someone after me. I think that's why we left the last camp so hurriedly. Someone is coming. You have to let me go."

"You must understand that you are Bear Hawk's woman now, Annie, and he won't give you up. He has gone through much trouble to bring you here, and he'll fight to the death for you," replied Soft Dove.

"I'm *not* Bear Hawk's woman, Soft Dove," began Annie, her face now suffused in anger. "I won't be held here against my will!"

At that moment, the flap of the teepee was thrown back and several women entered. One was very old with many wrinkles and long stringy gray hair. When she smiled at Annie, there were gaps where teeth had once been. The other two women were older than Soft Dove but younger than the ancient crone. All three were dressed in hide dresses decorated with beads and quills as was Soft Dove's dress.

One of the elder women carried knee-high moccasins which were decorated with bits of what looked like shiny glass or beads, and the other carried a dress of pliant animal skin, dyed yellow but with much decoration sewn onto the material. The old one carried a steaming bowl of water in a hardened clay bowl.

Soft Dove stood as the women entered and said a few words in her language. The old woman giggled as she pushed back her sleeves on which hung a long fringe down the back side.

"Stand, Annie," urged Soft Dove. "This is Sweet Water, my grandmother. And these are my aunts, Snow Bird and Warbler."

Annie rose and dipped into a small curtsy. As she was about to say 'how do you do', Soft Dove slipped behind her and swiftly lifted her torn and dirty dress over her head.

Sputtering with indignation, Annie fought the Indian women as her chemise and pantalets were summarily removed. While Annie tried to cover her nakedness with her hands, Soft Dove and one of the women caught Annie's arms from behind and pinioned them back. The old woman moved in front of Annie and began to thoroughly examine her.

The old crone felt Annie's biceps and thigh muscles, then she pulled back her lips to see her teeth. Annie was complaining loudly and thrashing at this outrage until Soft Dove spoke into her ear. "Just let her do what she has to do, Annie, and don't fight."

"Why are you doing this? Make her stop! Soft Dove, please make her stop," Annie pleaded as the old woman squeezed each breast and kneaded each nipple until they stood up like hard little pebbles. Annie struggled fiercely, but to no avail. The Indian women were strong and held her fast. Suddenly, the old woman dipped between Annie's legs and inserted her finger.

Annie screamed. The grandmother removed her finger, studying it as she rubbed the wetness between finger and thumb. Then to Annie's astonishment, the old woman stuck the finger into her mouth and smacked her lips. Then she laughed long and hard while uttering a barrage of words which caused the other women to giggle shyly.

"God's teeth, what's going on? Why are you treating me like this... and what's so damn funny?" Annie demanded as she kicked at the young woman.

"She paid you a great compliment, Annie," replied Soft Dove, as she and her aunts released the struggling girl. "She said that your wetness would greatly increase your pleasures on this night, and your husband would find much satisfaction between your legs. She also said you were built to carry many strong sons in your belly."

Annie was still trying to cover herself when the word 'husband' made its way into her outraged brain.

"Husband?" Annie turned to Soft Dove and asked timorously, afraid of the answer.

"I told you, you are Bear Hawk's woman now. He is to be your husband this night."

"Oh no, Soft Dove, you're wrong," stated Annie emphatically. "My uncle will be coming for me very soon. You have to stop all this nonsense right now. You can't treat a white girl like this."

Annie faced the Indian girl, forgetting her nakedness for a moment. When someone started rubbing her back with a hot rag, she shrieked. Again, Soft Dove and her aunt held Annie while the grandmother and the other aunt washed her thoroughly, ignoring Annie's loud complaints. Then her hair was combed with a teasel, pulling out all of the tangles along with bits of dirt and twigs.

After being dried with a soft fur, the yellow doeskin dress was slipped over her head, hugging her body as it reached her ankles; then the knee-high moccasins were tied on her feet. Throughout the humiliating experience, Annie continued to plead with Soft Dove, but her friend had stood mute, refusing to answer Annie's questions or help her in any way.

When Annie was dressed, the three older women left the teepee, leaving her alone with Soft Dove. "Sit, Annie, and we will talk now."

"You and your brother will be sorry for this, Soft Dove," Annie mumbled as she wiped frustrated tears from her eyes. "When I am rescued..."

"Annie, listen to me and heed what I say," Soft Dove's voice was steely. "You can *never* go back to the White world. That life is over. They will not accept you anymore."

"What are you talking about, Soft Dove? Of course my uncle and aunt will want me back. And I'm engaged to an important man who owns the Wolverine Mine," Annie stated petulantly.

"You will never be allowed back into your White society after they know an Indian has had you."

Annie blanched, thinking of the nights spent beside Bear Hawk, with only a breech cloth and a thin cotton dress between them. "But nothing happened, Soft Dove. He didn't do anything to me."

Soft Dove replied, "Bear Hawk was like a crazed animal after your uncle laughed at his offer and sent him away. He has risked much to bring you here, and he will not take no from you or anyone now.

"He wants you for a wife, Annie, and that is a great honor. He could keep you as a slave and use you as he wanted, but he wants to hunt for you, to give you children. He is the bravest and strongest of our hunters, Annie, and he will defend you with his life."

"This can't be happening. I don't love him; I-I love someone else, Soft Dove," whispered Annie miserably.

"No white man will want you once they know an Indian has bedded you, Annie," Soft Dove answered brusquely. "And even if you were free to leave now, no white man would believe nothing happened between you. Do you think your aunt would believe you? Would the man they have promised you in marriage believe you?

"You know what most Whites think of my People, that we are lower than dogs. You would be called a 'squaw' and considered beneath contempt. But here in these mountains with Bear Hawk, you will have status as being wife of a brave Ute leader who will love you and keep you safe. You will bear him many sons. Accept it, Annie, for this is how it is to be."

Annie thought over what Soft Dove had said. She didn't want to believe that her own people, her own blood-kin, would turn their backs on her for something she had had no control to stop.

But Annie remembered how quickly her father had abandoned her. And she pictured Aunt Marian's face when she had called Soft Dove and Bear Hawk 'savages'. Suddenly she knew Soft Dove was probably right. Even if she was rescued, no one would accept her back into polite society ever again.

And she shuddered when she thought of going back too J.C. Brashears. Would staying with Soft Dove and Bear Hawk be better than being the wife of a horrible man who terrified her? Would never seeing Will Redmond again be better than seeing him and knowing she could never be with him because he was married?

What choice did she have?

Soft Dove put her arm around her friend's shoulders, "You know what I say is true. We are your family now. Bear Hawk will have you, one way or another. Not even I could stop that. You might as well accept him as your husband. Face the facts, Annie, you have nothing to go back to in the White world."

CHAPTER FIVE

Soft Dove took Annie's limp hand and, resignedly, Annie allowed her friend to lead her out of the lodge. The tribe had gathered around the teepee. As they parted for her to pass, she saw Bear Hawk at the other end of the crowd.

He was clad in a long-sleeve hide shirt decorated with bits of bone and teeth braided into the fringe across his chest. Leggings covered his thighs, though he still wore the breechclout hanging from his waist. His sleek black hair hung loose, strands blowing lightly in the soft breeze of the dark night.

As Annie gazed at him, she asked herself what she had to go back to? Will Redmond, the man she loved, was forever beyond her reach. Marriage to the odious J. C. Brashears? A father who had thrown her away?

Annie realized that if she had to spend her life with a man not of her own choice, she would much rather it be Bear Hawk than J. C. Brashears. At least, she'd be with her friend, Soft Dove. Lifting her chin, Annie raised her chin and returned Bear Hawk's intense gaze as he walked slowly toward her through the darkness.

When Bear Hawk stood facing her, Annie thought she would drown in his smoldering black eyes. From somewhere behind her, beating drums matched the pounding of her heart.

Several gray-haired Elders surrounded the couple and began to chant. Someone took Annie's hand and turned it over. Before she knew what was happening, she felt the hot searing pain as a knife sliced through her skin. Gasping, she saw her own blood dripping to the ground.

But as quickly, Bear Hawk's hand was cut in the same way, then laid across hers as their blood mingled. Soft Dove was suddenly at Annie's side, speaking in a low tone as the chanting continued.

"Now you are of one blood, Annie, and you are his for all time. He will protect you, fight for you, feed you, and give you many strong children. You and Bear Hawk are one."

The singers stopped just as the drums were hit one last time, and the crowd uttered a loud 'whoa-ho' which made Annie jump. Then it was over and a sudden celebratory atmosphere spread throughout the tribe. The grandmother, smiling and wagging her head, wrapped a soft piece of leather around Annie's palm to staunch the bleeding, yammering words that Annie didn't understand. The aunts, Warbler and Snow Bird, hugged Annie, as did the rest of the Ute women.

Annie glanced back at Bear Hawk as he was being congratulated by the men and was surprised to see a boyish smile on his face. He looked younger, less terrifying, and a bit vulnerable.

"Now you are truly my sister," Soft Dove whispered into Annie's ear as she hugged her. "Please make my brother happy."

Annie pulled back to study Soft Dove's face. She saw the concern in the Ute girl's face. Was it for Annie? Or for Bear Hawk?

She didn't have long to wonder as Bear Hawk scooped her up in his arms and walked determinedly into the lodge. The crowd tittered behind them, and even though Annie didn't understand the words, the tone was unmistakable.

Bear Hawk stood Annie on her feet again once inside the teepee. He laced the door flap closed, then added a few sticks to the fire pit and the flames both warmed and brightened the interior.

Suddenly terrified to be alone with Bear Hawk, Annie shivered as he quickly rid himself of the beaded shirt and leggings. As he dropped the breechclout to the ground, she found herself staring at the man in front of her...her husband, a strong brown naked savage. Annie was suddenly mesmerized by his taut lean body, all muscle and sinew. And his need was most evident.

Will Redmond's face flitted before her for a moment, and she realized that after tonight, he would be lost to her forever.

Bear Hawk walked slowly around the fire to where Annie stood. He touched her hair gently, bringing a coppery strand to his nose and inhaling. He released her hair and traced her jaw line with his finger, his black eyes boring into her soul. Annie caught her breath as his hand moved down and caressed one breast.

Her heart beat rapidly and her breathing quickened. When Bear Hawk bent and grabbed the bottom of her dress and began to slowly pull it up and over her head, all Annie could do was to raise her arms in acquiescence. She stood before him, clad only in the knee-high moccasins as he raked her with glittering eyes.

Bear Hawk lifted Annie and lay her gently on the soft furs. Then using lips, teeth, and tongue, he proceeded to explore every inch of her body. Annie's breathing grew ragged as she became lost in the spiraling heat of his mouth as he seared her skin. His long soft hair left tingling caresses where it touched her, and she suddenly arched, crying out as waves of pleasure washed over her. Bear Hawk moved up her body, lifting her legs and entering her in one swift smooth movement.

Annie moaned as he filled her and began the slow sensual movements which she found herself returning. She wrapped her arms and legs around him, pulling him deeper inside of her.

Afterwards, they lay wrapped in a tangle of arms and legs while their heart beats slowed. Bear Hawk grasped Annie to him as though she might disappear if he let go. Annie was spent with pleasure, exhaustion, and shock at the events of the past days, but soon the two slept peacefully.

A few hours later, Bear Hawk took Annie again and just as she was drifting back into contented slumber, the weight of his body on hers shifted and cold air touched her finely sheened skin, making her shiver. She felt a soft slap on her backside and turned her head to see Bear Hawk leaning on his elbow, grinning. Annie found herself smiling shyly back.

He pulled her to him and held her tightly, murmuring unintelligible words over her head. A fleeting wish that it was Will Redmond holding her so tenderly passed briefly through Annie's mind, but she sadly pushed it away. Any hope of that life was gone forever.

After awhile, Bear Hawk released her, and as he put on his breechclout, Annie glanced around for her cotton dress. The only clothing she could find was the yellow doeskin dress. She reached for it and pulled it over her head, laughing suddenly when she realized that she still had on the moccasins.

Bear Hawk looked down at her and murmured, "*Kee-en.*"

Annie stared up at him as he repeated the word again, then made a laughing sound. "Does that word mean 'laugh'?" Annie mulled it over. She smiled back at the tall young Utw, her husband, glad that their first shared word had been a happy one.

When he untied the door flap and left the teepee, she followed him out into the early morning sunlight. As her eyes became accustomed to the brightness, she saw that the lodges around her had all been taken down and loaded on travois attached to horses. Everyone in the camp was busy at some chore, Annie noticed, and she scanned the dark-skinned figures for Soft Dove.

She spied her friend at a fire pit, stirring a container which steamed in the cool morning air and smelled deliciously. As Annie approached, she saw that it wasn't an iron pot which held the delectable aroma, but a bag made from the large stomach of a deer or elk.

"Doesn't it catch on fire?" Annie asked as she knelt beside Soft Dove.

"No, not if you soak it in water before putting it over the flame," replied Soft Dove, glancing at her friend with a knowing expression on her face.

Annie noticed the look and asked, "What's the matter? Why are you staring at me like that?"

Soft Dove smiled as she stirred the contents once more. "It is good to see that you have accepted your lot. I assume you and my brother came to an understanding last night?" She snickered softly.

"Stop that, Soft Dove, and tell me why you are laughing at me," demanded Annie.

"A lodge has thin walls, and from what everyone heard, my brother must be a very worthy husband indeed."

Annie put her head into her hands, too embarrassed to meet the eyes of the other members of the tribe. Their knowing looks would be harder to take than Soft Dove's.

"Don't worry, Annie, what goes on between man and woman in the furs is a natural, beautiful thing to my People, not shameful," Soft Dove replied when she saw Annie's reddened cheeks. "And our women enjoy it as much as the men. It would be wrong to feel shame for something the Great Spirit has given to his People as a wonderful gift."

As Annie pondered the difference in attitude toward sex by the Whites and the Indians, Bear Hawk approached. Annie's breath quickened as she stared up at the handsome young man, all male and musky. He pulled Annie to her feet and gazed sensuously into her face, rubbing her hair between his fingers.

Then he spoke a few words, never tearing his dark eyes from Annie.

"Bear Hawk says he is most pleased with his White wife," Soft Dove translated. "He thinks you might also be pleased with him. Is that not so?" She looked up at Annie.

Annie reddened at his apparent arousal in front of the entire tribe. She answered shyly, "Yes, tell him that I am pleased also."

Soft Dove translated and Bear Hawk smiled back at Annie. She marveled that 'home' would forever be with this strange and beautiful man who now knew her intimately. If only she didn't still wish that the eyes which looked back at her with so much passion were flinty green.

"The tribe is preparing to move," Soft Dove said softly.

"Why?" asked Annie, still mesmerized by Bear Hawk's piercing black stare.

"In case you are being tracked."

Annie jerked her eyes away and looked at Soft Dove. "Do you think there is someone out there searching for me?"

Though Bear Hawk didn't understand what Annie had said, he felt her go stiff in his arms. He spoke harshly to his sister who answered him back in the same harsh tone. Then suddenly he released Annie and stalked away.

"What did I do?" asked Annie, staring after him. Then she turned back to Soft Dove. "Tell me the truth, is there someone following us?"

Soft Dove watched her brother stride to his stallion, throw one leg across the bare back and gallop away. Slowly she answered, "I don't know, Annie, but if there is a White posse, then our tribe is in danger."

Stricken, Annie replied. "I don't want anything to happen to you or to any of the others because of me, Soft Dove. If there are people searching for me, and they catch us, what will happen to you and your People?"

"*We* are *your* People now, my sister, and we are used to moving around. If we are discovered, though, then we will be sent to the Reservation on the Uintah River like our relatives.

"These few of us who are free have eluded the White man for many years, and we will continue as long as we are able. We know these mountains better than the Whites, so do not worry. But remember what I said, Annie, Bear Hawk will never let you go."

Annie glanced into the surrounding forest, wondering if anyone *was* searching for her. And, for a moment, she wished with all her heart that it might be Will Redmond. But shaking her head, she knew it was only a pipe dream. She could never go back! It had been over a month since she had been taken by Bear Hawk. If anyone was hunting for her, surely they would have found her by now.

Quickly the lodge in which Annie and Bear Hawk had spent the night was dismantled and loaded. The tribe moved around the ridge of the mountain, crossing over the treeless tundra at the top. Bear Hawk and his friends had been scouting behind for any sign of a posse, and Annie did not see him again until the cook fires burned brightly that evening.

When he appeared out of the blackness of the starless night, Annie's heart beat faster as he devoured her with his eyes. As soon as they both had eaten, he grabbed her hand, along with a warm buffalo robe, and pulled her away from the rest of the tribe.

Throwing down the skin on a sheltered grassy area, Bear Hawk quickly slipped Annie's dress over her head. He was like a man gulping greedily at his first drink after a long drought as he quickly made her his. Annie's own passion surprised her as they came together in a heated, hurried, tangled joining which left them both breathless. Afterward, Bear Hawk pulled her close to his heart and wrapped the large buffalo hide around them.

Although Annie had accepted Bear Hawk as her husband, deep inside her heart, she couldn't help but wish that she could be sharing these moments of pleasure with Will Redmond. Tears ran down her cheeks in the darkness as Bear Hawk slept.

The Utes moved continuously, camping only for a few hours in the darkness. But as the days passed, Annie felt the tenseness of the People relax. Whomever they had been trying to evade, she thought, they must have succeeded. When no one was watching, Annie would glance back, wondering if it had been Will trying to find her.

Though Annie could still not communicate with Bear Hawk in words, she began to learn through signs and from Soft Dove's translations what was expected of her. Soft Dove had been right; Annie had status as Bear Hawk's wife.

She was treated with great respect by both the men and women, and the children often brought her small gifts of beads, soft furs, or finely sharpened awls for sewing as their shy mothers stood at a distance.

"Come, Annie, my brother expects you to make arrows for his bow. Sit here and I'll show you," Soft Dove said one bright afternoon when the tribe had set up a hunting camp. This would be a longer stay, probably two to three days or more. Annie had just begun scraping the bloody flesh from a rabbit fur.

"I'm learning so much, Soft Dove, but I didn't realize how much work daily life can be. I'm exhausted when it is time to sleep."

"You'll get used to it; you have lived the life of a spoiled White girl for too long, my sister," laughed Soft Dove. "This is how it is to be Ute. Mother Earth gives us everything we need, but we have to work hard to make it ours."

Annie leaned back on her outstretched arms, raising her face to the warmth of the sun. She tried hard not to think of her former life; it only brought back painful memories.

"Right now, if Bear Hawk had never taken me, I'd be married to that horrible J.C. Brashears," Annie thought, shuddering. She looked around, hearing laughter and conversation, seeing children at play, and was suddenly thankful that she was alive.

As her eyes wandered around the always busy campsite, she caught sight of Bear Hawk as he sharpened his knife and talked with several other Utes. He happened to glance her way and smiled warmly at Annie. She wanted to care for him as much as he cared for her, but her dreams were still achingly filled with Will Redmond.

Shaking her head to remove the memories, Annie turned to Soft Dove, "Teach me how to make arrows for my husband, sister."

Soft Dove could see that Annie was not truly happy. She knew that Annie had loved another in the White world, and she feared for her brother's happiness.

"First you must have the branches of the chokecherry; they make the best arrows. We peel off the bark and twigs, then it must be chewed."

Soft Dove worked as she spoke. Annie chewed on the sticks, twirling them round and round as the others did to make them straight, until her teeth ached. The Ute women laid the bare branches in a pile near the fire to dry. When they were dry, Soft Dove showed Annie how to split the ends and insert arrowheads, holding them firmly with sinew. On the opposite ends, hawk feathers were used to tip them.

After the women had assembled over a dozen arrows, Bear Hawk came over to inspect them. He and Annie were still only able to communicate through his sister. He had tried to say Annie's white name, but it came out as 'U-nay'. In the darkness, he often whispered her Ute name, Blood Hair, as if it were a prayer.

Soft Dove would often sit with the young couple in the evening and translate back and forth until Bear Hawk's physical desire became suddenly apparent under his breechclout. Then he would unceremoniously pull Annie away from the others and into his furs. Annie didn't mind except that the Ute were not a retiring race, and both men and women made plenty of obvious hand signals the next day. Though Annie didn't understand their words, the meaning was quite clear, and they seemed to love watching her pale skin blush.

One day as the tribe moved yet again, Bear Hawk rode up beside Annie's pony and lift her onto his big stallion.

"*Wan-zits,*" he said to Annie as he pointed to a small herd of antelope in the distance.

"*Wan-zits,*" she repeated. "Antelope?"

Bear Hawk nodded. Annie patted his sleek black stallion's neck. She turned to Bear Hawk and asked, "What is his name?"

"*Ka-va-hee,*" Bear Hawk replied as he rubbed his nose into her copper hair which was held back in a long thick braid down her back.

"*Ka-va-hee,*" she repeated, leaning into him and enjoying his warm breath on her neck.

Over the next few days, in the same manner, Annie learned that the huge brown elk which grazed in the meadows were called *pa-re-ah* and the shy long-eared deer was *ti-at*.

Bear Hawk would often go into a long oration in Ute, gesturing to the sky and the horizon. Annie would lean back against his warm strong chest and listen, just enjoying his voice. He would try to make her understand and sometimes became frustrated, but she could always make him smile again with a look or a touch which would rekindle his passion and produce a quick romp behind the cover of bushes.

One night, almost two weeks after their joining ceremony, Bear Hawk shook Annie awake, hurrying her to dress. The entire camp was awake and busily loading the travois.

Soft Dove approached while Annie was bundling the sleeping furs and cooking utensils. "Annie, you are leaving the tribe tonight. Bear Hawk is taking you far away for he believes that whomever has been tracking you has not given up."

"What about you?" gasped Annie as she stared into her friend's sad face.

"I hope that someday we will meet again, my sister," said Soft Dove stoically. "The tribe will continue in the opposite direction to give you and my brother a chance to escape."

Annie stood up and grasped Soft Dove's shoulders. "What if they find you? I can't let anything happen to your...my People. Maybe it would be better to leave me here and whoever is pursuing me will stop hunting you."

Soft Dove took Annie's hands in hers. "You don't understand yet. Bear Hawk will never give you up. He will die first."

Annie glanced at Bear Hawk who stood nearby and saw the fierceness as he stared at her. He wanted her...maybe even loved her. No one else in the world cared for her as desperately as Bear Hawk. She should be happy with him, she thought, and she had left nothing in the White world to which to return. Being wanted that much would surely cause her to love him back...eventually.

She turned back to Soft Dove. "But Bear Hawk and I can't talk to each other yet, Soft Dove; who will translate?"

"You will be forced to learn from each other, Annie," replied her friend softly. "Let us share our last meal together before we are parted."

The dry pemmican stuck in Annie's throat as she thought of what the future might bring. Bear Hawk was a renegade, an outlaw, so they would be forced to continue to hide. And other Indian groups, if there were any left who were still free, might not accept her.

Where would they go, she and Bear Hawk, separated from both of their races? And what if Bear Hawk tired of her? Would he abandon her in the wilderness to die? Or would he sell her to a trapper as was the fate of other White captives? Annie stared at Bear Hawk as he used his fingers to shovel in stew from a hardened clay bowl. Would he always want her and protect her?

Before she had time to contemplate more, Bear Hawk finished eating and lifted Annie to her feet.

"My brother has packed traveling food and what you will need in a parfleche. I wish you both safe journey," stated Soft Dove, sudden tears forming in her beautiful black eyes.

Annie hugged her friend for a long time, both of them sobbing. Then Bear Hawk and his sister spoke a few words. Bear Hawk hugged Soft Dove for only a moment, then helped Annie upon her sorrel pony.

Bear Hawk jumped upon the black stallion's back in one fluid movement, lifted his hand as a salute to his sister, and led Annie away from camp. Annie glanced over her shoulder once, and through her tears, saw that Soft Dove had turned her back and had her head in her hands.

Will had ridden hard for days and days, barely stopping to rest his weary horse, then pacing back and forth in frustration and eagerness to be going again. He didn't know if the smoke he had seen had anything to do with Annie, but a deep gut reaction made him feel the need to hurry.

Once aboard his rested horse again, he pushed the animal almost beyond its endurance as he climbed up and down the rocky slopes while searching for tracks. At each of their camps, Will had seen only one tramped down place where they had slept...on the same blanket.

"I'm gonna kill that bastard if he's laid a hand on her," Will steamed as he pounded a huge fist into his open palm. "Oh God, please let her be alive."

Seething, he jumped on his horse and rode on, stopping occasionally to study the rocky ground. He found where Bear Hawk and Annie had joined the tribe, and he reveled in the fact. He knew the tribe would slow them down.

Weeks passed as he found several abandoned camps where the tribe had stayed. A few days later, as the sun was overhead, he finally found the most recent camp. Rubbing the cold ash from a fire pit between thumb and finger, he mused, "They've only been gone a day at the most. I can easily catch a band of women, children, and horses with travois attached to their backs."

Will was forced to allow his winded horse to rest, crop some grass, and drink for a very long half hour while he paced and cursed. He planned Bear Hawk's death down to the last detail, praying that Annie was still alive. "I will find you, Annie Mitchell," he cried to the echoing mountains. "I have to tell you what you mean to me...how much I love you. If you'll have me, I'll make myself a free man and marry you. I'll never let you out of my sight again. And you can damn well guarantee that Brashears won't lay a hand on you ever. Oh, God, please let me find her!"

Will rode on and on, easily following the tribe as they crossed the "Child's Trail", named by the Utes because of its easy slope. The tribe was heading back toward Lulu City, he deduced, and he knew this territory like the back of his hand.

He was taken completely by surprise by the ambush. As he barreled down the trail like a madman, the long piece of sinew stretched between two trees caught him chest high, hurling him backwards off his horse. Lying on his back in the dirt, trying to get his breath, he was suddenly surrounded by five Utes aiming rifles at his head.

Before his breath returned, they hoisted him to his feet and led him to a hidden glade off the trail. Several Utes stayed to watch the trail behind, expecting more White men to come riding over the ridge.

Will's guns were taken, his hands were tied behind him, and he was suddenly surrounded by women and children who jeered at him and threw rocks and clods of dirt.

"WHO ARE YOU?" asked a commanding female voice. The taunting and attacks stilled as everyone, including Will, turned to look in the direction of the beautiful girl who had spoken. "I said, who are you?"

"The name's William Redmond, ma'am, and I'm the Undersheriff of Grand County. I'm tracking an Indian called Bear Hawk who abducted a White girl from Grand Lake." Will glanced around at the brown faces, searching for the pale one he sought.

"There is no White girl here," Soft Dove spoke imperiously.

"I think you might be lying, ma'am, no offense," drawled Will, dangerously slow.

"You may search all you like, but you will find no White girl here."

Though his hands stayed bound, they allowed him to walk among the crowd, his head almost a foot above the rest, as he scanned the faces and their belongings. His heart sank. He had tracked them to the Indian camp, then all of the signs had led here, so where was she?

All at once it dawned on him. Bear Hawk had used the tribe as a diversion, then had gone off in another direction. And Will, in his maddened state, had fallen for it. Now he'd lost another day or two.

"Damn," spat Will.

"Do you see that there is no White girl here?" asked Soft Dove, reading from his face the fact that he was aware of being duped.

"Yeah, so you all helped Bear Hawk spirit her away, but why?" asked Will, puzzled. "You knew someone was tracking them, and it could've been a whole posse who would have killed some of you and put the rest on a Reservation. Why would you risk yourselves for one White girl?"

"She is *his* woman now, and she doesn't wish to return to your White world," answered Soft Dove. "Bear Hawk loves her and will kill to keep her."

Will paled. He had tried not to think about their sleeping arrangements as he had tracked the two, but hearing the Indian girl's words left little doubt about Annie's plight.

"He can't keep her against her will," protested Redmond.

"*She* made the choice," replied Soft Dove, carefully watching the White man's face. She saw the agony her words caused him but continued anyway. "Did she have as many choices in your world? What did she have back there? The man she loved betrayed her. Her own father had thrown her away, and her uncle had promised her to one she hates. Why would she want to go back to the White world when she has a brave and honorable man who loves her?"

"But I love her, too," Will whispered before he thought.

Soft Dove's eyes widened. "It's you," she mumbled, realizing that this man must be the one Annie had loved.

"You've got to let me go, ma'am, so that I can find her," pleaded Will. "If she tells me that she'd rather be with Bear Hawk than return with me, then I swear I'll leave them alone. Please, give me that chance."

"She may already be carrying his child," said Soft Dove harshly. "Would you want her if she had a Ute baby?"

"I love her," he replied simply. "No matter what has happened, that will never change."

Soft Dove grew frustrated at this tall White man whose hurt and longing showed so clearly in his green eyes. "My brother is a fierce warrior, and he will *never* let her go! He will see you lying in your own blood first."

Will's eyes softened as he heard the pain in the girl's voice. "So Bear Hawk is your brother; that's why the tribe protected him." Then his eyes grew flinty again. "I will try not to kill him, ma'am, but if he's hurt Annie in any way, then I won't be responsible for my actions, and it might not be *me* lying in blood."

He and Soft Dove stared at each other for a long moment. Finally, Soft Dove said something in Ute, and Will's hands were released.

"No matter what happens, I want your word that you will not turn us over to the authorities. We would rather all be dead than be forced onto a Reservation. For giving you your life, I want your word," demanded Soft Dove.

Will scanned the scraggly group of few men and more women and children as he rubbed the circulation back into his hands.

"You can't hide forever," he said softly. "They'll find you eventually."

"I want your word," repeated Soft Dove.

"You have my word," stated Will.

Redmond's horse was brought to him; he mounted and began to retrace his path back to the camp where he could once again pick up Bear Hawk's trail. He mused that Bear Hawk must be quite a man to have a sister as courageous and noble as that pretty Indian girl who would risk her tribe and her own freedom just so he could have Annie.

A pang of jealousy gripped Will suddenly, making him bend double as he pictured Annie locked in the Indian's arms. 'She may already be carrying his child' the girl had said...Will couldn't bear to think of it.

Bear Hawk and Annie rode hard for several days, only stopping to rest and water the horses. A new tenseness permeated the silence between them. They left the towering peaks behind and headed west into flatter terrain with few trees. Red clay mesas dotted the desolate countryside as they rode toward the sunset.

As darkness fellon the fourth day, Annie felt herself begin to nod off several times. Bear Hawk had been riding ahead, peering into the blackness, trying to avoid prairie dog holes and hidden obstacles which might cripple the horses.

He glanced back just as Annie began to sway. Dropping back, he pulled her from her horse onto his. Drowsily, she leaned against him, secured by his arm around her, and slept. Her pony followed the big stallion obediently.

They rode on until dawn, when Annie awoke. She was still tired and felt that she had been on a horse forever. She begged Bear Hawk to stop, but he continued. Annie could see his fatigue which showed in the smudges of darkness under each eye and in the slump of his shoulders.

Trying to remember her geography from school, she figured they had left Colorado and had, by now, entered Utah and were continuing to move due west.

In the distance, she saw a stand of trees which, hopefully, indicated a water hole. The glare of the cloudless blue sky was blinding, and the baking sun, so much hotter than in the mountains, had beat down on Annie relentlessly, burning her skin.

When they entered the welcoming shade of huge cottonwoods and found fresh water, both Annie and Bear Hawk drank deeply of the cooling wetness.

They rested all that day in the shade by the pool. Annie watched as exhaustion finally overtook the young Ute, and he sank into deep peaceful slumber. His weapons were by his side, and Annie could easily have cut his throat as he lay there. But he trusted she would not try to run away or hurt him.

Annie wished she could forget the green eyes which continued to haunt her, and she wished she could come to love Bear Hawk instead. "What's going to happen to us?" she whispered before she curled herself around him and fell asleep.

The darkness was Will's enemy as his tracking ability was hindered. Even the coal oil lamp he had brought made it almost impossible to follow the trail at night. He was forced to stop, build a fire, and wait for daybreak. It was in those quiet lonely hours that Will was tortured most with pictures in his head of Annie and Bear Hawk.

Though he tried to catch a few hours of sleep, his dreams were filled with pale naked flesh intertwined with darker skin, her lilting laughter echoing in his mind. As soon as blackness turned to gray, he was back in the saddle again.

Will rode on as he crossed the dry flat land, following the two horses' tracks easily now. He thought of what he would say to Annie when he caught them. The gnawing ache inside was his fear of hearing her say she wanted to stay with Bear Hawk. But he *had* to find out.

Before dusk, he saw the grove of trees in the distance. Intuitively, he knew they were there. He dismounted and walked his horse quietly toward the copse. About five hundred yards from the shaded area, Will dropped the reins to the ground and piled rocks on it to keep the horse at bay. After he checked the load in his side arm, he strode silently towards the site, his heart in his throat.

Upon entering the glade, Will's first view was of Annie and Bear Hawk, peacefully asleep at the base of an old cottonwood. Bear Hawk's brown leg was thrown over Annie, his arm resting familiarly on her hip. Annie was dressed in a pale yellow deerhide dress with fringe on the arms and hem. Her feet were covered in knee-high moccasins. Bear Hawk was clad in nothing but a breechclout, and his long black hair was intertwined with Annie's burnished auburn locks.

As Will stared at their relaxed intimacy, his stomach churned, and for a brief second, he thought about turning around and returning quietly to his horse, to ride away and never look back.

Before he could act upon it, though, Bear Hawk had leaped to his feet, wielding a knife as he stood protectively in front of Annie. The action has roused Annie and she sat up, rubbing her eyes sleepily as she tried to comprehend what was happening.

When she saw Will draw his gun from his holster, she bolted into action.

"No, don't shoot him!" she cried as she tried to get in front of Bear Hawk. The young Ute pushed her behind him with one strong arm. "Will, please don't hurt him. Please."

Will's resolve disintegrated at her pleading, protective tone, and his gun hand dropped limply to his side. The three stood frozen for a tense moment until Will broke the silence.

"Annie, just tell me if you want to stay with him, and I'll go away," he said, trying to keep his voice from breaking.

Annie stared at Will from behind Bear Hawk whom she felt was tensed and ready to spring. Will's face looked differently, tired and vulnerable behind a stubbly beard. He had come after her. Will...with the green eyes, the one she loved and had dreamed of, was here and asking her if she wanted to stay with Bear Hawk. She almost shouted out her answer, then stopped.

She turned her head to look at Bear Hawk, who wanted her and would fight for her, even die for her. How could she just leave him like he meant nothing?

Annie moved from behind Bear Hawk and stood to the side, staring from his face back to Will's. What could she do? If she went with Will, he'd only take her back to marry Brashears. Will was only doing his duty as a lawman, after all, there was nothing personal involved. He was married.

And she belonged to Bear Hawk, pledged in blood. She glanced down at her palm. Bear Hawk watched her closely. Slowly he lowered the knife and turned toward her, speaking gentle words she could not understand.

"I love you, Annie," Will interrupted. Her eyes met his, and she saw all of the longing and wanting she had felt for him mirrored back in his eyes.

"But you deceived me; you're already married," she shouted back at him. "And now I belong to Bear Hawk." She bared her hand, showing Will the newly-scabbed cut on her palm.

"I don't want to live without you," moaned Will, feeling his control slipping. He wanted to make her a widow, and soon.

"It's too late, Will," cried Annie. "Don't you see? You and I can never be together, and I *won't* go back to that horrible Brashears!"

"I won't let Brashears near you, Annie, I swear. And I will get out of my marriage. Hell, it ain't much of one anyway, never was. I married young to a girl I'd grown up with. It was kinda forced on me when she said she was gonna have my baby. She'd lied, but by then the deed was done, so that's when my brothers and I came out west. Being married had left such a bad taste in my mouth, I didn't think anymore about it...until I met you."

When Will paused, Bear Hawk took Annie by the arm and spoke sharply to her again. Her confusion was evident, and she put her hands to her face. Bear Hawk turned away from her and faced Will once more, knife raised as he bent his legs in readiness.

Will unbuckled and dropped his gunbelt, then drew out his knife. The two men were each ready to kill the other for her. They circled, each eyeing the other and waiting for an opening. Will was bigger and had greater strength, but Bear Hawk had agility and speed in his favor to duck out of the way of Will's murderous passes.

"No, please don't do this!" Annie screamed as they thrust the deadly knives at each other again and again. Suddenly, Bear Hawk lunged at Will, making a swipe which caught the material on the front of his shirt and shirred it open, leaving a shallow bloody swath across the skin of Will's chest.

When Annie saw Will's blood, she dashed toward him. Standing protectively in front of Will, she stared into Bear Hawk's blazing black eyes and screamed, "No more; there will be no more blood spilled because of me."

Bear Hawk froze, staring at her, realizing in an instant he had lost her.

"Get out of the way, Annie," Will snarled, thinking Bear Hawk might take another stab at him and hit her instead. He roughly pushed her behind him, then saw that Bear Hawk had sheathed his knife at his waist. It was over in a moment.

The Indian stared hard at Annie, willing her to return to him, but Annie stayed closely behind Will, her head peeking out from behind, as tears coursed down her cheeks.

Sorrowfully, Bear Hawk recognized his defeat to the large White man. Without a word, Bear Hawk leaped onto the black stallion. After one soulful backward glance at Annie, he rode off at full gallop.

Will and Annie heard Bear Hawk's cry as he disappeared into the distance, "Uuuu-nayyy."

Annie sank to her knees, sobbing. "Oh God, I didn't mean to hurt him, but what else could I do?"

Will knelt in front of Annie and gathered her into his arms. As she had done once before at the edge of Grand Lake, she clung to him and cried miserably into his shirt front.

Holding her close, he stroked her hair. "You never belonged to him, Annie. He stole you. It's all over now. You're safe. I promise I won't let anything or anybody hurt you again."

The sun was sinking behind a mesa, leaving the sky a brilliant myriad of red and orange as darkness encroached upon the land. Will finally had Annie in his arms so he hated the dark a little less now.

"I'll make it right for you, Annie Mitchell, I promise," Will swore huskily.

He caressed the back of her neck until she raised her head and looked up at him with shimmering tearstained blue eyes. "I couldn't stay with him, Will, because I love you," she whispered.

Before he knew what happened, he was kissing her...deeply as she wrapped her arms tightly around his neck and met his kiss with as much intensity as he gave. On their knees in the sand, they clung to each other as shipwrecked victims might, each scared to let go, lest they be swept into a black nothingness from which there was no escape.

Only the two of them existed in the world, and when Will lay Annie down and pressed her into the sand with his body, she opened to him willingly. And he took her, fiercely, wanting to erase any vestige of Bear Hawk from her soul. Together, in an all-encompassing, tumultuous meeting of both body and spirit, they succeeded in eradicating all of the madness and uncertainty of the previous weeks.

Will held her tightly to him, feeling he would gladly die in her arms. Annie lay against him, inhaling the male scent, so uniquely his, and prayed that this moment would never end. How wonderful it is, she thought contentedly, to share my body with someone I love more than life itself.

"Did you love that Indian boy?" Will asked quietly after a time.

"I cared for him, Will, and I believe he loved me," she replied.

Will knew he had to accept her answer and be satisfied with it. She had chosen him; that was all that mattered.

"What's going to happen to us now, Will?" Annie asked, reality rearing its ugly head once more.

"I'm not taking you back to Brashears, if you're still thinking along those lines," he answered, a trace of bitterness in his voice. "I don't want you to go back to Daily's house either. That bastard was more worried about how your disappearance would affect his political career than about you. You can't share my bed at the Farview, but if Mrs. Young agrees, I'll give it to you. You can have the room I keep there. At least you'll be safe, in case Bear Hawk decides to come back for you."

"Will, there was a-a ceremony between Bear Hawk and me," Annie said in a tiny voice, fearing his rejection. "I'm married to him."

"It doesn't count in the White world, Annie, so it doesn't matter. You don't have to tell anyone what happened between you and Bear Hawk, if you don't want to," was his quiet answer. "It's just between you and me, and I'll take it to my grave."

He pulled her tighter and thought of the townspeople of Grand Lake. Would they accept her back into society, now that her reputation had been compromised? Some would, he was sure, and some would not. He'd fight for her, even die for her, but he felt ill-prepared to protect her from the vicious gossips.

While Will contemplated Annie's future, Annie was thinking about the wounded look she had seen in a pair of dark eyes before he had ridden out of her life as quickly as he had come into it.

CHAPTER SIX

Will and Annie lay in each other's arms until darkness completely covered them. Then Will got up and built a fire. After boiling some coffee, he forced a cup into Annie's cold hands. He wrapped a blanket from his bedroll around her shoulders and fried some bacon.

They didn't speak; Annie's thoughts turned inward as she pondered the past weeks. Will watched her surreptitiously as he made himself busy with the fire and food; he ached to take her in his arms again, but he knew she needed some time to put things in order in her mind.

He didn't want to think about what she and Bear Hawk had been to each other, but she was changed because of it. She seemed stronger, more mature.

After two cups of strong coffee, Annie began speaking in a low, monotone voice, "Bear Hawk abducted me from the pond, but in a way, he saved me.

"The reason I was sent to stay with Uncle Ben was because of a boy at school. I thought I loved him, and I thought he had loved me.

I disgraced my family and was expelled. So I was no virgin when Bear Hawk took me on the night of the joining ceremony."

"You don't have to tell me this," Will said tensely as he stared at his clenched fists. He didn't think if he could stand hearing it.

"I have to tell you, Will, if we are to have any kind of future. There should be no secrets between us."

In a dull voice, she continued on, telling Will every minute detail. Her eyes never left the fire during the narrative, and it was best she didn't see Will's stormy countenance as he pictured her with the banker's son who had taken her innocence so callously, her father who had thrown her away like so much garbage, to the apparent feelings she had had for that Indian boy.

"You need to know everything that has happened, Will," she finished, her head high, "so that you'll never have to wonder. And I won't blame you if you don't want me after you've heard it all."

The forlorn note in her voice wrenched his heart, and he moved to her quickly and gathered her onto his lap, as one might a child.

"Annie, I love you more than I've ever loved anyone in my life. I realized just how much you meant to me while out in those mountains searching for you," he said softly into her hair. "And though it nearly killed me to have to listen to what you've just told me, I needed to hear it. I don't want any secrets between us either. And don't think you can get rid of me that easy, Miss Annie Mitchell, because I'm here for the long haul...'til death do us part."

Annie gazed into Will's face and saw the raw honesty of what he said. She laid her head on his shoulder and listened as he began telling her about his own nefarious past.

"My folks were poor farmers, like your father, but I have cousins who are wanted outlaws back in Missouri and Kansas..." Although parts of Will's background was slightly unsavory, he bared himself to Annie as she had to him.

When he finished, he glanced at her sheepishly and grinned, "Now, you have to admit, my past has been much worse than yours; can you still look me in the eye?"

Annie hugged him hard as tears rolled down her cheeks.

"I love you even more, Will Redmond," came her smothered reply.

The next day, they started east again, back to Grand Lake. Before they left, Annie glanced around the small shaded glade which had changed her life so completely and asked, "Will, where exactly are we?"

Will pushed his hat back and said speculatively, "I'd say we're just over the border about ten miles into Utah." Annie didn't realize then how this shaded area would affect her life later.

Will and Annie took three full weeks returning to Grand Lake, leisurely relishing in their newfound discovery of each other. They knew that once they arrived back in the small town, they would no longer be free to physically share their love so openly. They spoke little of the past, concentrating on the present and their future together.

Dirty, bedraggled, and still clad in beaded moccasins and a yellow doeskin dress, Annie drew much attention from the townsfolk who happened to be on the street when she and Will rode into town. Will took Annie straight to the Farview House into the welcoming arms of Mrs. Young.

Soon though, word of their arrival spread and a curious crowd arrived at the boarding house. As speculations flew about from out in the yard and on the porch, Annie was whisked up to Will's room. Buckets of hot water were heated as Will dragged the big tub upstairs.

Alone for a moment, Annie clung to Will, panic overwhelming her.

"Why did we come back, Will? Why didn't we just keep going... away from here so we could be together? I'm suddenly so scared of people," Annie cried into his safe warm chest.

"I wish we *could* go away so we could stay together, darlin', but we've both got responsibilities to deal with first. You hold your head high, Annie girl, and show them what you're made of," Will whispered into her hair. "I'm gonna have a lawyer I know, George Miller, start divorce proceedings, and as soon as it's done, you and I will get married. Then we won't ever be separated again. I'll be right beside you until we're both old and gray, watching our grandchildren from the porch in two old rockers."

"I love you so much I feel like my heart might explode," she whispered.

He lifted her and kissed her soundly, making her ache for more. But she knew they couldn't make love now that they had reached civilization again.

Lydia Elder walked in on the intimate moment and cleared her throat.

Annie and Will turned their heads at the noise, so engrossed with each other they had not heard the door open. Immediately, Will lowered Annie to her feet and stepped away, reddening to his ears.

"You two must have gotten things worked out, I see," began Mrs. Elder as she laid out some clean 'white' clothes on the bed. "But I'd steer clear of that kind of behavior for awhile, until the furor over Annie's kidnapping dies down. Gossip is the only thing that keeps most womenfolk *in* this Godforsaken place, and Annie is the big topic right now. She needs you, Will, to dissuade the talk, not be the cause of more."

Will looked sheepishly at Annie, who had blushed even more than he. Lydia Elder had no idea what had gone on during the time Annie had been with Bear Hawk, but a blind man could see how things were with her and Will Redmond. The older woman smiled to herself. "Now get your things, Will, and go to your brother's cabin and leave us women alone."

After Will left, Annie gripped her stomach, fearing nothing would be the same again...ever. She moved to the window, desperate for another glimpse of his strong broad shoulders as he left the house. But a crowd was watching the window, hoping for a peek at her, so she quickly shut the curtains.

"I'm guessing you and the Undersheriff have come to an understanding," stated Mrs. Elder as she stood quietly, staring at Annie.

Annie could only nod.

"And I suppose this means you won't be marrying Mr. J. C. Brashears, is that right?"

Annie nodded again, a shiver running down her back.

"Annie, Will's right. You should not go back to the Dailys. I never did take to Marian, and Ben is a crook, in my opinion. You can earn your keep by helping me in the kitchen, so it won't be charity. And Mr. Will Redmond can call on you in the parlor like a gentleman."

Annie felt the tears well up when she thought of the time it would take to get a divorce, and polite society wouldn't allow him to 'call' on her at all until it was final. She burst into tears, and Lydia gathered her into her arms.

"Well now, you cry it out, if you want," the older woman said soothingly as she rocked Annie. "Soon you'll forget all about that nasty business with the savage who kidnapped you, and then you and Will can get married and start your lives over together, brand-new."

"That savage, as you called him, loved me," Annie sobbed. "And I hurt him deeply." Then she told her friend everything that had happened while she was with Bear Hawk.

Lydia had a feeling there had been more to Annie's abduction than was generally known, and she ached for what the young girl had had to endure. And Will's secret marriage had answered a lot of questions about his past indifference to the county girls who had set their caps for him over the years.

"Now dry your tears, dear, and take a soothing bath. Soon you are going to have to face the townsfolk, and you might as well look your best. And if Will Redmond said he's going to marry you, then you can take that to the bank. He's a man of his word, that's for sure. So, let's just get through the coming winter and then spring will bring good news, I'm sure."

She helped Annie strip off the yellow doeskin dress, holding it by a corner like it was something unpleasant. Annie grabbed the dress away and held it to her protectively.

"I'll take care of this, Lydia, you don't have to," Annie said as folded the dress carefully and placed it on a chair.

"You just take your bath in peace, honey, and call me if you need anything," Mrs. Elder replied as she stepped out of the room and quietly closed the door behind her. "I sure hope Will hurries up with that divorce," she muttered as she walked down the hallway.

Annie sank into the warm deliciousness of the water and leaned back against the metal tub's rim. She allowed her mind to sweep back over the past weeks, reliving every moment from her initial terror, to her gradual acceptance of Bear Hawk, and to the wrenching inevitable choice she had made.

As the water gently caressed and soothed her, she thought of her young Ute lover, his stormy countenance that could turn instantly into smoldering passion which had left her weak. She speculated where he might have gone, and prayed he was still free.

"I'm so sorry, Bear Hawk, I didn't mean to hurt you," Annie whispered as she gazed toward the darkened window. She doubted she would ever see either Bear Hawk or Soft Dove again, and she fervently hoped they would never be caught. To have their independence taken away would surely kill them.

Then Annie's mind turned back to Will. Her lover, her life, her hope for the future. She wanted his children...Annie sat up quickly in the tub and ran her hand across her flat stomach. What if she were already pregnant by Bear Hawk? Would Will be as accepting of a half-breed child as he was of her relationship with its father?

The gossip over Annie's abduction had humiliated Marian to such a degree she and Ben Daily had left Grand Lake and gone to stay just outside of Hot Sulphur Springs with Ronald Baker, a rancher and supporter of Ben's political ambitions.

Several days after receiving word of Annie's return, the Dailys beelined straight for the Farview House. Annie was warned of their impending arrival and stationed in Mrs. Elder's own quarters, pale even through the residual tan of the past weeks.

"Where's our precious girl?" Marian wailed as she sailed into the parlor, clutching a handkerchief to her eyes.

Mrs. Elder had managed to keep the local busybodies at bay, but Annie's aunt and uncle were another matter. She knew Annie would have to face them sooner or later. She led Marian and Ben into her quarters where Annie was sitting stiffly on a settee.

Annie rose at their entrance and turned a cold face toward them. She stiffly allowed Marian to hug her but refused to kiss the cheek put forward by the older woman. Ben watched Annie warily, trying to gauge if any change was apparent. He had no doubt she had been ravaged by the savage who had abducted her, and he luridly searched her face for confirmation.

When Annie stared back at him boldly, his answer was in her eyes whose depths showed a maturity which had not been there before.

"So, my girl, and how are you?" asked Ben jovially.

"I'm fine, Ben," Annie replied, dropping the familiar 'Uncle'.

He decided to ignore the slight. "It's time to go home with your aunt and me."

"No, I'm staying here."

Marian flapped her hands in agitation. "What is she talking about, Benjamin? She is supposed to return with us to the cabin."

"No, I'm not," Annie repeated to her aunt. "I've decided to board here at Mrs. Elder's and work for my keep. I appreciate everything you have done for me, taking me in when my father abandoned me, but I can't go back to your house."

"But what about your engagement to Mr. Brashears?" wailed Marian.

"I don't think Mr. Brashears would want me now, do you, Ben?" Annie replied simply as she turned to stare at her uncle.

"That's for him to say, my girl, not me," sidestepped Ben, ever the politician.

"Even if he still wants me, I will not marry him," Annie stated firmly.

"But you accepted his proposal and his ring," Marian railed, her face reddening in anger.

"I am not in possession of his ring, and I have changed my mind about his proposal. Oh, and you may keep my Hope Chest."

Ben watched Annie speculatively; she *had* changed, by God. She was a woman now, one with her own mind. He could see no more help coming from her for his career. It was best to cut familial ties, rather than be drawn into the scandal which surrounded her.

"All right, Annie, you stay here. But when you are ready to come back to us, we might not be so eager to take you in again," Ben said slowly, watching her reaction. He was disappointed when she only stared back at him blandly.

Ben and Marian Daily vacated the Farview House, to the avid curiosity of the people who had gathered to watch the exchange between Annie and her guardians.

Annie collapsed after they left, and Lydia sent her straight to bed. As Annie sank into the down-filled mattress, she thought of Will's big body which had so often slept in this bed. She wrapped her arms around the pillow, pretending it was Will. How she missed the feel of his strong arms which had held her while she slept each night of the journey back to Grand Lake! Tears rolled down her cheeks when she thought of how long it might be before he would hold her again.

The next morning, Annie rose early, pulled on a blue gingham dress and tied her dusky hair back with a blue ribbon which matched her eyes. She made her way down to the big airy kitchen at the Farview.

"Good morning, Annie dear," called Mrs. Elder pleasantly, as she busily flitted around filling platters with mass quantities of food. "Put on an apron, child, and start earning your board."

Annie quickly donned a crisp white apron. Feeding twenty hungry miners was a daunting chore, and by the time everything was ready, Annie could feel sweat running down between her breasts.

As she and the other hired girl brought in the first of the platters heaped with bacon, eggs, flapjacks, ham, warm homemade bread, and crocks of butter and jam, the loud noise of men's voices at the long wooden table was almost deafening.

But when the men saw Annie, suddenly silence fell over the room. Twenty pairs of eyes stared at her curiously, and Annie felt a blush run up her neck and into her face as it had on her first day in Grand Lake.

"Ahem, boys," drawled a much-loved familiar voice, "it's rude to stare at a lady. Pick up your chins and eat, unless you want to hurt Mrs. Elder's feelings after she worked so hard on all of this good food."

The speechless throng found their own faces reddening and turned back to the job at hand, cleaning their plates and clamoring for more.

But one face continued to stare. Charley Burn, Annie's first erstwhile suitor, couldn't tear his eyes away from her. He had heard the rumors which were circulating around town, about Annie and that renegade Indian spending all that time alone together out in the mountains.

Everyone was speculating about Annie's virtue, and whether or not it had been compromised. Charley and the rest of the town hadn't forgotten about her behavior on the Fourth of July with the Undersheriff, and then Will had been the one to rescue her. The two had spent many days alone on the journey back to the county. Everyone was anxious to know what had happened on the trail between the two of them.

Charley knew that most folks were thinking the worst, but he wouldn't believe it. To him, Annie Mitchell was an innocent angel, and he loved her madly. Already he'd blackened a few eyes of those who had had the misfortune to besmirch her name in front of him.

Annie, on the other hand, was careful not to meet Will's eye. If she had, she knew everyone would instantly see how she felt about him. And, because the whole town now knew Will had been secretly married during his time in Grand County, Annie didn't want to fuel the gossipmongers. To the town, Will Redmond was still the hero lawman who had gone after and rescued Annie from a 'fate worse than death'.

So Annie and Will each pretended there was nothing more than friendship between them, he thanking her when she refilled his coffee cup, and she demurely saying 'you're welcome' afterwards. Those at the table who were watching them closely were sorely disappointed by their cool exchanges.

Besotted Charley Burn was secretly elated.

Annie had been working and living at the Farview House for more than a week when an unexpected visitor arrived. She was kneading dough for bread, giving Lydia some much needed rest, and she had flour smeared on her apron and flushed cheeks.

When Annie heard the front door open, she quickly cleaned her hands, wiping the perspiration away from her forehead with her sleeve, leaving a streak of white in its wake.

She hurried into the parlor to tell the visitor to return later when Mrs. Elder was up from her nap. As she turned the corner, she caught her breath as she beheld Mr. J. C. Brashears standing before her.

The girl froze as she watched his cold silver eyes rake her from head to toe. Annie was glad she had on the voluminous apron or she might have felt naked under his scrutiny.

He doffed his hat in a courteous yet slightly contemptuous manner. "Good day, m'dear."

"G-good afternoon," Annie stammered, her heart pounding.

"It is due time we had a talk, don't you think?"

"I-I-I don't think we have anything to talk about, Mr. Brashears," Annie stammered.

He reached out, took her hand, and pulled her to the settee. As she sat stiffly on the edge as far away as she could manage, he continued in his cultured voice, "Oh, but you are wrong, my dear; we have *much* to discuss. Let's begin with your working here as a servant. This is not proper. You will cease immediately and return to your uncle's house."

Annie's courage returned at his arrogance. "I am not a servant here, sir; I work for my room and board. And I will continue to work here for as long as I choose."

Annie saw his eyes shift, as if an inner eyelid quickly opened and closed. She shivered.

"You are still my fiancé, Miss Mitchell, and I shouldn't have to remind you of our agreement before your unfortunate disappearance," he replied steely.

"I do not choose to be your fiancé any longer, and I believe your ring might still be in the knothole of a tree on my uncle's land," Annie declared, her pale face flushing with anger.

He suddenly gripped her arm brutally as he moved so close she could see the hairs in his nose. "Don't be flippant with me, girl; I told you what I would do to you if you tried to cuckold me."

With all of her strength, Annie wrenched her arm out of his grasp and stood up. Her copper hair was a fiery halo surrounding blazing blue eyes as she glared at him. "I don't know who you think you are, Mr. Brashears, but I am no longer the same girl to whom you so 'romantically' proposed.

"I was given a choice of coming back to you or staying with an Indian. Well, guess whom I chose! And the only reason I am back now is...well, that's none of your business. But my return certainly has nothing to do with you. So you can leave right now and never, and I repeat never, touch me again, or I will bash in your bloody English head with an iron skillet!" She ran over to the front door and threw it open, breathing heavily.

Brashears had paled at the start of Annie's tirade, but then his face turned mottled red. He stood up, donned his tall silk hat, and stalked to the door. Before he walked out, he spat contemptuously, "I now see your true colors, madam, and a slut will always be a slut. But an Indian's whore is far worse that any saloon slut. I wouldn't marry you, now that I know the real truth, if you were the last woman on earth. Consider my offer of marriage rescinded, as of this moment."

"Gladly!" Annie shouted after him. She slammed the front door as hard as she could, then collapsed against it, breathing hard. "What have I done?" she thought. "Now everyone will know what happened between me and Bear Hawk. I'll lose what little respectability I have left. The whole town will feel as Brashears does, that I have been "an Indian's whore". In a small community like this one, I might as well go work at the Dandy Saloon."

Mrs. Elder happened to come down from her nap to see Annie slide down the front door to the floor. Lydia rushed to her side. "Oh my dear, what's the matter? Are you ill? Or hurt?"

"J. C. Brashears has left," Annie began, anguish in her voice. "He tried to make me go back to Uncle Ben. He wanted to pretend as if nothing had happened. He still wanted to marry me, so I told him about choosing Bear Hawk over him, and now everyone will know! Soft Dove was right, I should never have come back to the White world."

Mrs. Elder put her arm around Annie. "Pride is a funny thing, and I'd be ready to take bets that your Mr. Brashears doesn't say a word about you and that Indian boy. His pride wouldn't allow it. Stop worrying about things that haven't even happened yet, child. There's enough trouble in this world today without vexing over tomorrow."

Sure enough, for the next few days, Annie anxiously awaited the deluge of innuendo and hurtful talk to be hurled her way...but all was quiet.

Several days later, Lydia called Annie downstairs. "It's time you got outside this house. I want you to walk over to the Mercantile and pick up some flour and coffee for me."

Annie blanched at the thought of leaving the security of the Farview. Her disappearance and recovery had been front page news in the *Prospector*. The newspaper was what Ben Daily had railed about as being started simply as the mouthpiece of George E. Miller, his political rival who practiced law in Teller. Ben and his supporters from Hot Sulphur Springs had always been supported by the *North Park Miner*.

Because the Redmond brothers and the sheriff were supporters of Miller, Will had managed to downplay the abduction in the *Prospector*, but Ben Daily had been more than happy to be interviewed again and again by the *North Park Miner*. He had used her disappearance to undermine the jobs done by the lawmen of Grand County in hopes of gaining more political power for himself.

"Don't be afraid, honey," Lydia said, taking Annie's chin in her hand. "Folks around here are a forgiving lot, and if you show your face to them, they won't think you have anything to be ashamed of."

Reluctantly, Annie threw a shawl around her shoulders, grabbed the shopping basket, and headed for town over the lake path. It was a lovely fall day, the aspens just beginning to lose their glossy green and melt into vivid yellow and orange. Annie breathed in the fresh alpine air and was glad Lydia had forced her out.

As she crossed the footbridge, she glanced to her right at the crystal blue water of the lake to Mt. Baldy, the rounded mountain directly across from the Farview. Though bare and treeless now, Annie knew that in a few months it would be covered in snow.

When she reached the business area of Grand Lake, she leisurely strolled down the wooden sidewalks, nodding her head and smiling at everyone she met. After passing someone, she'd feel their eyes on her back, but she kept her head high and walked on.

As she reached the Cane Mercantile, which was directly across the street from the courthouse and jail, she couldn't help but stretch her neck in that direction. She hadn't seen Will, except at mealtime at the Farview, since she returned, and she longed to feel his comforting presence.

"Excuse me, Miss Mitchell, can I help you?" asked a kindly voice behind her.

Annie spun around and was confronted by the shy young County Clerk, Jules Thermon. He'd removed his hat and was swallowing incessantly. "Good morning, Mr. Thermon," she replied politely, sidestepping his query. "How are you doing this fine day?"

Jules blushed to the roots of his fair hair. He still couldn't look her in the eye. "I-I'm just fine, ma'am. I-I'd like to say that I'm terribly glad you're safe, ma'am. My mother and I were very concerned about you."

Annie touched his arm gently, causing him to jerk as if he'd been shocked. "Thank you for your concern, Mr. Thermon. I'm glad to be back among friends again. Please give my regards to your mother."

Jules Thermon, still red, murmured a reply and backed away.

Annie glanced back over her shoulder at the courthouse but couldn't see through the glare of the windows. She entered the Mercantile to see several customers stop in mid-sentence to stare at her.

Gathering her courage, Annie smiled her best smile. "Good morning. Isn't it a lovely day?"

Mr. Cane, the proprietor, came quickly from behind the counter and took Annie's hand in his own. "Well, hello, Miss Annie. Yes, it is a fine day indeed, and it's wonderful seeing you looking so healthy and pretty. What can I get for you today?"

His friendly acceptance broke the mood and suddenly the other folks in the store were greeting her as if she were a long-lost relative. Annie relaxed, knowing she need not worry anymore about her acceptance back into the friendly little mountain community. Apparently Ben Daily and J.C. Brashears didn't have as much influence as they thought in Grand Lake.

A few days later, Will arrived at the Farview, and Annie met with him in the parlor, chaperoned by Mrs. Elder.

"I've spoken with George Miller about the divorce. He said I might have to go back to Missouri," Will told Annie, allowed only to touch her hands. He rubbed the tops with his thumbs, leaving a searing circle of heat. Both of them ached to hold the other, but until he was free, it was impossible.

"Why, Will, what good would it do for you to go back?" Annie asked, fearing a reunion with his wife if he returned to her state.

"Sarah's not being very cooperative by mail. I guess I need to convince her that this divorce is what we both need and want," Will replied, wishing he could sweep Annie into his arms and make proper use of that bed upstairs. "I don't want to go, but if I don't go before the snow falls, it'll be next spring before this thing is settled. And I want it settled soon before I bust."

Annie blushed at his sensual leer, afraid Lydia had overheard this last remark. She peeked over at her friend and confidant and saw that Lydia was extremely involved with her knitting, with just a hint of a smile on her face.

"Before I go, Annie, do you think...well, that we could go on a buggy ride or something? I'd like to take you out to Willow Creek to see my brother's spread," Will asked pleadingly.

They both looked over at Mrs. Elder and waited. Finally she put her knitting down and stared back at the two pair of yearning eyes.

"I don't suppose it would hurt for you to go out in the full light of day, but make sure you get her back before dark, Will," replied Mrs. Elder, chuckling at the looks of elation on the young couple's faces.

The next morning, Will was at the door half an hour after sunup. Mrs. Elder had filled a large picnic hamper with food as Annie's hands had shaken too badly to be of much use.

When Annie heard the knock, though, she flew toward the front door, her shoes sliding on the soft pine floor of the parlor. She jerked open the door and stared at Will, a brilliant smile spread across her face.

"Mornin', ma'am," drawled Will as he raked her with sultry eyes. "Are you ready to go?"

"Oh Will, I could hardly sleep last night, thinking about today," Annie blurted, then blushed to her roots at her brazen remark.

"That's what I love about you, woman," Will whispered, "you don't play any games with a man. What you say is exactly how you feel. Don't ever change."

Annie reddened again, then pulled Will into the shadow behind the door, throwing her arms around his neck and kissing him with abandon. He lifted her and answered her kiss with an intensity of his own. Dizzily, they broke apart when the door creaked open.

A small group of miners had already arrived for breakfast. Will grabbed the basket and Annie, heading toward the chaise he had rented for the day. They followed the lake path past the icehouse and over a little rise before turning left and heading south out of Grand Lake.

Annie lifted her face to the warm sun, enjoying the welcome heat as the mornings were already becoming cooler. Soon winter would close around the small community, making travel almost impossible except on snowshoes or in sleds pulled by sure-footed horses.

Thinking about the cold winter without Will, Annie asked plaintively, "If you go to Missouri, when will you be back?"

"I don't want to talk about that today, Annie," Will replied as he flipped the reins a bit harder than necessary on the horses' backs. "Today is just for us. Tomorrow can damn well wait."

Annie threw her arms around his neck, nearly sending his hat flying. The impact of her body caused him to drop one of the reins. Laughing, he reached down to catch the leather strap with one hand while throwing his arm around her and dragging her onto his lap.

Shrieking as Will settled her on his knees, Annie stared into his beloved face as she rubbed the stubble of his newly shaved cheek. His hat was crooked and pushed back off his high forehead. Will's eyes were squinty because of the bright sun, and he had a half-grin as if he were thinking of something humorous.

Annie's smile disappeared as the overpowering emotions of her feelings for the man washed over her, leaving her trembling as she clung to the material of his shirt.

"I love you so much it hurts, Will Redmond," Annie said as tears shimmered in her lashes. "Don't you ever leave me."

Will dropped the reins and let the horses have their heads as he suddenly felt an uncontrollable impulse to cling to her as well.

"By God, Annie Mitchell, we *will* be together this winter, I swear to you," Will's voice trembled as much as Annie's body. "I wouldn't want to live in this world without you."

Annie found his lips and the two came together fiercely until Will moaned and moved away. Lifting her off his lap and setting her firmly on the wooden bench beside him, he grabbed the reins again and turned the team off the road and into the forest.

"I can't be satisfied with kissing you, girl, I've been deprived too long," he growled, the half-smile returning.

Annie was breathing hard with need also, and made no brook of protest.

"Just hurry and find a private place," she whispered, still clinging to his arm.

As soon as they knew they wouldn't be seen by anyone passing on the road, Will stopped the team and tied the reins to a slender sapling. He grabbed a blanket from the back of the rig, lifted Annie down, and located a flat, rockless area in a copse of shimmering aspens.

Will spread the blanket and tore his shirt over his head. Already Annie was unbuttoning the front of her bodice. He moved toward her and tried to help, but his fingers were shaking.

"You start on my skirt, Will, I'll do this," Annie gasped as she nearly ripped the tiny buttons off the material.

Will turned her around and unbuttoned her skirt and let it fall in a heap around her ankles. Then he untied her pantalets and they fluttered to the ground. Annie finished unbuttoning the front of her bodice and threw it aside.

They stood facing each other. Will's smooth broad shoulders were tautly muscled with long thick arms which could tenderly hold her or ferociously fight for her. Annie was clad only in a thin chemise which reached the top of her thighs, with her dark coppery hair loose and curling past her shoulders down to a tiny waist.

Will gently pulled at the delicate ribbon which held the top of her chemise closed, then unbuttoned the three tiny buttons which opened just wide enough for him to slip his hand in and caress her breast. Annie's breath caught in her throat at his gentle touch, and she stared up into his face. Very slowly he removed her chemise.

He lowered her to the blanket, propping himself on his side with his elbow. His eyes coursed seductively over her body, down to her black stockings which reached the middle of her thighs. Very slowly he rolled each stocking down her leg, then removed her shoes until she was only shimmering skin from head to toe.

Annie raised up and pushed him onto his back. With her lips and tongue she traced his nipples then began a slow path downward as she heard him groan with pleasure.

Instantly, Will flipped her on her back and covered her body with his, filling her so deeply she cried out. The days and weeks apart had made him hungry for her, and he knew he couldn't stop, even if a gun had been put to his head. With only a few strokes he released into her as his fingers left bruises where he grasped her to him.

"Oh God, Annie, I'm sorry I couldn't hold out any longer,"Will panted, "but I thought I was gonna burst."

Annie smiled, pleased with her own power to overcome his commanding control.

He pulled back and looked into her half-closed eyes. "Don't go thinking this was the only time you're gonna be on your back today, Miss Annie Mitchell. I haven't even begun with you yet, darlin'."

Much later, and thoroughly sated, Will and Annie continued on the five miles to Gold Run on Willow Creek.

"Besides my brothers, there are about fifty men grubbing placers along here," Will explained to Annie as they began to see tents, lean-tos, and shanties along the rushing water of Willow Creek. "Out here, a man can homestead one hundred and sixty acres, but farming is too tough during the cold winters, so most folks come for the ore."

Annie stared at the families they passed, huddled around hurriedly thrown together board shacks. The women, thin and already worn out by life, were surrounded by dirty-faced children clinging to their skirts as they churned butter or washed clothes in cauldrons over open fires. Most of the men were bent over the creek, sluicing water, dirt, and sand around and around in flat metal pans.

"How can they live like this?" Annie asked, her heart pouring out for the poverty and desperation on the faces they passed.

Will replied, "The sheer hope of a glint is what keeps these people tied to an existence just above starvation. And it ain't any easier up in the mountains.

"Me and Bass had a mine up the Bowen. We called it the 'Sedalia' after our home town in Missouri. Most of the mines in the mountainsides have veins running from paper thickness to almost a half inch thick, but some tended to peter out after a few feet. It really ain't good mining up here. It's not only nearly impossible to get it out of the ground, but there's no easy way, except by mule, to get it down the mountain."

"Lydia told me about your mine. Didn't my uncle cheat you in some way?" asked Annie.

"Yeah, the bastard spread it around that our mine was petering out, but it wasn't. He scared away most of the buyers then bought it himself cheap and made a killin' off it. Damn, was Bass and me mad!"

Seeing his barely controlled anger at the mention of Ben Daily, Annie decided to change the subject. "Which brother is Bass?"

"I'm the oldest, and he's next," replied Will, a hint of pride in his voice. "His real name is Sebastian, but he gets real mad if anyone calls him that. Our youngest brother is Mann, short for Manilaus. Our ma picked names out of books, so I was lucky to be plain William."

Annie wrapped both her arms around his strong right one, laying her head against him.

"I like your name, Will," she said quietly.

He transferred the reins into his left hand and threw an arm around Annie's shoulders, pulling her close. He replied huskily, "You better like my name, darlin', 'cause I'm planning on giving it to you."

"As soon as the other Mrs. Redmond quits using it, right?" Annie looked up into his face, only partly teasing.

Will flinched, then squeezed her closer and said with his half-grin, "If I'd known I was gonna run into a redheaded wildcat with flashing blue eyes, I'd have gotten myself free a long time ago. The nights are mighty long now without you."

As they rode on, Annie lazed against Will, enjoying the peace and security she experienced when they were together. She found herself thinking of a pair of dark eyes as she watched an eagle soar between the closer peaks, circling and diving, adrift on the air currents.

She heard its raucous cry as it was joined by another, its mate no doubt, and they swooped and played among the clouds of the crystal clear day. She sent up a prayer that somewhere out in the surrounding mountains Bear Hawk was soaring still, as freely as that eagle.

Soon Annie and Will were approaching a small log cabin across the creek. Rough-hewn logs chinked with mud made up the one-room structure, and a thin wisp of smoke rose from the stone chimney. At the sound of their approach through the shallow ford, the door opened and two exact replicas of Will stepped out.

"Hey, Bass, Mann," Will called as he pulled the team up and jumped to the ground.

The three men, all over six feet tall, grasped each other's arms in greeting. Bass's hair was a tad bit darker, Annie noticed, and his mustache was fuller and bushier. His body was thicker, too, and he reminded Annie of a big friendly bear. Mann was leaner than either of his brothers. It was obvious he was the youngest.

Will came around the wagon and lifted Annie to the ground. He steered her toward the cabin and his brothers. "This is my girl, Annie Mitchell. Annie, these rapscallions are my brothers, Bass and Mann Redmond."

Bass, Mann, and Annie studied each other for a moment, taking inventory on what they saw.

"I can see now why you're so crazy about her, Will," Bass answered after a time. He doffed his hat and bowed. "It's my pleasure, ma'am."

Mann pushed Bass to the side, bowed lower, and said, "No, it's *my* pleasure, Miss Annie."

Annie blushed and curtseyed to the two Redmonds. They all had the same flinty green eyes and long straight noses. And their smiles were identical.

"I've heard a lot about the both of you, too, Sebastian and Manilaus," she said teasingly.

Mann only laughed, but Bass' face reddened as he turned his gaze on his older brother who was chuckling at his discomfiture.

"Now dammit, Will, why did you have to tell her our given names?" Bass swore, then he suddenly lunged at his brother, tackled him, and they rolled around in the dirt like small boys. Mann threw his hat on the ground and jumped into the fray of arms and legs.

Annie grinned when she realized they were only pretending to fight and weren't seriously trying to hurt each other.

"Don't make me cut a switch," she demanded after a moment, trying not to giggle.

Instantly, all three men stopped wrestling and stared at her, complete and utter astonishment on their similar faces.

"Did you tell her?" questioned Bass, as he helped Will and Mann to their feet.

"No, I didn't," answered Will as he used his hat to beat the dirt out of his pants and shirt. "Annie, our Ma used to say exactly the same words when we got into a ruckus as boys." He walked over to her and lifted her into the air, swinging her around. "See now, brothers, why she belongs in our family?"

Laughing, they all entered the small cabin. A square wooden table surrounded by tree stumps used for chairs dominated the room. The fireplace took up the entire right wall, and coals glowed warmly. Jars and crocks were lined up along a shelf, and barrels of flour and sugar were against the wall. On the opposite wall were bunk beds, one on top of the other built into the side of the cabin. They had sack mattresses stuffed with ticking, and colorful homemade blankets lay askew on the beds.

"Sorry it ain't much, Annie," Bass said, seeing the cozy room for the first time from an outsider's point of view.

"Do you all live here?" asked Annie.

Mann answered, "No, I live up in Teller City, most of the time. I work for George Miller, the attorney. It seems like an age since I've been with both my ugly brothers."

Will reached over and mussed Mann's hair proudly. "Yeah, this boy is moving up in the world. He can't take the time to visit his lowly brothers, can you, Manny?"

Mann blushed vivid red at Will's teasing. He retorted, "At least, I'm making more money than either of you two."

"Yeah, but doing what? Kissing Miller's ass?" asked Bass. Then he realized what he had said and glanced sheepishly at Annie, redder than his little brother. "I'm awful sorry, Miss Annie, for my language. I sort of forgot there's a lady present."

"No problem at all, Bass," Annie laughed. "I think I've heard worse from your big brother."

Will wrapped his arm around her shoulders and kissed her on the forehead. "Darlin', if you can't handle a little bit of cussing, then you don't need to marry a Redmond."

Everyone laughed as Annie threw off Will's arm and strolled around the small room to lay a hand on Bass' big arm. "The cabin looks very homey and comfortable, Bass. And you never have to apologize to me."

Will watched the exchange with his half-grin, knowing that Annie had made another Redmond conquest in Bass.

"I can offer you some coffee, ma'am, or cider," Bass sputtered, somewhat embarrassed at his reaction to Annie's intimate gesture.

"Let me fix it, Bass," Annie said as she found the large iron coffee pot and shook it, hearing the remains from breakfast slosh around on the inside. "Do you have a well, or should I fill it from the creek?"

"I'll fill it, Annie," Will said as he took the pot from her and disappeared out the door.

Annie, Bass, and Mann stood in the quiet room, all a bit shy without Will's comfortable presence.

Finally, Bass said quietly, "My brother is a good man, Annie. He was lied to by Sarah back in Missouri, and he's never quite trusted another woman. He seems mighty fond of you. Please don't hurt him."

Sudden tears pricked Annie's eyes at Bass' tender plea for his brother.

"I love him, Bass, with every breath in my body," she proclaimed softly, looking from Bass to Mann.

Both men reddened, and Mann said, "W-well, all right then."

Will reappeared at the door and broke the awkward silence. Annie found the coffee beans and grinder and went to work as the three men sat on stumps around the table.

They talked about mining and the local political scene as Annie bustled around the fireplace. She heard Will whisper, "Ain't it nice to see a woman in this place?"

And she had to smile to herself. More than anything in the world, she wanted a cabin just like this, where she and Will could live together and raise a family.

Annie joined the brothers at the table while the coffee boiled, after first sending Will out to the buckboard for the picnic basket. She laid out some of the provisions Mrs. Elder had provided. They all laughed, ate, and talked for several hours, thoroughly enjoying each other's company.

"Mann, what do you really think about Miller?" Bass asked after he'd poured a good size dollop of whiskey into his brother's coffee.

"He's all right, I guess," answered the youngest Redmond. "He pays me good wages to watch his back. I can't complain about that."

Bass shook his head, "I don't know, Mann. Sometimes Miller does things that just don't seem right. Just watch yourself."

Will replied, chuckling, "Don't worry about our little brother; he's a Redmond, ain't he? And Miller's all right, I guess. Not any more crazy than any other politician lately."

Bass rubbed his chin thoughtfully and said, "Well, I guess so. But just the same, Mann, you watch your own back."

Will was looser and more animated than Annie had ever seen him, and she reveled in the loss of reserve around his brothers that could so completely mask his naturally exuberant personality.

"We had best get started back to town before Mrs. Elder sicks a posse on us," Will said, sometime later.

Annie began to pack up the dishes into Lydia's hamper. She glanced up at both Bass and Mann. "I'm glad I finally got to meet you two. Why is it we've never seen either of you in town at any of the dances? There's plenty of town girls wishing for a big 'ole handsome Redmond to dance with."

"I think Mann's keeping the girls up in Teller occupied, Annie, and Bass doesn't dance. I think he's a little afraid of girls," Will said, smiling mischievously at his brother's scarlet face. "Besides, I've got the prettiest girl in the county, don't I, boys?"

Bass could only nod as he gathered up the cups and took them to the wash pan, trying to hide his embarrassment. He'd never been a ladies' man like his two brothers, and females had always seemed a little afraid of his bear-like size. So he had confined his time to the girls at the saloons who didn't care how big and hairy you were as long as you had money.

Mann scrutinized Annie up and down several times before Will playfully cuffed him on back of the head. "Keep your eyes to yourself, little brother. She's taken."

"I really wish you would both come to the next dance; I'd love to introduce you to some friends of mine," Annie said sincerely.

"If you have friends as pretty as you, Miss Annie, you can count me in," replied Mann jubilantly.

Bass said shyly, "I'm not one for dancing, ma'am, but maybe you could teach me a step or two, next time I'm in town."

Annie walked over to both men, so much like her Will. "And anytime you two come to town, please stop at the Farview to see me. Soon, I hope, you'll be my brothers, too."

Bass and Mann gazed at Annie's beautiful face, her ruddy hair, and her sky blue eyes.

"She's mine, boys, so don't get any ideas," Will snorted as he pulled Annie to his side.

After they had driven away, Annie asked Will how Miller was doing on his divorce.

"Annie, let's not talk about it now," Will urged.

"We *have* to talk about it sometime, Will, so we might as well get it out of the way," answered Annie hotly. She moved to the far side of the hard board seat and crossed her arms belligerently over her chest.

Will chuckled at her outthrust bottom lip, which angered her even more. She suddenly balled up her fist and punched him in the arm. "Don't you dare laugh at my distress, William Redmond! What *you* do has to do with *my* future, too."

Will pulled Annie across the seat and tucked her under his arm.

"All right, wildcat," he said softly, seeing the pain in her flashing eyes. "Bass and I are leaving on Monday next. It'll take us nearly a month, I suppose, if everything goes as planned."

Annie blanched. A MONTH? A month without Will? And he in Missouri with his WIFE? What if he decides to stay with her? What if he never comes back?

Tears fell on Will's hand as Annie turned her head away. He quickly removed his arm from around her and used both hands to tighten the reins and stop the horses. After pushing the brake lever forward, he turned to her.

Grasping Annie by the shoulders, Will turned her to face him. "Listen, girl, I don't want to see any tears from you. You're sitting here thinking I might not come back, aren't you?"

He peered into her face which she tried to avert. "Listen to me and heed what I'm saying, Annie Mitchell. Hell itself couldn't keep me away from you! And if something was to happen and I died, I swear I'll come back and haunt you until the day you join me! Nothing, and I mean nothing, is going to keep me from coming back to you. I swear it, darlin', and I always keep my word!"

Annie looked into his face as he spoke, and the tears became uncontrollable. He crushed her to him so she couldn't see the tears which formed in his own eyes. They clung to each other for a long moment, each trying to gain control of their emotions.

Finally Annie sniffed against his shirt and whimpered, "I-if something did happen, though, and you felt that you couldn't come back to me, I'd understand, Will."

"Damn you, girl!" Will exploded. "I'm telling you that *nothing*, not even death itself, is gonna keep me from coming back to you! So you better damn well be here waiting for me and not gallivanting around the mountainside again with no damn Indian buck!"

He pulled Annie's face up and covered her trembling lips with his.

On Monday, Will and Bass came by the Farview to say good-bye. Because of curious onlookers, Annie had to hold back her tears until she was alone in Will's old room. There she nearly made herself sick sobbing, deathly afraid she'd never see him again.

"When I do return, and I *will* return," Will had said quietly to Annie earlier in the parlor, "I would be honored if you would consent to be the LAST Mrs. William Redmond."

Annie had gazed adoringly at his handsomely rugged face and answered, "I will always be yours, wife or not, William Redmond!"

Will had squeezed her cold hands and wished they had been able to have some privacy for their good-byes.

"I'll be back sooner than you think, Annie, I swear!" was Will's answer. Then he was gone.

CHAPTER SEVEN

"Why is September so messy?" complained Annie, her chin in her hands, as she stared out the window at the interminable rain which seemed to have been falling for days. Heavy downpours had made the roads almost impassable, and gray skies matched Annie's gray mood. Day after unendurable day passed by slowly as she dragged herself through her daily duties.

"What you need is something else to think about," replied Mrs. Elder as she dipped flour into a big bowl. "Come help me with these biscuits."

"All right," Annie responded without enthusiasm. But she didn't move.

Wiping her hands on her apron, Lydia Elder turned to the girl. "Better yet, get a cloak and boots on and go into town. You need a change of scenery."

Annie dragged herself away from the window and put on the thick cloak which always hung by the back door. She pulled on a pair of large boots which fit over her own shoes. Covering her head with the hood of the woolen cloak, she slipped out the kitchen door into the dismal afternoon.

"Where are you right now, Will Redmond?" Annie asked aloud as she passed under dripping trees on the path which skirted the lake to town. "Are you thinking about me? Have you forgotten about me? Oh, how I wish I could see your face again! I feel like I might die of the want for you."

When she entered the Mercantile, there were several men sitting around the smoking woodstove in the corner of the store. The temperatures had dropped considerably now that autumn had come to the mountains. Already the aspens had turned yellow and orange and were falling as the nights dipped down into freezing digits.

"Afternoon, Miss Annie," called a familiar voice while Annie was removing her water soaked rain clothing. She glanced up to see Charley Burn bounding toward her, his hand outstretched.

"Good afternoon, Charley," replied Annie as Charley grasped her hand and shook it enthusiastically. It seemed he always happened to be wherever she was in town.

Pulling her toward the woodstove, Charley blurted out, "Come sit a spell and warm yourself, Miss Annie. It's mighty raw outside today. Have you heard the latest? We were just talking about what's going on with George E. Miller. Do you know who he is, Miss Annie? He's a County Commissioner from up at Teller. He's also a lawyer. Anyway, have you heard what's going on?"

Charley stopped to catch his breath as he gently pushed Annie into an empty rocker. The other men had been watching and listening to

Charley's breathless banter. When he stopped talking, an uncomfortable silence filled the room.

Annie tried to cover the sudden quiet. "Well, no, Charley, I haven't heard the latest gossip. Why don't you tell me?"

Beaming, Charley pulled up a barrel beside her and began. "George Miller called a Republican Convention here in Grand Lake on the second of this month. His hand-picked candidates were naturally nominated to several county offices, and he and Charles Barney were selected as Grand County's delegates to the Republican state convention in Denver."

Annie had never been much interested in politics but listened politely.

"Miller thinks he's got the county sewed up," said one of the young men Annie didn't recognize. "He even has Brashears from Georgetown backing *him* now, instead of backing Daily."

Annie sat up straighter when she heard Brashears' name. So, Uncle Ben had lost J.C. Brashears' support. Was it because of her, she wondered?

"Yeah, I heard that J.C. Brashears said he 'carried Grand County in his vest pocket'," exclaimed Charley, beaming at Annie while he spoke.

Charley was still trying to get up his nerve to call on Annie and proclaim his undying love and devotion. Putting down that slick dandy to whom Annie had been engaged seemed like the proper thing to say to try to impress her.

"I heard Daily say that the cabin where they held the convention was filled with so many 'democrats and bummers', that no member of his delegation could enter," put in Jim Calter, who had purportedly once been a scout for Custer, luckily before the Little Big Horn.

"Does calling a meeting affect my uncle?" queried Annie, her interest piqued.

Calter continued, "Yeah, earlier this month, Daily and his cronies from the Springs met and came up with their *own* opposition slate, with him and James Webb as the delegates."

Old Judge Wescott, Grand Lake's first settler, sat in the other rocker, a corncob pipe between his lips. He rocked back and forth a few times before muttering, "The Republican kettle of mule meat has finally boiled over, it seems." Being an longtime Democrat, he chuckled as tempers flared in the small store.

A week or so later, Annie was scrubbing the parlor floor when Charley Burn came barreling into the Farview. "Miss Annie, did you hear what happened? At the Convention?"

Annie wiped her forehead with her sleeve, then dropped the soapy rag into the bucket beside her. "Hello to you, too, Charley," she replied as she sat back on her heels.

Charley kneaded his hat in his hands, his Adam's apple bobbing excitedly. "Hello, Miss Annie, I didn't mean to interrupt your chores, but I thought you might want to hear what happened between your uncle and George Miller."

Sighing, Annie knew that whether she wanted to hear it or not, the gossip would soon reach the Farview. "All right, Charley, go ahead. What happened?"

Charley began, "Well, Miller and Barney took the stage over Berthoud Pass to the Republican Convention in Denver, but your uncle and Webb rode their horses over Rollins Pass, arriving first.

"Daily attended the Convention representing Grand County which made Miller mad as hell, oh 'scuse me, Miss Annie, when he arrived. They had an awful row on the steps outside the Brown Palace Hotel with your uncle accusing Miller of being a fugitive from justice in Mississippi.

"Daily said he could prove that Miller had been involved in the death of two political opponents there, and then Miller said he could prove that Daily had been involved in a shady murder back in Chicago."

Mrs. Elder, upon hearing the commotion, had entered the parlor. "What on earth is going on with those two? Something awful is going to happen if they don't settle down."

"Yeah, you're right, Miz Elder," Charley agreed, "I heard that George Miller told Ben Daily that they would 'have it out in Grand County sooner or later'."

Annie shook her head as she went back to her scrubbing. "I'm so glad I'm not a part of all that political turmoil. And I'm glad Will is gone and not involved in it either."

As October rolled around, Annie had heard nothing from Will, and her heart ached. On All Hallow's Eve, the Nickerson House hosted a costume ball. Annie didn't feel like going, but Lydia Elder encouraged her, even helping to air out the yellow doeskin dress and moccasins which Annie had carefully packed away.

"Don't you think this outfit might offend some people?" Annie asked as she turned this way and that in front of the long mirror in Mrs. Elder's bedroom.

Annie loved the feel of the soft leather against her bare skin, but it brought back memories of Bear Hawk's passionate lovemaking and haunted expression when he realized he had lost her to Will.

"Oh, pooh on them," scoffed Mrs. Elder as she stood back and admired the braids she had plaited in Annie's burnt red hair. "And if *you* don't wear it, then I *will*!"

Annie laughed and threw her arms around her friend, the one person who had become closer to Annie than any mother could. "Well, what are *you* going to wear then?"

"I've got a Spanish shawl and comb that my husband bought me on our honeymoon," Mrs. Elder replied, wistfully recalling younger days with her long-dead husband. Then shaking off her melancholy, she proclaimed, "I'll be a fine Spanish Lady."

At the dance, Annie was the center of attention in her Indian dress which hid little of her natural curves. Shyly she accepted dance after dance, her knee-high moccasins sliding easily over the scrubbed pine floor.

Charley Burn anxiously awaited his turn for a dance with her, and when it was finally his time, he nervously held her in his arms as he swept her across the floor. He was decked out in the apron of an assayist, with his sleeves rolled up and banded on the upper arm. The visor cap, worn low on his forehead, made his unruly brown hair stand up in sprigs above the visor rim. It was all Annie could do not to laugh at the boy.

"I-I-I've been waiting to dance with you for awhile now, Miss Annie," began Charley, his round face blotched with shyness. "I've been wanting to see you alone sometime, too. You see, I wondered it you'd mind i-if I-I c-called on you."

The music, costumes, and dancing had all been on Annie's mind when what Charley said filtered through to her consciousness.

"What did you say?" she asked, thinking she hadn't heard him right.

"I want to court you, Miss Annie, with marriage as the consequence," Charley blurted out the rehearsed line.

Annie stopped dancing, removing her arms from Charley's hand and shoulder. Her look of pity angered the young man.

"Don't look at me like I had the rabies," the boy rasped harshly. "If you don't want me to court you, just say so."

"Charley, I'm so sorry. I feel extremely flattered you think of me in that way," Annie began, sick at the hurt expression on his face. "But I don't think of you as anything more than my dear friend. I hope I haven't done anything to lead you to believe otherwise."

Charley stared down at his feet, the visor hiding his flaming face. "No, you never led me on. I just thought that you might not be against getting to know me, that's all. Maybe you'd grow to love me as I love you."

Annie felt tears gather behind her lashes. She reached for Charley's hand and held it in her own until his eyes met hers.

"Charley, if things were different, I would be most honored to have you court me. If things were different, I know it would be you whom I might come to love. But I can't, Charley. I just can't."

Jerking his hand away, Charley asked angrily, "Is it true, then, what they've been saying about you and the Undersheriff?"

"I'll answer that, if you don't mind," came a deep voice from behind them.

Annie spun around and there stood Will... dirty, bearded, and with that half grin she had come to love so well. It took all of her willpower not to hurl herself into his arms as she stood there beaming at him.

The crowd had become silent when the two tall Redmond brothers had entered the room. Charley and Annie had been so deep in conversation they had not noticed the approach of the Undersheriff.

Glancing around at the expectant crowd, Will whispered to Charley, "Let's you and me take this outside, Charley, so we can have some privacy."

As Will turned to go, Charley shouted back, "No, I want to hear your answer right now, in front of everyone. I happen to love Miss Annie and want to marry her. What do you have to say about it, you being already married yourself?"

Annie watched Will's face redden in anger rather than embarrassment. She saw his fists clench, then Bass put his hand on Will's shoulder as a reminder of the avid witnesses.

Will fought to physically control himself then shrugged off his brother's hand.

"In two weeks time, I'll be a free man, and then I'm gonna ask Miss Mitchell to be my wife," Will said loudly, wanting everyone to hear. "And if you or anyone else here has anything to say about it, step on outside and we'll discuss it further."

An audible murmur crisscrossed the crowded room, then Annie did what she had wanted since his arrival. She jumped into his arms and kissed him soundly in front of everyone.

"Well, it's about time," stated Mrs. Elder loudly.

The audience broke into cheers and raucous applause as Will and Annie lost themselves in each other. Finally, hearty slaps on Will's back broke their hypnotic spell, and they were congratulated by all at hand. Annie was kissed by man after man until Will put a stop to the uproarious celebration by firmly escorting her out into the cold night air.

As they passed through the throng, all faces were smiling...but one. Charley Burn watched angrily as the Undersheriff took *his* gal away.

Once outside, Will grabbed her into his arms again, nearly squeezing the life from her.

Annie's tears flowed freely as she kissed him all over his bearded face, saying over and over, "You came back, you really came back!"

"Now quit your frettin', darlin', I told you Hell itself couldn't keep me from you," Will replied huskily as he gazed at her beautiful face which he'd kept locked in his heart on the difficult journey.

"Why didn't you write, or let me know what was happening? I've been sick with worry," Annie cried.

"Well, it doesn't look like you sat at home and pined over me, now does it?" Will drawled as he took in her clingy leather dress which had nearly driven him crazy on the trail home after her rescue. "I guess I can't be gone a measly sixty-five days without you dancing all night, getting proposed to by some young kid, and wearing your Injun clothes like you were waiting for that renegade to come whisk you away again."

Annie saw the side of his mouth twitch as he fought the grin which was aching to appear. She pulled him to her and whispered seductively in his ear, "While everyone is dancing, no one will notice that you've escorted me home. The Farview is empty and there's a warm bed waiting for us."

"I'm filthy, darlin', since I nearly killed my brother and my horse on the trail trying to make it home sooner. I want you, Lord only knows, but I wanted to smell a bit more human before getting naked with you again."

"I happen to like the way you smell, Undersheriff Redmond," Annie murmured as she rubbed herself against him.

"Oh darlin', you are gonna be the death of me yet," he whispered huskily, "but I can't think of a better way to die."

Will climbed on his horse with Annie still in his arms and galloped around the lake to the darkened boarding house. Indeed, all of the inhabitants were still at the dance... and would be until dawn. Jumping from his horse, he took the steps three at a time until he reached his old room which Annie now occupied.

He flung open the door and unceremoniously dumped her on the bed. Tossing his hat to the side, he slammed the door shut with a backward kick of his foot.

After tearing each other's clothes off, Annie and Will came together in a fury of passion, his lips and hands bruising her tender skin as he ravished her again and again.

When at last they were spent, Will pulled her close and wrapped a long leg over her, wedging her tightly to his slick skin. "I hope you have given me your child tonight," she whispered, barely audible.

"Well, not 'til we can make it legal, you little wanton," Will murmured sleepily, "but after that, I hope we have a babe every spring."

"Now you're trying to kill *me*," Annie exclaimed, smiling at the thought of Will's babies at her breast.

As they lay entwined, Will told Annie about the trip to Sedalia. "I visited our old farm, and everything seemed so much smaller."

"That's probably because you are so much bigger than when you left, Will," teased Annie as she snuggled against him, playfully twirling the hair on his chest while he spoke.

"Sarah looked old, too, and I guess no one else ever wanted her, that's why she never tried to get a divorce. She cried when I told her why I'd come, and it made me feel something awful. But I kept seeing your face, and I knew I had to make her understand."

"You didn't...didn't want to... to be with her, did you?" Annie asked in a small voice.

"Not hardly, woman, when I knew I had you waiting here for me. But I talked to her, and talked, and talked, trying to make a divorce sound like something she would want, too. I guess I ought to be a politician, Annie, because I finally got her to see it my way. When she promised to sign the papers, I knew we were home-free. I was so damn anxious to get back, I had to nearly drag Bass with my bare hands."

Annie smiled sleepily as she imagined standing in front of a preacher with Will at her side. Just before dawn, Will arose and dressed, stealing out after one last look at Annie's contented face.

Her hair was spread across the pillow in a dark curtain of copper and one arm was out of the warmth of the covers. He carefully placed it under the blanket, trying not to wake her, then gently kissed her parted lips.

When Annie awoke, the sun was streaming in the window, the grayness of the past two months miraculously gone. As she rubbed the cold sheet beside her, she smiled as she remembered their night of pleasure. Stretching leisurely, Annie felt her flat stomach, hoping Will's child would soon be growing beneath her heart.

Life resumed in Grand County as November dawned. Sheriff Tom Roberts and Undersheriff Will Redmond had divided the duties for the coming winter since traveling back and forth in the deep snow was next to impossible. Tom took Hot Sulphur Springs, leaving Will in Grand Lake. Besides breaking up a bar fight occasionally and dealing with claim jumpers and drunks, Will's time was frequently spent at the Farview, rather than at the jail.

On Election Day, November 7, 1882, Will had his hands full keeping the two Republican factions from an out-and-out brawl. Daily's man was elected state senator over Miller's chosen candidate, and Rogerson from Gaskill (also Daily's man) had been elected County Commissioner. Toward the middle of November, Emma McLeary called at the Farview. Annie welcomed her friend, and they sat in the parlor with steaming mugs of hot tea, the leaves of which were a rare delicacy doled out only on special occasions or for special friends.

"Emma, I'm so glad you've come," Annie exclaimed. "I've missed you and working at the school."

"It's good to see you, too, Annie, but this isn't just a social call. I have a request."

"Anything, Emma," replied Annie warmly.

"I want you to take over in my place at the school."

Annie gaped at her friend, confused. "I don't understand, Emma."

"You see, Robert and I have decided to be married at Christmas."

Annie jumped up and threw her arms around Emma. "Oh, that's wonderful! I'm so happy for you. But can't you still continue to teach, too?"

Emma did not look at Annie. "No, we're leaving Grand County, just as soon as the snow melts next spring."

"Leaving Grand Lake? But where will you go? Isn't this Robert's home?"

"He wants to go somewhere we can farm the land. It's too harsh up here even for a garden in the summer," Emma exclaimed.

"I didn't know Robert wanted to be a farmer," mused Annie. "Is this what *you* want? To be a farmer's wife?"

"No, it's not," retorted Emma unhappily. "I love Robert, and I love our life here. But the mines aren't producing like they were, and Robert is worried that they might close down."

"I understand, Emma, but I didn't finish my own schooling or get a teaching certificate."

"That's not a problem, Annie. There's going to be a teacher test given here later in November. If you pass it, I'm sure the Board will approve your application. You're the only one even remotely qualified. It pays forty dollars a month, and the students already know and love you."

Annie thought it over. When Will received his divorce, they were to be married, but until the babies started coming, why couldn't she do what she had always wanted to do?

"I'll do it, Emma, but what's on the test? Will I be able to pass?"

Emma spent time with Annie each afternoon, tutoring her in geography, literature, and mathematics as they prepared for the teacher test.

Will was less than enthusiastic about the upcoming examination. "Why do you want to teach a bunch of raggedy-ass varmints anyway?" he asked petulantly one cold November evening as they sat in the warm parlor of the Farview while the wind and snow blew outside.

"Someday, one of those raggedy-ass varmints might be a little Redmond," Annie teased. "Don't you want our children to have an education?"

"I only finished the sixth grade, Annie, and I've done pretty well, now haven't I?" Will asked, belligerently.

Annie moved closer to Will on the settee and took his wide roughened hand in her own. She brought it to her lips and gently kissed the knuckles. "I wouldn't care if you were completely illiterate, Will Redmond, I would still love you madly.

"But our children *will need* an education. The world is changing so fast. Did you know there is already a thing called a 'telephone' in Denver? You could actually talk to someone who is across town from you. I want our children to have every opportunity to understand when new things come their way, don't you?"

Will frowned as he thought about the 'telephone' and other newfangled inventions he'd heard of lately. It bothered him to think of Grand County changing. He liked it just the way it was...a bit wild at times, but comfortable and reliable.

And he really hadn't had time to give much thought to his children. He thought back to his own childhood, growing up in Sedalia, Missouri, during the War Between the States.

"When I was a kid, I remember wanting to run away and join the War, but I was too young. It seemed so romantic for a boy then, to fight for your state's rights. I didn't really understand the horror of it all until it was over, and I watched my kin and neighbors coming back with terrible injuries and missing arms and legs. Some didn't come back at all.

"I remember telling my Pa that I didn't want to be a farmer like him. I wanted to see the world. He was real upset that I, being the oldest, wouldn't take the farm he'd sweated over his whole life.

"When Sarah said she was pregnant, my Pa figured that I'd settle down on the farm. And I did, for a few months, until it became obvious that Sarah wasn't going to have a baby after all. I remember feeling so trapped. She left our farm and went back to her parents. That's when me and my brothers headed out west to look for gold.

"I had a great childhood, Annie. We weren't rich, by a long shot, but Ma always had something good cooking over the fire, and having my brothers around never left me feeling lonely." He grabbed Annie's hand and gazed into her eyes. "I hope we have lots of kids. And yeah, I want 'em all to be as smart as their Ma."

She glanced around to make sure they were alone, then leaned in. Moving his long hair out of the way, she kissed his neck, making him shudder with pleasure.

"Don't get me started, darlin'," he muttered thickly as he gently pushed her away.

"You started it, Mr. Redmond, if you recall," Annie stated playfully, feigning indignation.

He stood, stretching his back, and put on his hat, gloves, and overcoat. "Guess I'd better do my rounds in town and make sure some jackass ain't causing a ruckus."

Will had been sleeping in the jail on a cot since the snow started falling as it was too far to travel each night to Bass' cabin. "You study for your test, darlin', and who knows, maybe you can teach me a thing or two." The twinkle in his eye as he boldly raked her body left his meaning quite clear.

Annie threw on her shawl and quickly dragged him out onto the darkened porch, brightened by the white snow covering the ground. She stood on tiptoe to put her arms around his neck, and he easily lifted her up to eye level. As they stared at one another, his arms supporting her, neither noticed the biting cold as they made their own warmth.

Annie easily passed the teacher test and made plans to be the new teacher the next summer.

George Miller informed Will that it was only a matter of getting the paperwork from the lawyer in Missouri before the divorce was final. Since it was nearly impossible for mail to be delivered to Grand County during the winter, it might take longer than had been expected.

On Thanksgiving night, Will and Bass Redmond escorted both Annie and Mrs. Elder to the Ledman Ranch located on the South Fork of the Colorado River. The week before, Bass and Will had moved the furniture to the corners of the parlor at the Farview, and Annie had spent hours teaching Bass the popular dances of the day.

When the four arrived at the dance, a local musician, Jack Mitchell, was playing the fiddle and calling square dances.

"Come on, Sebastian," Annie said as she dragged the shy man toward the nearest eligible young girl. "Hetty Spender, this is Mr. Bass Redmond, the Undersheriff's brother. He doesn't know many people so I was wondering if you could introduce him around."

The pretty young blonde blushed and giggled. "Very pleased to meet you, Mr. Redmond. I'd be happy to help him meet people, Miss Annie."

Annie left her future brother-in-law in Hetty's capable hands. As Will swooped her onto the floor for their first dance, they saw that Bass was twirling his partner first in the Quadrille and later in a rousing rendition of the Virginia Reel. Will and Annie laughed as they danced the night away.

Will particularly enjoyed "Sweet Little Susie" , a singing dance he remembered from Missouri where the men kept time on the wooden floor with their booted feet as they circled the line of girls. Will and Bass, with their deep baritone voices could be heard above the rest, singing lustily:

> *"Where oh where is sweet little Susie?*
> *Where oh where is sweet little Susie?*
> *Where oh where is sweet little Susie?*
> *Way down yonder in the paw-paw patch.*
> *Come on, boys, let's go find her,*
> *Come on, boys, let's go find her,*
> *Come on, boys, let's go find her,*
> *Way down yonder in the paw-paw patch."*

This went on until the men, nearly breathless from their singing, had found all their sweet little Susies, and Promenaded home, ending the dance.

When the sun began to rise, the revelers set out for the long ride home, tired but still exhilarated from the dancing. Will lifted Annie and Mrs. Elder into the cutter, tucking in warm blankets around the ladies' laps.

Then he put heated stones from the fireplace wrapped in burlap at their feet. The sure-footed horse knew enough to stay on the road since the terrain was one smooth white blanket which hid rocks and holes that could be tragic in the icy desolation.

In the middle of December, Will came to the Farview, his face a mask of pain.

"Oh, God, what is it? cried Annie when she saw how pale Will was.

"It's Jules Thermon, Annie."

"What about him, Will, what has happened?" asked Annie as she pulled Will's overcoat off and sat with him on the settee.

"A snowslide," began Will, his voice trembling. "He was killed in a snowslide up at the Hidden Treasure Mine."

"When did it happen?" asked Lydia Elder quietly, hearing Will's last statement as she walked down the stairs from her afternoon rest.

"Being the superintendent of the mine, Jules was trying to break a new trail for his miners to get from the bunkhouse to the mine easier, and a slide started somehow," Will began. "And because his body is covered with hundreds of tons of snow and debris, getting him out is next to impossible until the thaw."

"Oh, that poor boy," gasped Mrs. Elder as she dabbed her eyes with her apron. "Annie, we need to take some food to his mother, Minnie. Oh, that poor, poor boy." Mrs. Elder left the parlor and went to the kitchen.

Annie stayed by Will's side, the two lost in their memories of the young man. "At my first dance in Grand Lake, I danced with Jules. He wouldn't look at me, and I remember stomping on his foot to get his attention. What a shy, kind boy he was! Besides my own mother, he's the only other person I have ever known who has died," Annie stated solemnly as Will's strong arms gave her a measure of security which she felt had slipped a bit from her world.

"Death is inevitable, darlin', especially up here in the mountains. He's not the first of my friends to die, and he sure won't be the last. But it never is easy for the ones left behind."

Annie, Lydia, and the rest of the ladies of town took food and comfort to Mrs. Thermon. In times of trouble, the women of Grand Lake bonded in sorrow.

"My boy is lying out there all by himself," sobbed Mrs. Thermon. "I wish someone would bring him home."

"Just as soon as it thaws, Minnie," replied Lydia softly. "Just as soon as it thaws." Annie stood by, completely at a loss to say or do anything to relieve the woman's pain and anguish.

The loss was hard on the small close community, but life went on.

On Christmas Eve, the Ledman's hosted another party. Will and Annie went alone because Mrs. Elder had a head cold. When they arrived in the cutter, Annie was much impressed by the five decorated Christmas trees which stood in the huge diningroom, one in the center and one in each corner.

Red paper balls and gold streamers twined through the green branches, and candles lit each tree. The party opened with all present joining hands and dancing around the central Christmas tree.

As Annie and Will sat out one of the dances, drinking punch and enjoying a well-earned rest, she confided to Will. "I never knew people could have so much fun at Christmas.

"When I grew up, everything was so solemn and serious all of the time. I was never allowed to have friends over to play or to go to anyone's house, and we never celebrated any holidays, not even birthdays.

"My father read the Bible story each year, and I always thought Mary might have wanted a bit of celebration when her little baby, Jesus, was born. People came to see them, according to the scriptures, like the shepherds and Wisemen and all, and they even brought presents. But my father never saw it my way. We spent the entire Christmas day in Church, praying for the redemption and forgiveness of our many sins. When I was little, I didn't see how I could have so many sins already."

Will squeezed her hand. "I guess I haven't helped much...in the sin department, that is. But surely God will forgive us for loving each other so much. I guess He'll be mighty happy to see me make an honest woman of you."

Annie glanced at Will, seeing his half-smile. "Well, if loving you makes me go to Hell, then I'll have to say it was worth it."

Will reached into his hip pocket and pulled out a small leather bag. "I guess this is just as good a time as any. Annie Mitchell, even though I'm not a free man yet, I want you and God and the world to know how much I love you."

He opened the pouch and held out a small wad of tissue paper. Then he got down on one knee, holding Annie's hand in his own. "Annie Mitchell, please consider this a token of my undying respect and affection."

With shaking hands, Annie carefully unwrapped the soft paper. Inside was a gold ring with an beautiful green emerald sparkling in the middle. Will took the ring and placed it on Annie's third finger of her left hand.

"Annie, darlin', will you be mine forever?" Will asked quietly.

Breathlessly, Annie replied, "Yes, yes, forever and beyond. Not even death could keep us apart, William Redmond."

Unaware of anyone else in the room, Will pulled Annie to her feet and kissed her. The other occupants of the the party had all witnessed the romantic scene and suddenly started clapping and cheering.

Annie and Will broke apart abruptly, reddening at the applause of their friends and neighbors. Will squeezed Annie's hand as he gazed down at her shining face so filled with love. He swept her off to the dance floor, twirling her to the music.

"When I was a boy, we decorated a Christmas tree every year. We'd go out into the woods and chop down the biggest one that would fit into our cabin. It was always a special time in my family, filled with us noisy boys. I remember when I got my first pocketknife, my first gun, and other times when I got longjohns and socks," he chuckled.

"Promise me we will always have loud and noisy Christmases, Will," Annie pleaded as tears formed in her blue eyes.

"I promise you, my love, because wherever the Redmond brothers go, there's sure to be lots of noise."

On New Year's Eve, The Grand Lake Dramatic Society presented 'Our Boys' in the newly-built Opera House which was followed by a dance at the Grand Lake House. But a pall had darkened Annie and Will's mood. Though some mail had been able to get through the rough snow-packed roads, nothing concerning his divorce was among the parcels.

He and Annie had planned on being married before the New Year, and Will had even bought a small log cabin on the west shore of Grand Lake from Judge Wescott's initial claim. Mrs. Elder and others had been donating furniture, dishes, and whatnots to the young couple's future home.

"1883 will be a year which will change our lives, Annie, don't fret now," Will said soothingly as her long face twisted his heart. They were standing by the window of the Grand Lake House that overlooked the frozen lake beyond. "All we are waiting on is for Sarah's lawyer to send the papers so George Miller can take it to a judge to sign. Then we'll be free to get married. Just have some patience, darlin', it'll happen, I swear. Nothing is gonna keep us apart, Annie, trust me."

"I know, Will, it's only that already Emma is married, and I wanted us to be, too," Annie pouted. She watched as the dancers swirled past. "And what if I get pregnant? What will happen then?"

Will thought for a moment, a myriad of emotions crossing his face, then answered solemnly, "I guess we can't take that chance, can we? We'll just have to quit being together until we get married. I won't have any child of ours being labeled a bastard."

Annie's look of horror almost brought a grin to Will's serious face. "What are you saying? Not be together? I couldn't stand it, Will. It's the only time I have you all to myself," she cried.

"My little wanton," whispered Will as he gently pushed her against a wall and discreetly squeezed her backside. "It would only be for a couple of weeks at the most. And if I can stand it, you should be able to."

"I don't think you *could* stand it, Mr. William Redmond," she smiled innocently up into his eyes, which were darkening with passion.

Will quickly moved away from the heat of her before anyone could see the tightening of the front of his britches. "You might be right, Miss Mitchell, after all," he said thickly. "Do you want to go for a ride around the lake to a certain log cabin I happen to own?"

"Yes, I do, but not until you kiss me properly at the stroke of midnight, my big handsome Undersheriff," Annie whispered in his ear as she rubbed her breasts seductively against his arm.

"I'll do more than 'kiss' you properly if we can leave now," he answered huskily.

"Later, now dance with me," Annie said, her blue eyes flashing.

"Wait a minute, Annie, or the whole town's gonna know what a lucky girl you are to have a man with big feet," Will grinned as he tugged at the front of his trousers.

A few moments later, he swung Annie out onto the dance floor until the countdown to the New Year began. Then everyone went outside, and as 1883 arrived, fireworks exploded over the lake. As Annie stood in front of Will, his long strong arms around her, they watched the colorful glowing flashes in the darkened night, both dreaming of the coming year's happiness in store for them.

While everyone was engrossed in the show, Annie and Will stole away and went to the tiny cabin in the woods on the west side of the lake. In each other's arms they did a bit of celebrating of their own.

Hours later, as Annie and Will slept peacefully wrapped in each other's love, a murder was about to occur at the Grand Lake House.

The owner, Wilson Waldron, a Grand County Commissioner, had celebrated the New Year a little more than he should have.

Couples were still dancing in the big diningroom of the Grand Lake House when Waldron staggered upstairs to the apartment he shared with his wife and new baby. "Why don't you dance with me, Mrs. Waldron?"

Amanda Waldron was nursing their son. "You need to sleep it off, Wilson. Leave me alone and go to bed."

"Nobody tells me what to do, woman," Waldron growled. He took the baby from his wife's arms and put the screaming infant in the crib. Then he grabbed his wife and began slinging her around the small room in a drunken dance..

"Stop it, Wilson, you're hurting me and the baby is crying," Mrs. Waldron cried, drawing the attention of Robert Plummer, a boarder who happened to be walking by their rooms.

Robert, a young man new in town, stuck his head in the door, seeing immediately that Wilson was irritating his wife. Thinking he could be of assistance, Robert said with a smile, "Mr. Waldron, why don't you let your wife tend to that baby. He's awful upset."

Waldron's wife used the interruption to break free and run to the child, cuddling him to her breast and trying to stop his hysterical sobbing.

"Just what the hell do you think you're doing in my house?" bellowed the intoxicated Waldron. He swung his attention from his wife to Robert Plummer, who stood in the doorway. "What are you looking at? I think you're just a might too interested in my wife, boy."

Mrs. Waldron grabbed Wilson's arm, pleading with him, "Stop this, Wilson, and go to bed. Robert is just trying to help."

Wilson Waldron jerked away from his wife and grabbed the rifle off the mantle. When Plummer saw what was happening, he backed out of the doorway and walked rapidly toward the stairs.

Over his shoulder, Robert called, "Settle down, Mr. Waldron, I'm not interested in your wife."

But, Wilson followed Robert down the stairs and stumbled out into the street, cursing at the young man. And, as Robert Plummer crossed the street, Waldron shot the Plummer in the back.

Will was roused out of a sound sleep by Bass. Everyone who was still dancing had rushed outside to see Wilson weaving around in the street waving the rifle, and Robert Plummer face down in the dirt.

Annie, sat up sleepily when the warmth of Will left the bed. "What's going on, Will? Where are you going?"

"Bass is outside. There's been a shooting in town and I have to take care of it."

Annie sat up, suddenly wide awake. "Who was shot? Will, please don't go; you might get hurt."

Will walked over to the bed and gently patted Annie's bare shoulder. "Don't worry, darlin', nothing will happen to me. All of the ruckus has already happened. It was Wilson Waldron, Bass said, who killed that young Plummer boy. I've got to lock him up."

"Oh, how horrible!" Annie exclaimed. She reached up and clung to Will. "Your job is too dangerous, Will. I would die if anything happened to you."

"Don't you worry, Annie girl, I'm mighty careful when guns are drawn. Get dressed and I'll see you back to the Farview before anyone knows you're missing."

The next day, Charley Burn was the first to share the news of how Waldron's arrest sparked several controversial political results. "Waldron was gonna retire, soon, as County Commissioner in favor of Rogerson of Gaskill. John Kinsey already resigned *his* seat as County Commissioner because he was so perturbed at all the political turmoil in the county."

"So what's the problem? asked Mrs. Elder.

Charley continued, "Rogerson of Gaskill plead himself ineligible for some reason, and Governor Pitkin stepped in and replaced him with none other than Ben Daily! Well, you know how much that irritated George E. Miller. Tensions between Miller and Daily seem to increase every minute. It's all anyone can talk about."

"It doesn't sound like Miller is any better than my uncle, does it?" harrumphed Annie.

Within a week, the incumbent county treasurer and new county clerk (both Miller's men) encountered difficulty in securing bonds for the coming year.

Will Redmond and Sheriff Roberts were kept busy stemming would-be lynch mobs who were aching for Waldron's skin while Ben Daily and George Miller continued to vie for control of the county. The cauldron of politics in Grand County was certainly boiling over.

CHAPTER EIGHT

The beginning of 1883 proved to be a bitter one, not only because of the severity and frequency of blowing snowstorms but also because of the unusual number of tragedies and political unrest in the county.

As January, waned, Will had still not heard any word on his divorce. He and Bass snowshoed the seventy miles to Georgetown in a blizzard just to send a telegram to Sarah's lawyer back in Sedalia. Will spent two long days at the Ennis Hotel waiting for an answer. When it finally arrived, he was crestfallen.

Sarah had changed her mind about granting the divorce. And Will was stymied unless he made another trip back to Missouri.

"Damn her hide, Bass!" Will stormed after reading the wire. "What am I gonna tell Annie? I can't go back to Sedalia now, in the middle of winter. I'll have to wait 'til the snow melts, and that might not be until June. If I can't have Annie all to myself soon, I'll explode, Bass, I'll just explode!"

"Will, Annie loves you," began his brother calmly. "She'll wait no matter how long it takes, you know that. Sure, she ain't gonna be happy about it, but she loves you, Will, and you're a lucky man."

Will grinned sheepishly at his brother while nodding his head. "You're right about that, Bass, I *am* a lucky man. Now let's get on the road and get back to her."

Early in February, Annie snowshoed to the General Store for some much needed supplies. As she was taking off the bulky snowshoes, she couldn't help but overhear the conversation around the woodstove.

"I heard County Commissioner George E. Miller went to the new governor, Grant, and requested the cancellation of Ben Daily's nomination as Commissioner."

Another said, "Yeah, I heard MIller's claiming Daily's appointment by Governor Pitkin was illegal and should be canceled. Grant ain't a supporter of anyone in Grand County, so he told Miller that he couldn't UNappoint a Commissioner. He told George Miller that we mountain folk need to clean up our own messes."

Charley Burn piped in, "Miller sure was pissed, I heard, but he can't kick Daily out of being a Commissioner."

Mr. Cane, the Mercantile proprietor, said, "Ben Daily's gonna be right put out when he hears what old George is trying to do to him." He looked up and saw Annie standing at the door. "Oh, Miss Mitchell, I'm sorry, I didn't see you there."

"It's all right, Mr. Cane, as I have no love for any of the men you're discussing. But, just for argument's sake, what do you think my uncle will do about it?"

Charley Burn jumped to his feet when he heard Annie's voice. "I can tell you what he did, Miss Annie."

Everyone turned to the boy, and he puffed up with pride at being able to tell the best gossip. "Well, that Ben Daily was real mad, and he went to his friend, Webb, in Hot Sulphur Springs. I heard tell he told him to relieve two of Miller's appointees as county attorneys, then replace them with one who was in Daily's pocket."

"Can he do that?" asked Annie.

"Oh yeah, he can," stated Charley adamantly. "Daily drew up a paper which proposed all manner of reforms with the help of *his* appointee. It surely is coming to a head between Miller and Daily."

Annie harrumphed, "I think all of this political brouhaha is sheer nonsense. Two grown men... acting like children. There ought to be a law against men being allowed to behave so stupidly."

The faces of the men around the woodstove were aghast as they stared back at Annie. No woman had ever ventured an opinion on the state of the political scene. And the derisive tone in Annie's voice shocked them all to their bootstraps.

Annie ignored their reactions and went about the business of purchasing the items from her list.

Later that month, Annie was at the courthouse visiting Will when Sheriff Roberts stumbled in, pale and shaking.

"Oh God, there's been another snowslide," barked the Sheriff as he moved to a cabinet and brought out a bottle of whiskey. He put it to his lips and downed several big slugs.

Annie and Will watched and waited, horrified by his statements.

"Who, Tom, who was it this time?" asked Will quietly.

Sheriff Roberts sank into a chair, his head in his hands. "I saw it all. It was awful, Will, just awful.

"Early this morning, Stokes and me was shoeing up to the cabin by the Toponis Mine when the slide started. We could see it heading for the cabin, but the roar of it prevented our voices from reaching the poor bastards inside. We skittered behind a large tree, watching the slide take all the timber in its path. The upper part took the roof of the cabin and partly covered me and Stokes. I thought we were goners, for sure.

"But we were able to dig ourselves out, then we tried to get to the cabin. But we couldn't make any headway so I went for help, leaving Stokes to keep trying to reach the men inside. A bunch of the boys from the Wolverine came to help us, and about ten in the morning, we found Mike Flynn, still alive, lying on his back with his head resting on a log and another log on his chest. He was the lucky one.

"The others weren't so lucky. Doc Duty was found at Flynn's feet, still sittin' on a stool. His body was bent double with the weight of the snow. Mike said he had heard Doc moaning for awhile. Close to Doc was Thomas Booth, his back broken and his face smashed. He must have been killed instantly." Tom took another swig of whiskey.

Annie and Will exchanged horrified looks.

Then Tom continued. "Jack Williams was found a little distance from the rest. He was probably killed instantly, too. The bodies were all sledded to Gaskill. I guess they'll bring 'em back here for burial."

Annie put her cold hand into Will's, and he squeezed it hard enough to make her wince. "Doc, Jack, and Thomas were my friends. What's wrong with this damn county?" he cried. "It's like there's a curse or something."

Jack Williams and Thomas Booth were hurriedly buried in Gaskill, but Doc Duty was brought back to the Grand Lake cemetery and given a decent sendoff. Everyone in town attended, the wind blowing through the pines and the snow laying wet and heavy on the black veils of the women.

Snowstorms continued to wage battle through February. Fifteen hundred cattle were lost during that winter, and still the political turmoil became more and more fractious.

In late February, Ben Daily and James Webb issued a call for a special Commissioner's meeting at Grand Lake. Ben and Marian had moved to property outside Hot Sulphur Springs, so whenever he had early business at the Lake, he'd sometimes ride in the night before and board at the Farview. Annie did her best to avoid him.

When he and Webb walked from the Farview over the lake path to the courthouse, George E. Miller and Will's youngest brother, Mann, were waiting along with Will and Sheriff Tom.

"I have to go over to Teller on business," announced Miller. He was a few inches taller than Ben Daily, but around the same age. His stiff black mustache hung down on either side of his mouth and reached below his long chin. Mann Redmond had become his right-hand man and principal body guard. Though not as tall as Will or Bass, the resemblance between the three brothers was remarkable.

Miller turned to Will and the Sheriff, who had foreseen trouble between the two Commissioners. "I expect you two, as the law in these parts, to keep these men from having their meeting without *all* of the Commissioners present."

As Miller rode away, Ben Daily and his cohort, Webb, immediately tried to enter the courthouse anyway. Will drew his pistol, leaned casually against the frame of the door, and calmly made a show of spinning the cylinder and checking it for cartridges.

"Are you threatening me with that revolver, Redmond?" Daily asked while he anxiously eyed the deadly weapon in the Undersheriff's hand.

"No one's threatening nobody," Tom retorted irritably as he stood between Ben and Will. "Ben, you know as well as I do there ain't gonna be no meeting today. Not when everyone ain't accounted for, is that clear?"

The crowd which had gathered to watch the interchange muttered among themselves. Daily and Webb studied the two lawmen, then finally decided to withdraw.

"It's obvious whose pocket you're in, Sheriff," stated Ben Daily loudly. "But no matter. We will adjourn to the Nickerson for a bite of breakfast."

He and Webb went to a private room at the Nickerson, ordered breakfast, and proceeded to elect Daily chairman of the County Commissioners. The two men then wrote up a paper certifying the *North Park Miner*, which was anti-Miller, to be the official newspaper of Grand County.

Later that day, using talk of a possible lynching as an excuse, Daily ordered Sheriff Roberts to remove Wilson Waldron from the jail in Grand Lake for his own safety and move him to the Jefferson County jail at Golden.

As soon as Will and Sheriff Roberts left town with Waldron, the *North Park Miner* published a scathing letter authorizing Grand County citizens to 'cease all payments to anyone claiming to be the County Treasurer'.

"I don't understand what all of this means," Annie said later as she read the newspaper Charley Burn had brought by the Farview.

Lydia was up to her armpits in wash water, scrubbing the sheets for the occupants of the Farview. "It means Ben Daily is a skunk, Annie, pure and simple. *He's* decided, on his own, that the County Treasurer, who happens to be a supporter of George Miller, was not legally appointed. So your uncle is telling everyone not to pay any taxes or fees to him. I tell you, I'm getting so sick of all this politics. They should *all* be taken out and shot, in my opinion!"

The political clincher came on March eighth, when Daily and Webb announced a special Commissioner's meeting at Grand Lake for March twelfth, and rumor had it that Daily had drafted an ordinance to transfer the county seat back to Hot Sulphur Springs. This was the straw that could divide Grand County irreparably.

The repercussions caused by his actions soon left Ben Daily slightly paranoid. "That damned Miller and his friends are becoming dangerous. I've heard about some threats against me," he told Marian. "If I attend that meeting, some fool might try to kill me. Well, Miller can't hold a meeting without a quorum either, so Webb and I just won't attend."

"Ben," said Marian, worry lines across her forehead, "I think we might need to go back to Chicago. I fear for you every time you leave this house anymore."

Ben used Marian's fear, and his own, as an excuse not to attend either the meeting on March twelfth or the regular meeting which was scheduled for the first Monday in April.

The County Treasurer, Joe Flannagan, finally secured an adequate bond and in mid-May designated Gilman Martin, one of Will's closest friends, as his Deputy Treasurer. Over dinner at the Farview, the conversation was dominated by the local politics.

"Gil Martin has begun collecting delinquent taxes," Jim Calter began.

"Isn't that his job?" asked a young miner, new to the area.

"Sure, it is," chuckled Calter, "but he's specifically taxing James Webb's saloon in Hot Sulphur Springs and a sheep farm belonging to one of Ben Daily's strong supporters, Ronald Baker."

Charley Burn broke in, "It pissed off Baker so bad that he swore out a warrant on Gil and Flannagan for illegal taxation. They were tried in the Springs last week, but the judge found some legal reason to release them. I suppose the judge was in Miller's pocket, too."

The war was on between George E. Miller and Ben Daily. At the end of May, Ben sailed into the courthouse, glanced around to make sure Redmond wasn't around, then confronted Sheriff Tom Roberts. "I have here some damn incriminating evidence about George E. Miller's indictment back in Mississippi." He threw a sheaf of papers on the sheriff's desk.

Tom Roberts opened the papers and leafed through them quickly. He leaned back in his chair and asked, "So what do you want me to do about this, Ben?"

His face livid with anger, Ben shouted, "I want you to do your job for once, Tom Roberts, or else next election, you might not be sitting so pretty in this county."

Tom sat forward in his chair and stated in no uncertain terms, "Daily, I think you'd better get out of this office before I find evidence on you and throw you in the back room. And don't you ever threaten me again, is that clear?"

Ben backed toward the door, seething. "Does this mean you are *not* going to act on the evidence I've brought you against Miller?"

Sighing, Sheriff Roberts replied, "Yeah, yeah, I'll look into it."

Ben Daily stormed out of the office, infuriated the Sheriff would most likely do nothing with the information against Miller.

The snows continued late into the spring, and when the roads became passable, Will arranged for he and Bass to journey again to Georgetown. He wanted to try and settle the matter of the divorce with Sarah by wire without having to make the long trip back to Missouri.

While the two brothers were discussing the trip over dinner at the Farview, Mrs. Elder made a startling suggestion. "The Mercantile is running mighty low on supplies right now. I could sure use some staples, but I really can't go myself. Would you mind taking Annie to Georgetown with you and helping her with my shopping?"

Both Annie and Will jerked their heads in Lydia's direction, seeing the small smile on her face. Then Annie and Will looked at each other, their eyes locked together with the promise of the coming days...and nights together.

Will cleared his throat and tried to keep his voice from showing the excitement he was feeling. "Sure, Mrs. Elder, Bass and I'd be happy to take Annie along. How much trouble could she be?"

Even when the snows began to melt, the the county was continually punished with downpour after downpour of incessant rains. The trio set out for the Springs, the first stop on the way to Georgetown. The ride was miserable; rain and fog prevented any enjoyment of the scenery as Will drove the team while Annie and Bass dripped uncomfortably beside him.

When they arrived in Hot Sulphur Springs, Will arranged for an overnight stay for the three of them at the Stagecoach Inn. He had some business to take care of, so he got two rooms, one for Annie and the other for he and his brother. Later, Will planned on leaving Bass to sleep alone.

While Will was tied up at the Sheriff's office, Bass took Annie to dinner at the Inn diningroom. As they enjoyed their food, a tall buxom woman with unusually bright yellow hair and orangey-red cheeks approached their table. She stopped a moment, a look of confusion on her face as she stared at Bass and Annie. Finally she stomped over to their table.

"Hey Bass, I thought you were your brother for a minute," the woman stated, her voice loud and nasally. Then she looked Annie up and down and asked rudely, "Who's this?"

Bass had reddened at her approach, and now he looked as if his face would burst into flames at any moment. He glanced around nervously to find the patrons curiously watching the unfolding scene. Finally he answered, "E-evening, Marcy, this here is Miss Annie Mitchell from Grand Lake."

"Oooo, now, it's *Miss* Annie Mitchell, how quaint!" the woman spat sarcastically. Then she bent down into Annie's face. "Are you the bitch who's been keeping my Willie occupied at the other end of the valley?"

Annie's eyes widened at the woman's crassness and sour breath. She turned in confusion toward Bass, but he just shrugged his big shoulders in exasperation.

"Would you like to sit down, Miss...?" Annie asked finally, curious and slightly perturbed that the woman had referred to Will as 'hers'.

Marcy jerked out a chair and flounced down in it, an ugly snarl on her face. Annie thought the older woman might have been pretty once, if she didn't wear so much paint on her face. "The name is Adams, Marcy Adams. Now that I'm sittin', answer my question. Are you the one who I've been hearin' about over at the Lake?"

"I am the fiancé of the Undersheriff, yes," Annie said quietly, showing the emerald ring on her third finger.

"Listen, you, I've been with Will Redmond a lot longer than you, in fact, I've probably had *more* of him than you ever have." The prostitute tossed her yellow hair smugly. "Hell, I've been his favorite gal since he came to the Springs, and I ain't ready to give him up to no milquetoast like you, you hear? I'll fight you for him, right outside in the street, right now."

Annie sat back in her chair astounded. This whore with whom Will had apparently frequented wanted to fight her!

"Miss Adams," Annie began slowly, not knowing quite what to say, "Will and I are going to be married. I have no desire or reason to fight with you because Will Redmond is *not* yours anymore, if he ever was. He's mine, and you need to understand that."

Marcy pushed back her chair roughly, sending it crashing to the floor. By this time, all of the participants in the diningroom had lost interest in their food. Bass, feeling terribly inadequate, stood up and put his hand on Marcy's arm, which she immediately flung off.

"Dammit, Bass, stay out of this," Marcy shouted. "This is between me and her." She turned on Annie who was still seated, staring boldly at the angry prostitute.

Marcy grabbed the front of Annie's dress with both fists and dragged her out of her chair. Annie tried to wrench Marcy's hands from her clothes but was unable to break free. Instinctively, Annie brought up her knee, right into Marcy's lower stomach, doubling the woman over long enough for Annie to jerk herself free. Then Annie clenched her fist and cuffed Marcy in the face. The prostitute fell backwards to the floor.

Annie's face was suffused in anger now, and she was breathing heavily as she stood over the prostate woman and gasped, "Will Redmond is *mine* now, Miss Adams, so you had better get that through your thick painted skull. And I don't take kindly to being rough-handled by a woman or anyone else."

Will had entered the restaurant just in time to see Annie knee Marcy, then he watched in shock as Annie had balled up her fist and punched Marcy right in the mouth, sending her sprawling to the floor.

Will hurried to the table and helped Marcy to her feet as Annie rubbed her knuckles, her blues eyes fiery.

"All right, girls, that'll be quite enough," Will said in his lawman voice, trying hard not to chuckle. Marcy was still stunned by the blow, and her eyes didn't quite focus.

"Willy?" she asked in a little girl voice. "Have you come back to me, my sweet Willy?"

"Marcy, listen to me, I told you before that I ain't ever coming back," Will said gently.

The prostitute's eyes teared up and the kohl on her eyelids began to run down her face in ugly black smears. She looked from Will to Annie and back again, then stood up and ran from the building.

Will turned to Annie as she sucked on the broken skin of her knuckles. Bass just stood there, dumbfounded.

"Well, damn, darlin', I can't leave you alone for a minute, can I?" Will grinned at the memory of Annie's infamous knee which had nearly crippled him last summer in Gaskill. Then he pictured her again rarin' back and punching Marcy with a strong right fist. When he realized everyone was still staring, he quickly ushered Annie out of the door, leaving Bass, who was still speechless, to take care of their bill.

Annie was trembling now as Will hustled her up the stairs to the door of the room they would be sharing. As soon as the door was closed behind them, he pulled Annie onto his lap as he sat on the edge of the bed.

She continued to suck on her knuckles, shaking, until he pried her hand out of her mouth. He examined the broken skin and decided it wasn't so bad.

"You little wildcat, do you realize you just fought over me?" he asked, grinning from ear to ear.

Annie stared at his grin, realizing she had actually knocked the girl to the floor. She began to smile, too, as she remembered. Then she thought of all of the times Will must have been with that painted floozy. Suddenly her smile faded, and she reached around and slapped Will soundly across the face.

"Why'd you do that?" Will exclaimed as her finger marks shown brightly on his cheek.

"That's for sleeping with that whore!" Annie cried, jumping from his lap and stomping over to the window across the room. She stared out into the dark night, furious with herself for being so eaten up with jealousy.

"Hell, Annie, what was I supposed to do? A man can't live like a monk, can he? And I didn't even know you back then," he cajoled.

Annie twirled on him, fire blazing from her darkened blue eyes, "Did you love her?"

Will crossed the room in two strides and stood in front of her, his arms not reaching for her like they usually did whenever she was near.

Calmly, he replied, "No, she was just a whore."

"And what am I?" Annie screamed back at him.

"You're the woman I love and plan to marry, darlin', haven't you figured that out yet?"

Annie stared at his solemn expression, then threw herself into his arms. He hugged her to him as he moved toward the bed. Lifting her in his arms, he lay down on the bed with her pressed close to his chest. He stroked her hair as he held her, and her shivering finally subsided as his words soaked in.

"I'm sorry, Will, that I have such a temper," Annie's voice still shook a little.

"That's all right, just as long as you'll promise me one thing," Will answered.

"Anything."

"Promise me you'll always fight for me, even if the odds don't look good," Will whispered in her ear. "Because I promise I'll always fight for you."

Annie's reply was lost in his kiss.

The rest of the trip from the Springs over Berthoud Pass was uneventful though extremely wet. Four miles past Empire by way of Union Pass across the Columbia Mountains, they entered the three walled valley of Georgetown. Bass told Annie a little history about the boom town, which lay in a pocket of hills at the foot of the climb to Argentina Pass.

"It was called the Griffith District first when gold was being sought. Then in 1864, silver was discovered up the Argentine. They called it the Belmont Lode, and it was quite a find. Me and Will heard about it when we were passing through Denver, and that's how we ended up in Colorado instead of going on to California."

As they drove past the depot and on into town, Annie saw how much bigger it was from Grand Lake. She thought back to the previous summer when she had first boarded the stage which had taken her over Berthoud Pass to Grand County. How long ago that seemed now!

Bass pointed up to the steep mountains which surrounded them. "The sun rises behind the Saxon Mountains, peeks over the top of Woodchuck Hill, and lights up the tips of the Columbia and Democrat

Mountains across the valley. The higher reaches of Mount McClennan, away up in the Argentine, will be brilliant long before any warming beams strike the center of town."

The threesome made their way through the crisscrossed streets to Taos where they registered at the Ennis Hotel. They used the same ploy as at the Stagecoach Inn, Bass and Will in one room, and the one next door for Annie. Switching rooms was easier than they had thought it would be.

As soon as they had changed clothes, Will escorted Annie downstairs to dinner and on to the Cushman Opera House while Bass hit the saloons. Annie, who was unused to alcohol, drank entirely too much champagne.

The next morning, Annie awoke with a tremendous headache.

"God's teeth, who hit me?" she whimpered as Will lay a cool compress across her forehead.

"You, my dear, are a very cheap drunk," Will chuckled as he pulled on his boots.

"How did we get back here?" Annie asked as she opened one eye. "I don't even remember leaving the Opera House."

"You passed out before the last act," Will drawled, "so I hefted you over my shoulder and brought you back to the Hotel. And don't worry, I didn't take advantage of you 'cuz it wouldn't have been any fun making love to a corpse."

"Oh Will, my reputation is ruined!" Annie wailed.

"Don't worry, no one knows you here," Will stated as he put on his hat and headed for the door.

"Where are you going?" Annie cried.

"To the telegraph office, and I'm gonna stay there until Sarah changes her mind about the divorce."

"Do you want me to come with you?" Annie asked as she squinted from the light of the window.

"Naw, you get some more sleep," Will said. He took some coins from his pocket and laid them on the dresser. "If you get hungry, just go across the street to the Eatery."

"Is it proper for me to go out alone?" Annie asked innocently.

Will laughed out loud. "You punched out a whore in the Springs, you got drunk last night, and you're laying around half-naked in *my* bed. Ain't it a little late to worry about what's 'proper', darlin'?" He turned on his heel, still chuckling, and walked out the door.

Annie slept until noon, then awoke ravenous. She dressed, took the coins, and walked out of the hotel. As she looked left, then right, she noticed stores down the street. When Annie had been at Miss Mary Flynn's School for Young Ladies in St. Louis, she had often stared at the displays in the windows of stores. She had never had money with which to buy anything.

At last she had money in her reticule, so she headed down the street, her hunger forgotten for the moment.

An hour later, after buying a ridiculously expensive new hat, Annie headed back to the cafe across from the Ennis Hotel. Upon entering, she spied an empty table and sat down. Though small, the place was clean and each table was covered in a smooth linen tablecloth with a single red rose in a small vase. A large woman in a voluminous apron took her order and brought her a hot cup of tea while she waited for the food to cook.

Annie ate leisurely, enjoying herself immensely but wishing Will's large frame would come through the door. Suddenly she heard a voice behind her which sent shivers down her spine.

"How nice to see you again, Miss Mitchell," J. C. Brashears said in his cold, crisp speech.

Terrified, Annie looked up into his scary silver eyes. She had so completely put him out of her mind that she had forgotten Georgetown was his home.

"May I sit down?" he asked imperiously as he pulled out a chair without waiting for her answer. He waved over the large woman and ordered a cup of tea for himself. "It's been such a very long time since last we met, my dear, and you don't look any worse for the wear from your unfortunate abduction. I understand you chose not to live at your uncle's house again."

Annie squirmed as if he might rip off her clothes with his scaly gaze.

"Have you lost the ability to speak, my dear? The last we met, you weren't so shy with your words."

She found her tongue and her courage, "Yes, I speak, Mr. Brashears, to people whom I have something in which to say. You, however, are not one of them."

"What? But we were engaged once, my dear, or have you forgotten?" replied Brashears, slickly.

Annie gathered her gloves and parcels, preparing to leave. All at once, she felt his steely grip on her arm forcing her back into the chair.

"I am not finished yet," Brashears growled, his voice still polite, but with an edge to it.

His eyes were glittery and lacked any compassion. Annie became frightened, searching the room for a would-be rescuer. To her despair, no one else in the room seemed to be looking their way. In fact, it seemed like the other diners were purposefully avoiding the interaction between her and Brashears.

It must be true, Annie thought, he *is* the 'Boss of Clear Creek County', a powerful man with his hand dipped into everything vile or otherwise in Georgetown.

"Let go of my arm, Mr. Brashears," Annie demanded a bit shakily. He still had the power to terrify her.

He rose, twisting her arm behind her and began forcefully escorting her toward the door. In her ear she heard him hiss, "I'm not finished with you yet, miss. You thought you could make a fool of me, didn't you? You need taming, my dear, by a man who knows how women should be treated."

Annie began to struggle in earnest and call out for assistance, but the people in the cafe averted their eyes. One man began to rise from his chair, but J. C. Brashears glared at him until he sat down again. He yanked her arm, pulling it up painfully until she knew he would think nothing of breaking it. She was helpless and could do nothing but go forward as he steered her out of the Eatery and up the sidewalk.

As J. C. Brashears forced Annie around the first corner, they came face to face with Bass and Will. Will's face was expressionless, which Annie knew was more dangerous than any show of anger.

"Get your hands off her right now, Brashears, and I might not kill you," Will said quietly. "If you don't let her go, you'll be the deadest son of a bitch in Georgetown in about two seconds."

Annie couldn't see the Englishman's face, but she felt the pressure slowly release on her arm. When he let go completely, Will pulled her roughly toward him.

"You aren't the law here, Redmond," Brashears was breathing heavily now as he watched the two big men fingering their gun belts. "If you harm me in any way, my men will hang you."

"You were trying to abduct a woman in broad daylight, with witnesses," Will told him calmly. "I don't think *we're* in the wrong here. Now turn around and move on down the street, and if you ever come near Miss Mitchell again, I swear I'll kill you, is that clear?"

Annie saw J. C. Brashears back away as he threatened, "You're in *my* territory now, Redmond, and the Sheriff here is *my* man. You, your brother, and that slut will all be hanged."

Bass growled and moved forward which caused the Englishman to turn and walk swiftly away, glancing back occasionally in fear.

Will turned to Annie, a look of frustration and anger marring his handsome features. "I can't leave you alone for a second, can I? You are one walking piece of trouble. Now we'd better get out of here fast or that bastard will have Bass and me arrested, leaving you all to himself." He grabbed her arm roughly and walked her hurriedly across the street to the hotel.

"It's not my fault, William Redmond," Annie argued. "I only went there to eat. It's not my fault he's a crazy man."

"Well, it doesn't matter, Annie, none of it matters anymore," Will stated, storm clouds in his eyes. "We were gonna go back to the Lake today anyway because Sarah has left town and no one knows where she's gone. Without her signature, I can't get a divorce, and I can't marry you."

Annie stared at him in astonishment as he half-lifted her up the stairs at the hotel. He pushed her into their room then went over to the window. She stared at the floor, all of her hopes and dreams suddenly dashed to pieces in front of her.

"What are we going to do, Will?" Annie asked in a tiny voice.

"Pack up and head back to Grand County. What else can we do?"

Annie woodenly did as he said, tears trailing down her cheeks as she stuffed her clothes and hair brush into the carpet bag she had brought. Afterwards, she sat on the bed, staring at nothing.

Finally Will turned to her. "Maybe this is for the best, Annie. Maybe you should find some man who can marry you and take care of you properly. Maybe it was never meant to be between us."

Annie stared at him, suddenly seeing a stranger standing before her.

"If that's what you think, Will, then maybe I should."

He stared back at her for a moment. Then he said, "I'll get the horses hitched. Go to the General Store and start doing Mrs. Elder's shopping. I'll pick you up in the wagon."

Annie walked slowly to the Mercantile. With her heart a leaden lump, she looked over Lydia's list before she handed it to the clerk.

> 100 lbs. of coffee beans @ 10 cents a lb.
> 25 lbs. of bacon @ 8 cents a lb.
> 50 lb. sacks each of shelled yellow corn, flour,
>   meal, and sugar @ 5 cents a lb.
> 2- 50 lb. boxes of dried apples @ $2.00 a box

Will and Bass, silent, were waiting in the wagon to load up after Annie had settled the bill. The ride back to Grand County was slow, sodden, and sad. It was all Annie could do not to cry, but she had decided that if Will didn't want her anymore, then she wouldn't allow him to see how much she hurt inside. Another man had thrown her away, she thought angrily, I should be used to it by now.

Three days later, the silent threesome drove into Grand Lake. The return trip had taken longer due to the loaded wagon. Annie had spent the first lonely night at the Peck House in Empire and the second at the Gaskill Inn atop Berthoud Pass and the third at the Stagecoach Inn. Miserably, she had wondered if Will had gone back to the Antlers Bar in search of Marcy.

When Will pulled the rig up to the Farview around dark, Annie jumped down and dashed inside, unable to control her tears any longer. Mrs. Elder met Annie at the door and watched her streak past, taking the stairs two at a time.

"Will, what happened?," Mrs. Elder asked.

Will grunted as he began to untie the tarp over the provisions bought in Georgetown.

"There's someone here to see you, son," Mrs. Elder continued.

Will looked up, the pain evident in his big handsome face. "Who?"

"It's me, Will," Sarah Redmond said, standing at the door. She was a farm girl, stocky and solid, and time hadn't been kind to her. Approaching thirty now, Will tried to remember why he had ever wanted to bed her.

Will stared at her as if he were seeing a ghost. "What the hell are you doing *here*? I've just been a hundred and forty miles trying to reach you."

"I think we should talk in private," Sarah replied, blushing, aware that Mrs. Elder and Bass were still standing on the porch.

"Go into the parlor, you two," Mrs. Elder stated as she hustled them into the warmth of the front room. She prayed Annie would stay in her room.

Sarah sat on the settee, but Will paced around the room like a caged animal, his frustration from the past days nearly at overflow. He had deliberately pushed Annie away on purpose because he knew he would never be free to marry her, though it had cost him dearly.

"Won't you sit with me, Will? I've traveled a long way just to see you," Sarah said, her flat voice irritating Will's already tightly-strung nerves.

"Dammit, Sarah Horton, I want a divorce," yelled Will, no longer able to control himself. "Why didn't you sign the damn papers?"

"I don't think I want a divorce, Will. I think it might be God's will that we stay married."

"How can you say such a thing?" he hollered. "I don't love you, and don't tell me you love me, 'cuz you don't. You haven't wanted to live with me since we were kids. Why are you making me so miserable now? Didn't I marry you when you said you were pregnant? And wasn't it a lie? Hell, Sarah, Bass told me about you and him. Didn't you think he would?"

Sarah continued to stare at Will solemnly. A noise on the stairs caused her to turn her head. Annie stood on the bottom stair, staring at Sarah with wide blue eyes. Then she looked at Will.

"Oh God, Annie," Will moaned, unable to deal with the confrontation about to happen.

Annie walked slowly over to Sarah, and the two women eyed each other appraisingly. Then Sarah asked, "Are you the one he wants to divorce me for?"

"I was," Annie replied. Then she looked at Will, questioningly.

Will stood, helplessly, gazing from one woman to another. Finally he answered, never taking his eyes off Annie, "I want to marry her, Sarah, more than I want to live right now. If you don't give me the divorce, Annie and I can't even see each other anymore. It just wouldn't be fair to her."

He turned to Sarah. "Do you understand how much I love her?"

Sarah looked from Will's face to Annie's.

"All right, Will," Sarah said resignedly, "I just had to make sure. Find a lawyer and we'll get it straightened out now. You're right, I never loved you, but you were such a wild handsome boy, and in my youth, I burned for you as much as she does now. I'm sorry to have come between you two; I never meant to cause any hurt."

Annie and Will stared at Sarah, then at each other. With two great strides, Will had Annie in his arms as she sobbed happily into the front of his shirt.

Two weeks later, Will and Sarah were legally divorced by special decree, and Sarah was on her way back to Missouri. Annie and Will set their wedding day for the afternoon of July Fourth, at the Farview

House. Much preparation was needed, and Mrs. Elder began altering her own wedding dress for Annie.

Ben and Marian Daily still felt threatened in Grand Lake so they sold the cabin above Grand Lake and moved permanently to a ranch on the lower Fraser River. Ben had heard that George E. Miller, the lawyer who had arranged Will's divorce, was saying a 'vigilance committee' had been organized and that Ben and his cronies would be 'encouraged' to leave the county within the next few months.

Annie and Will were in the Cane General Store in Grand Lake picking out some curtain material for their cabin when Charley Burn rushed in and breathlessly stammered, "W-Will, Ben Daily s-swore out a warrant against you and Alonzo Coffin for making threats against him."

"What?" asked Annie as she stared into Will's face.

Will turned toward Annie, anger and disgust clearly mirrored in his eyes. "Don't fret, darlin', it's nothing. Alonzo and I ran into Ben at the Springs a couple of weeks ago and the bastard started in on you. He said some pretty nasty things, and well, you know I ain't gonna stand for that. So I backed Daily into a corner and told him how well he'd look with several vital parts of his person laying on the floor in front of him, and if he ever said another word about you, I'd lay him out on the street like the dog he was."

Annie blanched at the cold-blooded threat, sure that Will meant every word. No wonder Ben was frightened. "So what will happen now? Will you have to go to jail?" asked Annie, a wrinkle of worry appearing between her blue eyes.

"Tom won't arrest you or Alonzo," stated Charley, secretly hoping the Undersheriff *would* be arrested and removed from Annie's life. "But

I heard that William Zane Cozens from Fraser has been appointed special constable, and he might do something about it."

"Well, we'll cross that bridge when we come to it," replied Will.

But luckily, continuing high water from the heavy rains kept Cozens in the Fraser Valley and unable from carrying out the arrests.

On July second, two days before Annie and Will's wedding, Ben Daily left his ranch in the early morning, a bit nervously. Things in the county had been too quiet lately.

Ben had told Marian before he left, "I have it on best authority that Miller is not even a legal attorney. I made some inquiries, and his name is not on the list of graduates from the school of law he said he had attended. I am going to bring this to the attention of the Board and get him railroaded out of the county."

"Maybe you shouldn't go, Ben," Marian fretted as she pawed at his jacket sleeve. "I believe Miller is insane, and he seems to have the Sheriff and that awful Undersheriff in his back pocket. I have a strong feeling that he'll either rule or ruin."

"Don't worry, I'll be in the company of James Webb and Ronald Baker. Even though things have been said and done in the heat of anger, I feel everything can eventually be worked out satisfactorily in my favor."

When Daily and his business associates arrived in Grand Lake, they registered at the Farview.

"Hello, dear niece," Ben said jovially when he saw Annie.

"Don't try and make up to me, Ben Daily," Annie railed. "I heard the terrible things you said about me. Then you swore out an arrest warrant against the man I'm going to marry just because he defended me. You are beneath contempt." She refused to serve him and stayed in the kitchen while he and his friends ate.

Later that day at the Commissioner's meeting, George Miller and Jim Carney asked to be excused as they said they had pressing business on a divorce case in Gaskill.

"Of course, George, by all means, do go," replied Ben jocundly. "We'll just confine our activities to the preparation of routine matters until we can all meet together."

Overhearing this exchange between the rivals, Charley Burn replied to a friend, "It looks as though peace has finally dawned."

And peace would have dawned, had the deceitful Daily and his friend, James Webb, done what they had implied. But on July third, the two men met in secret and drew up eight summonses, addressed to a number of county officers of Miller's sympathies, including Sheriff Tom Roberts and Undersheriff William Redmond.

The summons required their appearance before the board at ten A.M. on July fifth to show cause why they should not be required to give new bonds with 'sufficient' security.

Later at the saloon, Ben and Webb relaxed over a whiskey.

"I guess raising the bonds to twenty or thirty thousand dollars will make it next to impossible for our poorly paid law officials to meet the high bonding rate," said Daily, smiling conspiratorially. "Miller's main 'yes-men' will be ousted for insufficient bonds since there's no one in the county who would be able or willing to put up a cash bond of that exorbitant amount.

"Then we'll appoint our own men and establish bonds through my connections with the moneyed people in Chicago who own the

Wolverine Mine. I can't wait to see Miller and Redmond's reaction. Those bastards will regret ever crossing Ben Daily."

When George E. Miller returned to Grand Lake from Teller, he heard of Daily's latest and most horrendous treachery. At the jail he met with Sheriff Tom Roberts, Will, and Will's youngest brother, Mann.

"That bastard," Miller growled, "has gone too far this time. Let's put a scare into him that will send him packing from the county for good. We'll sneak up on him, wearing masks, and scare the tar out of him."

"Now wait a minute, tomorrow is my wedding day," argued Will. "I hate Daily probably more than any of you, but I'm getting married tomorrow. I don't want anything to mess that up."

"Don't worry, Will, we'll do it right after he's eaten breakfast," answered Miller. "He, Webb, and Baker will be heading for the courthouse, and they'll be on the footpath by the lake. We'll hide by the icehouse and when they come over the ridge, we'll surprise them."

"And do what, George?" asked Tom nervously. He was just as angry as the rest of the men at Daily, but he and Will were also the elected law officials of the county.

Miller rubbed his hands together and replied easily, "Don't worry, I'll do all the talking; you just enjoy the sight of that skunk and his toadies scrambling out of Grand County forever."

"Just so long as I'm back at the Farview in time for my wedding," said Will, and the other men poked him in the ribs and slapped him on the back in camaraderie.

"Trust me, son," smiled George E. Miller.

CHAPTER NINE

The Fourth of July in 1883 dawned sunny and warm. The town of Grand Lake was jubilantly expectant of the celebration, not only of the country's Independence, but of the much awaited wedding between Undersheriff William Redmond and Miss Ann Millicent Mitchell, which had been announced in the *Prospector*.

As Annie rose from her bed at the Farview, she hugged herself when she realized it was the last night she'd ever have to spend without Will by her side. She stretched her arms over her head and gazed out the window at the lake. It was smooth as glass, unmarred by any skiffs or early fishermen. The surrounding mountains glistened with the early morning dew not yet burned away. The sky was a brilliant blue, with a few wispy clouds floating lazily by.

"What a glorious day!" Annie mused happily. "And today I will become Mrs. William Redmond of Grand Lake. We'll go to *our* cabin on the lake and start our life together. I can't believe this day is really here. What a long winter it was!"

There was a short rap on the door.

"Are you up, dear?" called Mrs. Elder.

Annie threw open the door and hugged her friend. "I can't believe it has finally gotten here! I'm so excited; I can't wait until two o'clock! Have you seen Will? Did he come for breakfast? Can I see him before the ceremony, or is it bad luck?"

"Questions, questions, child, you are full of them today," laughed Mrs. Elder. "Now get yourself dressed because we have a lot of hungry men to feed today. And just because it's your last day here doesn't mean you get to be lazy."

Annie threw on a calico cotton dress and quickly packed the rest of her things in a satchel. She reverently laid out Lydia's wedding dress on the bed. It was an ivory satin, with hundreds of seed pearls sewn on for decoration. The bodice was high and the sleeves reached her wrists and then buttoned with tiny buttons. The skirt was long and the train trailed behind gracefully. Annie couldn't wait for Will to see her in the beautiful dress.

When she arrived downstairs, her uncle, James Webb, and Ronald Baker were finishing their breakfasts. She sailed past them without a word into the warm kitchen.

"I really can't stand the sight of Ben Daily," Annie spat, donning a clean white apron.

"Annie, dear," began Lydia kindly as she opened the big woodstove door and removed a plate of steaming biscuits, "this day is a new beginning for you. Why don't you let bygones be bygones? Do you want animosity between you and Ben to spoil your wedding day?"

Annie sighed, "You're right, I suppose, I shouldn't be so hateful on today of all days. All right, I'll take out the biscuits and try to be civil to the old bastard."

She pushed open the diningroom door with her hip and entered the room. The other diners at the table rose politely, all except Ben Daily and his cronies who glanced her way then continued their whispered conversation.

Deciding to ignore the snub, Annie painted on a beautiful smile and set the plate on the table. "Good morning, Uncle Ben, gentlemen. I hope you all slept well last night."

Ben Daily turned to stare at Annie, his bushy eyebrows raised. "Well, so it's 'Uncle' again, is it, girl? Don't you think it's a little late for family reunions? I don't think Marian will ever forgive you for all the trouble you've caused us. And I don't remember any invitation to your wedding, now do I?"

Annie tensed at his sarcastic tone, then bit back the retort which was on the tip of her tongue. "I was just saying 'good morning', not asking you to take me back into the bosom of your love. The fact is, I wanted to try and make peace with you on this special day, but you continue to be the insensitive bastard you've always been. So I take back anything I said that might have even remotely sounded like polite conversation. And you, my dear uncle, can just go to Hell."

She stormed out of the room, hearing Ben Daily's smirking laugh behind her.

Less than an hour later, Annie and Lydia were busily icing the tiered wedding cake when she heard popping sounds from outside. Both women turned their heads toward the window.

"Isn't a bit early to start shooting off fireworks?" Annie asked.

Later that evening, a grand fireworks display had been planned over Grand Lake in celebration of America's Independence Day. But by then, she and Will, legally wed, would be climbing out of bed to see the show from the window of their cabin across the lake.

Suddenly, Annie heard a commotion out on the porch. She wiped her hands on her apron, as did Mrs. Elder, and they went through the now-empty diningroom to the parlor. As Lydia Elder opened the front door, she and Annie saw the men who had been smoking their pipes and enjoying the morning air chaotically rushing toward the lake path.

Jim Calter, on horseback, was shouting, "The shootin' has started, boys."

Annie paled, "What shooting? What are you talking about?" She dashed off the porch in the direction of the footpath.

"Wait, Annie, it could be dangerous!" yelled Mrs. Elder. But the girl kept running.

When Annie arrived at the scene, she was horrified by what she saw. Ronald Baker, the sheep farmer from Hot Sulphur Springs, was staggering toward her, blood covering his face and body. Someone caught him as he fell.

A man's body lay half in the lake, but the head was submerged, so Annie couldn't tell who it might be. She gagged as the blood colored the deep blue water an ugly rust.

On the rise was another man's body, his face covered in a flour sack mask. Holes had been cut out for eyes and mouth and a cord held it tied around his neck. Annie saw grayish brain matter mixed with blood ooze through the bullet hole left in the mask.

Unable to move, Annie watched in horror as Mack James, the deputy from Teller, removed the mask to reveal the staring dead eyes of George Miller. "The God-damned son of a bitch should have been killed long ago," Mack spat in disgust.

The body in the lake was pulled out by several men to reveal James Webb, shot directly through the heart.

"Miss Annie, you shouldn't be here," cried Charley Burn when he noticed her. He had just found Ben Daily over the rise two hundred feet north of the icehouse.

Although not dead, Daily had been shot in the right lung, and the papers he'd been carrying were soaked in blood.

"W-Who?" Annie sputtered to Charley, grabbing his shirtfront. "Who did this?"

"I don't rightly know, but someone said they saw three masked men hurrying off into the woods. And one of them was shot because there's blood on the ground. Don't you worry, they'll be found... and hanged for sure."

"Where's Will?" asked Annie, as she scanned the faces of the men running around chaotically in the area.

Charley looked uncomfortable as he replied gently, "I'm sorry to be the one to tell you, Miss Annie... but someone said that one of the masked men might have been him."

Annie whirled on Charley, her eyes defiant, "No, Charley, you're wrong! Will wouldn't have killed anyone like this! You're wrong!"

Charley's jealousy reared its ugly head. "Then where *is* he? Where are the Undersheriff and the Sheriff? Nobody seems to be able to find them!"

Annie began beating the young man on the chest with her fists, tears streaming down her face, "No, Charley, I won't let you say that about him! He wouldn't do this; I *know* him! You're wrong, and you're just saying this to hurt me because I love him and not you!"

Charley gathered Annie into his arms and led her back to the Farview as she continued to sob and maintain Will's innocence. Even though it was true what he said, Charley couldn't stand to see the girl he loved in so much pain.

Seeing the distraught Annie in Charley's arms, Mrs. Elder rushed toward them. "What's happened, Charley?"

"There's been a shoot-out!" Charley told the wide-eyed, frightened woman. "Miller and Webb are dead, and I think they're bringing Daily and Baker here."

As soon as he spoke, a spring wagon carrying the two survivors rolled into view. Ronald Baker was carried upstairs and put in the room he had rented while Ben Daily was laid on the settee in the parlor, his blood dripping on the soft pine floor beneath.

Annie watched in horror as Mrs. Elder tried desperately to staunch Ben Daily's wound, but to no avail. Dr. H. F. Frisius of Teller, who happened to be in town for the celebration, had been summoned but held little hope for Daily.

Where is Will, Annie screamed over and over to herself.

Ronald Baker, though shot through the bridge of the nose and in the hip, was coherent enough to recount what happened. Annie followed Mack James, the only lawman available, upstairs and stood with her back plastered against the wall just outside Baker's room, her eyes wide with horror.

Baker, though in extreme pain, gasped, "We were walking over to the courthouse, and just as we crossed the rise, I heard a shot ring out. I heard Ben say 'I've been shot'. I looked over at him and saw red spreading over the papers as he fell. "I saw the shooter; he had a rifle and a mask covering his face. With him were two other masked men.

"Before I knew what had happened, I was shot in the face while I was drawing my revolver. One of the masked man shot me in the hip with his side arm, then started beating me with the butt of the rifle Somebody, I guess it was Webb, shot him, and the masked man went pitching over on his face.

"Through all the blood on my face, I saw Webb try to hide behind the icehouse but another masked man came around the other side. Webb shot at him, and the pistol flew out of the masked man's hand. Then Webb was shot by another masked man and fell into the lake. I was sure I'd be killed next, so I started trying to crawl away."

"We know the dead masked man was George Miller, but who were the others?" asked Mack James.

"I-I couldn't tell for certain," was all Baker would say.

Annie went to her room, sick to her soul. Could Will have been involved? Could he have been the one who shot Ben Daily? Everyone knew how much Will hated Ben. Was Will out there somewhere hurt?

The distraught girl, forgotten and alone, sat on the edge of the bed beside the ivory wedding dress as the hours slowly ticked by.

Around noon, Mrs. Elder, disheveled and pale, entered Annie's room. She gently removed the wedding dress and laid it over a chair. Then she sat by Annie and put her arm around the girl's slumped shoulders. "I've got some bad news, Annie, but I believe you need to hear it. Will might have been involved in the shooting. He, Mann, and Sheriff Tom were seen riding toward Willow Creek earlier. You had better face facts, dear."

Annie looked at her friend, making Mrs. Elder blanch at the complete despair in Annie's bloodshot blue eyes. "Will wouldn't kill anyone in cold blood, and you know it as well as I do," was all the girl could say.

"Well, I know it, child, but if he *was* involved, then it had to be that snake, Miller, who brought him in on it. I never did trust him. But Annie, listen to me, if Will was involved, he can't ever come back here, or he'll hang for sure. People are gonna want someone's blood for this."

A hurried inquest was conducted that same afternoon, and the results were soon spread throughout the little town. A six-man jury found that the 'deceased had come to their deaths at the hands of some unknown persons in a felonious manner', even though it was common knowledge that Miller had been one of the attackers.

Annie was prostrate with grief. This was supposed to be the happiest day of her life...her wedding day, and now the groom was missing and under suspicion of murder.

When Annie's bleeding hadn't come last month, she hadn't been too concerned, knowing that she and Will would be married long before the baby began to expand her waistline. Now she lay on the bed in which Will had once made love to her, wrapped her arms around her belly, and cried for him and his child which she carried. And she prayed, harder than she had ever prayed before, that Will and Tom were only in Gaskill or Lulu City, dealing with claim jumpers or drunks, instead of being on the run.

The people of Grand Lake, though shocked by the events of the shootout, were even more sympathetic for Annie. They came and went throughout the day, only to be turned away by Mrs. Elder. Men gathered on the porch, discussing the sinister repercussions of the unhappy incident as the fireworks and celebration were abandoned.

"I heard the men from Teller are going to come here and wipe Grand Lake off the face of the earth," reported Charley Burn, eager to do something, even if it meant fighting. "We need to get ready for an all-out war, too, with the folks from the Springs."

"Maybe we need someone to wire the governor for militia," spoke up Ike Talden.

"Naw, we can handle any trouble that comes our way, boys, just like we did when old Colorow and his Utes messed with us at Junction Ranch," muttered Jim Calter.

"Do you really think Sheriff Tom and Will were the masked men?" asked young Billy Smart.

"If they weren't, then where in hell are they? And where is Will's brother, Mann? I think a lot more might have been involved, too," stated Harry Sanders.

The men mulled over the events, each one not wanting to believe anything bad about their friends, but each remembering how many justifiable reasons Will Redmond had for wanting Daily dead.

Two hours after dark, Annie, who had been lying on the bed staring at the ceiling, heard a staccato of taps on her window. She rose and went to it, peering into the dark moonless night as another barrage of pebbles lightly spattered the glass. She could just make out a form in the cover of the trees. She raised the window and immediately recognized the huge hulking form of Bass Redmond. He motioned her down without saying a word.

Annie quickly ran over and locked the door, then climbed through the window onto the gabled roof. Bass rode his horse under her, and she jumped from the second story, landing in his arms.

"Where's Will?" she asked in a desperate whisper as she threw her leg over the saddle and settled in front of Will's brother.

Bass glanced anxiously around, touched his finger to his lips to insure her silence, and the two rode off into the night. They kept to the trees as they went south from Grand Lake.

"Is he all right?" cried Annie when they were well away.

"He's shot, Annie, but he's alive," Bass said, his voice husky with feeling.

"Oh, God, he was involved in the shooting, wasn't he?" Annie moaned.

"Yeah, and the sheriff and my brother Mann, too."

The two worried riders only stopped once to rest the horse. Bass took off his big jacket when he felt Annie shivering in her light cotton dress against the cold night and shock.

Around two A.M., Ben Daily died without regaining consciousness. When Lydia knocked on Annie's door to give her the news, she received no answer. She tiptoed away, thinking Annie was finally getting some much needed sleep.

When Annie and Bass reached the cabin on Willow Creek, several horses were tied outside, and she could see light inside.

She vaulted off Bass' horse before it had stopped and ran toward the cabin in the dark. She stumbled and fell once but rose again, oblivious of her scraped knees. She threw open the door and was confronted in the crowded room by eight to ten burly men.

Quickly scanning the faces, she recognized Mann and a few others as she pushed through the mass of unwashed bodies until they parted. There at the table was Will, with a blood-soaked sleeve and meanly bandaged arm. His shoulders were slumped as he nursed a half-empty bottle of whiskey.

When he looked up, Annie's stomach lurched at the total defeat on his ashen face.

"Will," she gasped.

In a breath, he was on his feet and she was clinging to him. The injured limb hung uselessly at his side as he used his strong left arm to hold her to him.

The men filed quietly out of the cabin leaving the two alone.

"Oh God, Annie, I was so afraid I wouldn't get to see you before I had to lea....," he began, his voice hoarse with longing. Then he moved back to the table and sat down, keeping Annie on his lap.

"Don't talk, just hold me," Annie whimpered against his neck.

"I'm so sorry about our wedding," he said softly as he kissed her hair. He pushed her away so that he could look into her face. "Annie, listen to me, I didn't know anyone was gonna get shot, I swear it. The only reason the boys and I went was to scare Daily. We didn't know Miller had planned to kill him." His voice broke.

"Will, what's going to happen now?" Annie asked as she stroked his hair, which hung in dirty strands around his face. Big tears slid down her cheeks and glistened in her lashes.

"I have to get out of the territory, but I couldn't go without seeing you first. I had to tell you how it really was. I swear, I didn't even fire a shot. Webb shot me, and my gun went flying," he said as he held his injured arm up.

"Don't, Will, don't think about it. I'll come with you. We can...."

He cut her off harshly. "*No*, Annie, you *can't* come with me. I'm a wanted man, now, and the law's gonna be after me for the rest of my life. It's no life for you, darlin', I've ruined everything for us."

"But I'm strong, Will, I could...," she began tremulously.

"No, dammit, now stop it, Annie, you'd just get in my way and hold me back!" Will had known he would have to use Annie's love for him against her. She wouldn't insist on coming if she thought it would be bad for him.

He'd had hours to think about the two of them. He was no good for her now, and he needed to cut the ties between them so she could get on with her life.

The thought swiftly crossed Annie's mind of telling him about the baby, but she quickly discarded it. He was right; even if she wasn't pregnant, she'd only be a burden to him.

"Where will you go?" she asked, her stomach knotted with pain.

"I don't know yet, somewhere far away, I guess." His voice was dull as if he didn't really care anymore.

To hide her desolation, she began to examine his wound. The bullet had broken the bone in his right arm above the wrist. Although the break looked clean, she busied herself with removing the dirty bandage and heating more water over the fire. She slipped out of her pantalets and tore them into strips, dipping them in clean water. She gently washed the wound where a shard of bone stuck through the skin.

"Drink more of that whiskey, Will, because I have to stick the bones back together so they can heal properly, and it's going to hurt like hell."

Her ministrations so far had made him break into a sweat, so he took a couple of big swallows of the whiskey and gritted his teeth, preparing himself for the excruciating pain he knew would follow.

Annie used a clean wet cloth to gently but firmly press the bone back under the skin, lining it up with the rest of the remaining bone as best she could. She wished she had *boneset*, an medicinal herb she had learned about from Soft Dove, but she gratefully remembered her Indian friend had said that bones knitted over time if splinted correctly.

Annie scanned the small crude room, and her eyes rested on the logs stacked by the fireplace. She peeled the bark from one of them, using two pieces to wrap around Will's arm. She tied strips of cloth tightly around the makeshift splint. If Will was going to have a chance of survival all alone in the wilderness, he needed his right arm...his shooting arm.

Neither of them had spoken during the procedure, and when she sat back to examine her handiwork, she smiled slightly.

"It's good to see you smile," Will said softly.

Annie raised her eyes to his, her smile quivering.

"Can we lie down?" Will asked, feeling a bit queasy from fighting the stabbing agony racing up and down his tired body.

Annie gently pulled him over to the bunk after he had doused the kerosene lantern, the fire the only illumination on what should have been their wedding night.

Carefully, so as not to hurt him anymore, Annie peeled off his shirt which was stiff with dried blood. Then she unbuttoned his trousers and let them fall around his knees. Though he was in much pain, a part of him was still able to express his appreciation.

Smiling, she pushed him down on the bunk and knelt before him, her face hidden in the darkness. As she struggled to remove his boots, he reached out with his left hand to touch her wild coppery hair which was being backlighted by the flames. Rubbing the silken tresses between his fingers, he knew he would never again see anything as beautiful.

When she had succeeded in removing his boots and pants, she stood before him and slowly removed her own clothing as he leaned back on his good elbow and watched with a slight smile, the first she'd seen.

Their lovemaking was slow and sensual, Annie on top trying not to jostle his injured arm. She massaged his chest as she sat astride him, his hardness straining against her. She knew he was anxious to be joined, but she wanted this brief time together to last so she could burn it into her memory.

Both of them realized that this would most likely be the last time for them, so they touched each other tentatively, afraid for it to be over. When Annie leaned down, her breasts brushing the curls on his chest, he used his left arm to pull her mouth close to his.

They kissed, lightly at first, but intensifying as they strained to get closer, tongues dancing and intertwining. Will moved down, caressing her ear lobe and sucking on her neck until he left reddened marks in his wake. He lifted her hips until he could enter the secret place which was his home.

Will loved Annie's first gasp whenever he pushed deeply inside her, and he watched as she sat up and threw her head back in pleasure. Using his left hand to touch her breasts, he noticed how large her nipples had become. As he raised his head to take one of the hardened tips in his mouth, Annie drew back as if his touch had hurt her.

They stared at each other a moment until their hips began again the slow dance of love. He wrapped his good arm around her and carefully flipped her over, pulling her body under his as he nestled between her legs.

Afterwards, as they lay still joined, Will whispered into Annie's hair all of the love he felt and would always feel for her. She, in turn, covered his chest with tiny kisses as they basked in the afterglow which was so intensely bittersweet, it brought tears to both their eyes.

"Annie, don't believe what they're gonna say about me in town," Will whispered huskily. "You fought for me once, remember back at the Springs? Please fight for me again, darlin'. I know my involvement was wrong, but I'm not the villain they are going to paint me to be."

"The people of the county are going to want to blame someone, but I swear on my life, that I'll make them know the truth," replied Annie as she tried to memorize his scent and taste. "You all were duped by George Miller into a situation which escalated out of control. The one responsible is dead, and you aren't; that's the only thing that matters to me, my love."

Will drew her closer and kissed her desperately as Annie felt him begin to harden inside her again.

Much later, still tightly wrapped together, Will whispered, "No matter what you hear, Annie Mitchell, remember that I'll always love you. Even death won't ever change how I feel about you!"

A few hours before sunup, Bass knocked on the cabin door. "Will, you have to leave now, and I need to get Annie back before anyone misses her."

Annie and Will dressed, a miasma of depression permeating the gnawing emptiness in both of their hearts. She checked his wound, then rebound it, tearing the rest of her undergarments into strips for him to use on the road.

As they moved toward the door of the cabin, Will suddenly pulled Annie back into his arms, leaving her breathless at the intensity of his hopelessness. "I love you Annie, more than my own life. I'd take you if I could, you know that, don't you?"

"I know, Will, but I'd only slow you down. This is the hardest thing I've ever done, letting you go, but you have a chance without me. I give you that chance at life, Will Redmond, as my final gift to you," Annie cried.

Will replied thickly. "I signed over the cabin to you. Bass will take care of the legal side of it, but it's yours. I want you to find someone who will be good to you and take care of you. Promise me you will live life, not sit around and be lonely pondering on what might have been."

Annie couldn't answer through her sobbing. She could only cling to his shirt and cry for the child who would never know what a wonderful man its father was.

Will tipped her chin up and gazed in her eyes. "Promise me, Annie."

"I promise. And you promise to stay alive."

"I'm a pretty hard character to kill, darlin'," Will's half grin turned her heart to jelly.

Bass lifted Annie onto his horse, then climbed up behind her. Will and Annie stared at each other as Mann and the others looked on, embarrassed at witnessing the intimate moment between the two who were being parted forever.

"I will always love you, Annie Mitchell."

"And I will love you, William Redmond, forever."

As Bass spurred his horse away from the cabin, Annie heard Will call out, "Remember your promise."

Annie sobbed inconsolably on the ride back.

"Don't worry, I'll make sure you're taken care of," Bass said, tears just behind his eyelids.

He dropped her off in the back of the Farview, but she didn't have the energy to try to climb back in the upper story window. Instead she walked slowly around to the front door, beyond caring what anyone thought.

In the parlor was a crowd of people and a sheet covering the body of Ben Daily. Annie hardly noticed as she walked passed, her eyes dull and red.

All the voices went silent at her appearance, her hair matted and tousled and her thin cotton dress showing clearly she was wearing nothing beneath. She walked as if in a daze, and Lydia Elder was the first to regain her composure at the sight of the bedraggled girl.

"Oh my stars, Annie, where have you been?" cried Lydia as she rushed to Annie's side. "I thought you were sleeping. Were you out walking in the cold night? My God, you'll catch your death."

But Mack James, the deputy from Teller, immediately noticed the smudges of whisker-burn on her pale face. "Miss Mitchell, I need you to answer some questions. Do you know where the Undersheriff is?"

"Deputy James, can't you see she is beyond exhausted?" Mrs. Elder spoke harshly. "Let her sleep, then you can interrogate her."

"No, Mrs. Elder, I can't wait. Every minute is vital if we're going to catch the murderers."

His remark brought Annie out of her daze. She turned on the deputy and all of the other blurry faces in the room. "Will didn't shoot anyone; none of them knew what Miller was planning," she shouted vehemently. "Will is not a murderer, and I won't allow you or anyone else to say it about him!"

With that, she collapsed to the floor in a dead faint.

"Now see what you have done," groaned Mrs. Elder.

Charley Burn, rushed forward and lifted Annie's limp body. He took the stairs two at a time as Lydia followed.

Annie's door was still locked so Charley brought her back downstairs to Mrs. Elder's own quarters. He laid Annie gently on the star-patterned quilt then stood back, staring at her beautiful pale face.

Charley's heart swelled; even if Redmond came back, he'd be charged with accessory to murder and sent to prison or hanged by vigilante friends of Daily's. Charley smiled at the thought because then there would be nothing in the way of his suit for Annie. Eventually, with Redmond permanently out of the way, Charley was sure she'd come to love him.

In the parlor, the men continued discussing Will and the others until the sun came up.

"It's obvious she's been with Redmond, so he can't be far," Mack said. "I'd say we ought to check out the Gold Run camp on Willow Creek. They're probably hiding him and the others. And I don't think Sheriff Roberts is as completely innocent as he says. Where was he when the shooting started? He says he was taking a drunk, Heck Ames, home, but someone said they saw Heck at the Dandy Saloon right before the shooting."

"Well, he *is* still the sheriff, so we need to talk with him first," stated Joe Hoffton.

Mack James turned on him angrily, "Will Redmond is Tom's best friend. Do you really think Tom will bring him to justice? He hasn't even formed a posse. And didn't Ed Fisty say he saw him in the company of the wounded Redmond rushing away from Grand Lake right after the shooting?"

"Well, that downpour yesterday afternoon has washed all of the footprints away, Mack," retorted Harry Snader. "So how are we going to be sure who did it?"

Mack James steepled his fingers and replied, "We'll just have to catch the bastard."

When Annie regained consciousness, Mrs. Elder was sitting beside the bed, a worried expression on her gaunt face.

"Will..." Annie whispered before she realized where she was. When she opened her eyes and saw her friend, tears welled up in her blue eyes.

"Annie, dear, don't say anything about Will," Mrs. Elder said quietly as she glanced at the closed door.

"But he didn't do anything," whimpered Annie.

"That may be so, but there are factions in this county that don't care whether Will shot anyone or not; they want someone to pay, and Will is the one," replied Mrs. Elder.

"They won't find him!" Annie cried miserably as she sat up. "He's gone, and he'll never come back." She broke into heavy, heart-wrenching sobs. "What am I going to do without him? How can I go on living?"

Lydia drew the wretched girl to her bosom. "You'll find a way, dear, trust me. He wouldn't want you pining away for him, now would he?"

"He-made-me-promise-to-go-on-living, "Annie sobbed. "Why do I just want to die?"

"Maybe he'll come back for you after things cool down?" replied Mrs. Elder.

Annie's head jerked up, and she suddenly brightened. "That's true; when all of this is over, he'll send for me and we can start over somewhere else. Oh, Lydia, thank you for giving me back some hope!" Annie wrapped her arms around her belly, not wanting to tell anyone her secret just yet. When Will comes back, she'd have his child.

Annie was forced to speak with Sheriff Roberts later that day. Mack James, still suspicious of Roberts, stayed in the room during the interrogation.

Tom pulled up a chair and sat in front of Annie, who was perched stiffly on the settee in Mrs. Elder's private quarters. His face, which had always had a smile just under the surface, was ravaged by emotions barely held in check. Annie recognized the sorrow and regret in his eyes and voice at having to question her about Will.

"Annie, the men said you showed up early this morning under suspicious circumstances," Tom began gently.

Mack James interrupted, "She had obvious whisker-burn on her face, and she wasn't wearin' anything under her dress. And besides that, her door was locked but the window was wide open, and there were fresh horse tracks under the window leading off to the south. She started telling everybody that Redmond didn't do it, and that he'd been shot. How would she know he'd been shot if she hadn't been with him?"

Tom looked back at Annie's stony face. "Well, Annie, what do you have to say to Mack's charges? Were you with Will?"

"Yes, Tom, I was, and he didn't shoot anyone," she answered quietly. "And *you* know it, don't you?"

The wretched expression on his face was Annie's answer.

"Tell me where he is so he can come back and answer the charges against him, Annie."

"I can't do that, Tom. With the way people are feeling, someone would lynch him, guilty or not."

"No, I won't let that happen, I swear," Tom said sincerely.

"You can't protect him, Tom, I'm sorry," Annie finished. She crossed her arms over her breasts and lifted her chin a notch. The interview was over.

Mack James' face was livid with anger. "Dammit, Tom, she's in contempt for not cooperating."

Sheriff Roberts whirled on the deputy, "What do you want me to do, James, throw her in jail?"

"Yeah, that's a good idea," Mack answered as his eyes lit up. "Then Redmond would come out of hiding for sure."

"Well, I ain't doin' it, Mack," replied Tom tensely.

The rest of the day found the Farview House the hub of avid curiosity and speculation. Marian Daily and Fred Baker, Ronald's grown son, arrived later in the afternoon.

"Your aunt is here, Annie," Mrs. Elder announced through the door. Annie had chosen to stay in her room after Charley Burn had climbed through the window and unlocked the door.

"I don't care," replied Annie bitterly, clutching the pillow closely to her as if for protection. She wasn't sorry Ben Daily was dead, and she had no feelings of sympathy for Marian. Her only concern was for Will's safe getaway.

"Honey, she just lost her husband," Mrs. Elder whispered through the door. "She needs family around her."

"I am *not* her family!" Annie screamed.

Ben Daily was to be taken back to the ranch on the Fraser River to be buried. Annie could hear Marian crying loudly downstairs, but it did not move the girl. When Lydia reported that Annie was not feeling well, or she would be comforting her, Marian made a hissing noise.

"I don't want any sympathy from that ungrateful hussy," Marian railed, loudly enough for everyone, inside and out, to hear. "It was because of her that that blackhearted Redmond killed my Ben. I told him not to come to Grand Lake. I knew Redmond was gunning for him." She began sobbing loudly into her handkerchief.

Annie wanted to run out of the room and testify to Will's innocence, but if she did, then people would know that he wasn't out of the county yet. Someone might find him, so she stayed mute.

"I'll fight for you, Will, but not until you have a chance to get away," Annie breathed.

Ronald Baker still lived, though the doctor gave him little hope of survival due to infection. Neither of the bullets could be removed, so the injured man remained at the Farview. He called for a lawyer and legally turned over all of his assets to his son, Fred.

George E. Miller was buried in the Grand Lake cemetery but few attended the burial. The townsfolk of Grand Lake were on the alert for mobs from Teller City or Hot Sulphur Springs to come after those responsible. Women and children were warned to stay indoors, and local men took turns on patrol day and night, walking the streets heavily armed.

Mann Redmond, Gil Martin, and Lon Coffin showed up in town several days later and were promptly arrested by Mack James, but later released by Sheriff Roberts for insufficient evidence. After their release, Mann went to the Farview to speak with Annie.

She was in the kitchen, trying to keep her hands busy though her mind was with a tall man with flinty green eyes and soft lips whom she hoped was far away by now. When Mann opened the door to the warm homey room and peeked his head in, Annie's hands flew to her face as she gasped. The big ceramic bowl she had been holding in one hand shattered to the floor sending the contents splattering in all directions.

"Will," she whispered. Then she saw that it was only Mann.

The youngest Redmond glanced around the kitchen to see if anyone else was there, ignoring the mess on the floor. He took Annie by the arm and led her to the corner by the back door.

"Will got away," Mann whispered. "Bass and I are to see to you and make sure you get the cabin, then we'll meet him later, when everything dies down."

"Thank God he made it out," Annie breathed a sigh of relief. Then her head came up. "Are you going to take me with you?"

"No, Annie, I'm sorry," Mann answered sadly as he saw the naked pain in her eyes. "Will gave me strict orders to get you settled here. He doesn't want you to come with us."

Mann saw her tears and pulled her to him, allowing her to cry while he held her.

"Tell him to come for me after it's all over, Mann, please, tell him," Annie pleaded as she sobbed.

"Maybe he will, Annie, after it's all over."

The next day, Sheriff Tom Roberts left Grand Lake for Georgetown. Thirteen days after being shot, Ronald Baker, former county clerk and friend to Daily, died from his injuries. He was transported back to Hot Sulphur Springs and buried there. In the mean time, Marian Daily quietly sold the ranch on the Fraser and disappeared, leaving Ben's body buried somewhere on the property.

Annie spent many sleepless nights after Baker died of infection from his wounds, worrying about Will's injury. Had she cleaned it well enough? Would it fester and kill him, too?

Life has a way of going on after tragedy, and so the little town of Grand Lake continued, mostly because the overflowing rivers kept the hotheads who wanted revenge from traveling.

Annie was given the title to Will's cabin on the west side of the lake, and she moved into it, though she still worked for Mrs. Elder at the Farview. A new schoolteacher had been hired for the school. Mann and Bass also bought Sugar from the livery in Gaskill where Ben Daily had sold her and delivered her to Annie.

Charley Burn haunted the Farview at every meal. He even moved into a tent at the rear of the boarding house. He made it a point to be outside each evening after dinner was cleaned up, just as Annie began the short ride around the lake to her cabin.

"May I escort you home, Miss Annie?" he'd ask night after night.

"Thank you, no, Charley," Annie would reply each time.

Toward the end of July, Annie was in the kitchen at the Farview when Jim Calter gave everyone the bad news. "Sure is a shame, that's all," he was saying as Annie came through the door with another platter of fried potatoes. She waited for him to continue, but when he saw her, he suddenly began to pay close attention to his plate.

The room went silent. Annie looked from face to face but no one would meet her eyes. She set down the bowl, placed her hands on her hips, and asked, "What news? Jim? Charley? Ike?"

Charley looked up at the woman he loved more than anything in the world and replied, "Jim just came from the Springs. Seems Sheriff Tom shot himself at the Ennis Hotel in Georgetown. We figure he was eaten up with guilt because he and the Undersheriff were involved in the shootin' of the Commissioners."

Annie paled, and Ike Alden, who was closest to her, quickly rose and ushered her into his chair.

"Oh, God, not Tom, too," Annie moaned. Then it registered what Charley had said, and she turned on him and the others viciously. "Tom felt guilty because *he* was the one who shot James Webb, who had been his friend. But the only reason he shot him was to protect Will. And Miller was the one who started shooting in the first place. The others were just going to scare my uncle so he'd leave the county. You see, it was Webb who shot Will, and Will didn't shoot anyone! So I don't want to hear any of you saying he did, do you hear me?"

Lydia Elder had heard Annie shouting from the kitchen and entered the diningroom. "What's all the noise in here?"

Annie lay her head on the table as the news was shared again for Lydia's benefit. Annie said a prayer for Tom, a good man who, like Will, had gotten caught up in Miller's evil scheme. The death toll had now reached five.

Sorrowfully, Annie rose from the table and walked out onto the wide porch of the Farview. She gazed up into the star-filled night, wondering if Will was sharing the night sky with her, wherever he was.

"If only I knew you were all right, Will," she whispered into the soft night air.

"Who are you talking to?" Charley had followed her...again.

Wiping tears away, Annie answered quickly, "No one, Charley, no one."

"I'm sorry about Sheriff Tom; I guess we all are," Charley said kindly. "And I'm sorry about bringing up the Undersheriff and making you all upset, Miss Annie."

Annie turned to the tall lanky young man, her eyes immediately drawn to his prominent Adam's apple bobbing as if it were alive. "Tom Roberts was a good man, and this tragedy just doesn't seem to end, does it?"

Charley moved toward Annie as if to take her in his arms, and she instinctively drew back, her eyes narrowed.

"Hell, I ain't gonna hurt you," the boy avowed. "I just want to be the one to comfort you."

"Thank you, Charley, but I don't need comforting,"Annie replied too quickly, moving away from him.

"Wait, I've got to know." Charlie's voice cracked with emotion. "Will I have a chance with you, once you've had some time to get over Redmond, I mean?"

Annie turned back and gazed into his young face, remembering another darker one which had once looked at her with the same yearning.

"No, Charley, I'll never get over Will," she answered honestly. And in the depth of her soul, she held on to the the hope that Will would someday come back for her.

"Well, I ain't gonna give up, Miss Annie, because I love you so much I can't think of nothing else," was Charley's heartfelt reply.

Annie watched as Charley strode off the porch toward town over the footpath which had been the bloody scene of the Fourth of July massacre on the shores of Grand Lake.

CHAPTER TEN

Ore had never been easy to get out of the mountains, and the quality of the ore in the first place had never been great, so the boom became a bust. The mines began to die after the shoot out.

The mines, especially the Wolverine, suffered terribly after the shooting of the Commissioners. The moneyed men who had supported Ben Daily suddenly pulled out their financial backing. Men who had depended on the mines for their livelihood were suddenly laid off, and the boom towns of Gaskill, Lulu City, and Teller began to slowly decline as the miners abandoned the Never Summer mountains in search of work elsewhere.

Charley Burn was laid off, too, but he refused to leave Annie, so he got a job at the sawmill. Like an annoying puppy, he continued to follow Annie wherever she went.

Annie tried to ignore him, but he made it impossible. He followed her to town for supplies from the Mercantile, and he waited outside in order to carry her basket back. Everytime she turned around, he was there.

As she and Lydia unloaded the groceries, Annie complained. "What am I going to do about that boy? I can't seem to make him understand that I'm not interested in him...or anyone."

"He's got it bad, that's for sure," chuckled Mrs. Elder. "Maybe you should just marry the boy and put him out of his misery."

Annie was appalled by her friend's suggestion. "How can you suggest that? You said yourself that Will would come back for me. I don't think he'd appreciate it if I was married to someone else... again."

"'Might', honey, I said 'might come back'. What if Will doesn't send for you? What if he can't?" asked Mrs. Elder seriously. "Are you going to dry up into a lonely old maid...waiting forever as your youth and beauty fades? Is that what Will would want you to do?"

Tears sprang into Annie's eyes. "I'd rather be an old maid than be with anyone else, and you well know it."

"What about the baby? Doesn't it need a father?"

Annie froze. "How did you know?"

"Dear, I've born three, two that lived," replied Mrs. Elder. "I can recognize the symptoms. You've been losing your breakfast for weeks now."

Annie slumped into a chair. "What am I going to do? I couldn't tell Will before he left. Soon everyone will know; I can't hide it forever. I have to believe that Will will come back for me before anyone knows."

"Maybe you should think about marrying that Charley, then, so's folks don't know."

"I couldn't," Annie replied softly. "Not when there is a chance that Will will come back for me."

"I understand how you feel, Annie, and I'll support your decision. But folks around here haven't forgotten Will's part in the killings. Once they find out you are going to have his baby, they might not be so forgiving."

Tears spilled down the girl's cheeks as she hugged her belly. "Oh, Lydia, what am I going to do?"

"Don't worry, honey, we'll figure it out when the time comes," Lydia replied kindly as she patted Annie's back.

The relentless rain had finally quit, and the days grew warmer as August arrived. Annie had had no news of Will or his brothers, and her skirts had had to be let out to accommodate her expanding waistline, though not enough to cause gossip just yet.

On the sixteenth of August, Annie had just finished hanging a load of laundry on the drying line in back of the Farview. Mrs. Elder came to the back door.

"Annie, dear, would you come in?"

"Be right there," answered the girl as she threw the last of the wet blankets over the line, spreading it to dry in the warm bright sun.

As Annie entered the back door, she heard voices in the parlor. She passed through the kitchen, inhaling the sweet-smell of fresh bread baking in the iron woodstove. She had finally gotten over the nausea which had plagued her, and now she was constantly ravenous, nibbling often throughout the day. Annie opened the door and moved through the diningroom, table scrubbed and ready for the evening meal still a few hours away.

As she entered the front parlor, her eyes shifted immediately to the pine floor under the settee which still was darkened with the stain of Ben Daily's blood. No amount of scrubbing had been able to remove that telltale spot.

Then she saw Lydia, standing beside a man Annie didn't recognize. Mrs. Elder was agitated, bunching her white apron in her hands as she stared at Annie, a worried crease between her brows.

"Are you all right, Lydia?" Annie asked, concerned by her friend's state.

"Yes, dear, I'm fine. Why don't you sit down?" the older woman began, sitting beside Annie as she looked from the man's face back to the younger girl's. "Annie, this is Mr. Henry Shoch."

"How do you do, sir," Annie replied politely, dazzling him with her fresh-faced beauty which had blossomed with the pregnancy.

"How do, miss," replied Mr. Shoch, clearly uncomfortable.

"Mr. Shoch owns a ranch and has come here from Utah...and honey, y-you've got to be brave," Mrs. Elder stuttered.

Annie felt a sudden stab in her stomach. "What's wrong? Is it about Will? Tell me," she demanded, the color suddenly draining from her face.

"Well ma'am, as I was telling Mrs. Elder, while me and the boys were out rounding up strays, we come across a body on the trail. We believe it was that of Undersheriff Redmond." stated Henry Shoch stiffly.

Annie grabbed her middle, doubling over as an excruciating pain flashed through her. She clutched Lydia's arm and gasped, "What makes you think it was him?"

"The name, William Redmond, was scratched in the saddle nearby, miss, and it was also written in the sand beside the body."

"N-no, b-body, it can't be, h-how, where...?" Annie whispered raggedly, as the pain in her lower abdomen became agonizing.

"We found the body about ten miles over the border in Utah, ma'am. It was in a cottonwood grove by a stream of water. We thought he'd been murdered at first, but a Colt revolver was found under him with one spent chamber. He was just laying on a blanket like he was goin' to sleep, but there was one bullet hole in his right temple. It's been ruled a suicide."

"It can't be," Annie wailed as Will's words reverberated through her being: 'I wouldn't want to live without you'. "No, no, no, no, no, I won't believe it, I can't. He's coming back for me and the baby. He wouldn't leave me, he woul..."

Annie suddenly collapsed in a heap on the floor, a pool of blood reddening her skirt and apron.

"Oh my God," shrieked Lydia as she bent to the girl. "Mr. Shoch, help me!"

Henry Shoch, more used to heifers than women, lifted the unconscious girl and followed Mrs. Elder upstairs. After he lay Annie on the bed, Lydia turned to him, "Go into town and find the doctor."

Henry stood staring at the pretty young girl, pale as tissue paper, until Lydia shoved him out of the room. "I *said*, go get the doctor!" she screamed.

The news of Will Redmond's suicide caused a miscarriage, and afterwards, a high fever left Annie writhing and incoherent for days.

When the fever finally broke, she fell into a deep coma-like sleep from which the doctor offered little hope of recovery.

Lydia Elder had made the doctor swear on his oath to keep silent about the loss of the child.

The ladies of Grand Lake, upon hearing the news of the Undersheriff's death and Annie's apparent illness brought on by the shock, flocked to the Farview and took turns sitting vigil at the girl's bedside. Charley Burn, though not allowed in Annie's room, camped outside her bedroom door, to Lydia's dismay, and refused to budge.

"I'm staying right here, Mrs. Elder," Charley stated belligerently. "I want to be here when she wakes up."

Lydia touched the boy's arm tenderly. "Charley, dear, Annie's very ill. Dr. Telius says she might not wake up."

Charley stared over Lydia's head, his Adam's apple still for once. "I don't care how long it takes, I ain't leaving. She *will* wake up. I know it!"

For three weeks, Annie lay on the brink of death. Then one morning in late September she awoke, confused and disoriented. It took all of her energy just to turn her head. Lydia was asleep in the rocker by the bed, her knitting hanging off her lap.

Annie's slight movement brought Lydia awake with a jerk, and the knitting fell soundlessly to the floor. Tears welled up in the older woman's eyes as she clutched Annie's hand. "Oh, thank the Lord, you're back."

"W-what do you mean...back?" Annie rasped weakly.

"You don't remember any of it, do you? Well, that's a blessing, I suppose."

The door burst open and Charley Burn, his hair standing on end, rushed into the room.

"I knew she'd make it," Charley cried, beaming ear to ear. "Didn't I tell you? I just knew it."

Annie felt boneless and was unable to ask any more questions, though she had many. She drifted off to sleep again, but this time it meant recovery was near.

"Charley," Lydia instructed, "run get Dr. Telius. He's not going to believe this."

By the time the doctor arrived, Annie had awakened again. "You gave us quite a scare, young lady. But it seems that you're on the mend," blustered the little man as he lifted her limp wrist and checked her pulse.

"Lydia," Annie managed, her lips cracked and dry.

"Don't talk, child." Mrs. Elder was wiping away tears with her apron. "It's going to be all right now, you'll see. Everybody has been so concerned about you. Just rest, we'll talk later."

Annie closed her eyes and slowly sank back into oblivion. She heard Dr. Telius, from very far away, say, "Well, there's no damage, I don't believe. She'll be able to have other children."

Tears seeped from under Annie's closed lids. The doctor's words had brought back the horrible reality: Will had killed himself in the place where he had rescued her from Bear Hawk, and she had lost his baby.

It took Annie several more weeks to gain enough strength to be allowed to sit up in bed. Her depression continued, making her recovery slow, and she absolutely refused to see anyone but Lydia.

Will's final effects were turned over to her since Mann and Bass had mysteriously disappeared from the county. The effects included the Colt, the saddle which had his name scratched into the pommel, fifty dollars which had been sewn inside his shirt, and a pair of worn field glasses covered in buckskin.

"Oh God," wailed Annie as she hugged Will's possessions to her breast. "How can I go on living without him?"

Lydia winced at the anguish in Annie's voice. "Honey, don't think on it anymore. You need to start looking forward instead of backward. It won't bring him back."

"I don't want to look forward," Annie sobbed. "I want to die! Tell me again how he was found."

Lydia sat on the edge of the bed and recalled what had been related to her by Henry Shoch. "Henry said that William Stong and Harry Golden were with some cowboys, following some cattle which had strayed from the Ouray Indian Agency.

"They were aiming to water their horses at a stream surrounded by trees. The b-body, Will, was laying in a grassy area under a big cottonwood. One of them went to fetch Major Minnis at the Uintah Reservation, and he returned with a dozen or so Utes. Everyone thought he'd been murdered, you see. Oh, Annie, do you have to hear this again?"

"Yes, go on," Annie said, her eyes dull.

"The Indians found the writing in the sand. He had written his name, I suppose, so if someone found him, they'd tell you."

"So I'd know he wasn't ever coming back for me," Annie wailed raggedly.

Her heart-wrenching cries echoed throughout the Farview, and Charley Burn, still outside her bedroom door, felt tears spring to his own eyes at the sound of her agony.

The final death toll from the ambush on the lake path was now six...six men who had come to their ends over politics. Grand County would never forget the tragedy and not a day went by without someone speaking on it.

Grand Lake almost disappeared from the map, as did Gaskill, Lulu City, and Teller, when the mines failed one after another. The Denver newspapers vilified the brutal murders by referring to Grand County as 'Bloody Grand'. The only thing that kept the small village on the banks of the lake from drowning was the money from the curious tourists who traveled to see the spot where the horrific deed was committed.

As the winter of 1883 closed in on the slowly healing mountain town, Annie grew a little stronger though her spirit seemed broken.

On a cold day in November, she finally crawled out of bed at the Farview, dressed, and stated she was going home.

"Now Annie, I can't let you do this," Mrs. Elder argued. "You're not ready. You're too weak yet. Who will take care of you? Please Annie, be reasonable."

Annie turned to her friend and smiled wanly, the first smile in over three months. "Lydia, thank you for everything, for taking care of me, for being my friend. But it's time I went home. It's all I have left of Will. Please understand and don't try to stop me."

"Well, I'm going to have Charley go over everyday and chop wood and shovel snow then. I know I can depend on him not to let you die."

Charley Burn bundled Annie into a borrowed cutter and hitched Sugar to it. When they arrived at the cabin, Annie went in alone while Charley shoveled a path to the shed and took care of the horse.

The tiny cabin had only one room with a stone fireplace on the left, a table with two chairs, a rocking chair, and a big empty four poster feather bed on the right. Annie sank into the rocker, staring at the bed and thinking of the many nights of lovemaking she and Will had shared and would never share again. She thought of all the plans they had made for their future together...the home, the family, the love.

When Charley entered with an armload of freshly cut firewood, he saw the tears streaming down her cheeks. He quickly went to work building a fire which soon warmed the room, then he went back to the sleigh and brought in the stew Mrs. Elder had sent. After pouring it into a pot and hanging it over the fire to simmer, he quietly slipped out.

Charley Burn did exactly as Lydia had said...he kept Annie alive. He made sure her cabin stayed snug and warm, with a gigantic pile of wood stacked both inside and out. He never intruded on Annie's solitude, and she barely acknowledged his presence when he was there. But he was content just to be in her company.

Around Thanksgiving, Annie had an unexpected visitor. Mack James, who had all but arrested her in his rabid pursuit of justice after the shooting of the summer before, showed up at her door. In the absence of lawmen in the interim, he had become the new Sheriff of Grand County.

"Miss Mitchell, I don't mean to intrude on your privacy, but I wanted to say how glad I was to hear you are up and around. You had quite a bad spell there for awhile, or so I heard," said the attractive man whose bushy blond mustache dipped low on either side of his mouth. Though a few inches shy of six feet, every inch was honed muscle. His blue eyes were rimmed in deep smile lines from the many days out in the cool dry air of the mountains.

"Please come in, Sheriff James," Annie invited politely, though still suspicious of his motives. "Would you like a cup of coffee?"

"Thank you, ma'am, don't mind if I do."

Mack James removed his big-brimmed hat and sat at the table, watching Annie closely. He thought she might have become even more beautiful than when he had seen her on the day after the ambush, wearing next to nothing under her thin dress. Having lost so much weight, Annie's creamy skin was almost translucent. Her lips were full and red, without the paint of rouge, he noticed, and her hair had regained its glossy sheen and was a dusky copper which made a man to want to run his fingers through it.

Annie had avoided all company since her return to the cabin, and she wasn't exactly overjoyed to see the man who had so vehemently wanted to pursue and punish Will Redmond. When she had filled their cups and placed a plate of small cookies on the table, she sat down opposite the Sheriff and asked plainly, "All right, Mr. James, what do you want?"

Mack James' blue eyes grew large. "Why, nothing, Miss Mitchell. I only wanted to call on you. I have no ulterior motive other than to be neighborly."

Annie narrowed her eyes. "You're not here on official business?"

"No ma'am, I'm not. The case is closed now, as you know, so I'm here on a social matter. To be honest, Miss Annie, I'm here to ask if I might escort you to dinner at the Nickerson this coming Saturday night."

Dumbfounded, Annie sputtered, "I-I don't think so, Mr. James. I'm not ready..."

Mack leaned over the table and covered her hand. "I understand, Annie, and I don't want to pressure you. But you have to eat, right? So why not let me buy you a nice relaxing dinner? I promise I won't accost you in any way. What do you say? It's only dinner. And I'm pretty darn pig-headed, I might add. I won't take no for an answer."

Annie stared at the hand which covered hers. Blond hairs crisscrossed the back of his long fingers. Without thinking, she found herself comparing Mack James' hand to Will's large strong hand, and sudden tears appeared in her eyes.

Shaking her head, she removed her hand from under his and wiped the wetness away. She knew Mack James meant what he said. He wouldn't go away quietly like Charley had.

She heard Will's voice telling her to live her life and not be lonely. She looked at Mack James and realized how lonely she was! And it was only dinner...only dinner. "All right, Mr. James, I'll have dinner with you. But remember, it's *only* dinner."

Mack stood, a confident smile on his face. "Fine, I'll pick you up around six. Is that all right?"

Despite herself, Annie had an enjoyable evening on Saturday with Mack James. Though a bit arrogant, the Sheriff *was* entertaining. She actually was able to put aside her overwhelming grief for a moment as he regaled her with stories of his life and experiences. And after that evening, Mack James began to actively court Annie, much to Charley Burn's dismay.

Charley showed up at Annie's cabin on Christmas Eve with a small, delicately wrapped present.

"You shouldn't have," replied Annie, her eyes drawn to his ever bobbing Adam's apple. "I didn't get you anything."

The young man's ears reddened as he stared at his feet, twisting his wide-brimmed hat in his hands. "Miss Annie, I didn't expect anything from you. But this is something real special. I went all the way to Denver to get it, and I-I hope you like it."

She quickly unwrapped the rectangular package and inside was a pearl necklace. Her eyes widened when she thought of the price of the beautiful piece of jewelry. "Charley, I can't accept this! It must have cost you half a year's wages."

Looking up at the smitten boy, Annie saw bright tears form in his eyes. Quickly she added, "It's the nicest gift I've ever received, Charley, but it's too expensive. Please return it and get your money back. With the mines closed, you need that money."

"No, ma'am, I want *you* to keep it. And when you wear it, think of me," replied the young man. Suddenly, he dropped to one knee and took Annie's hand in his. "I-I love you so much, Miss Annie, and I always have. I'd like you to consider this necklace a token of my intentions. You see, I-I want to marry you."

Annie tried to speak, but Charley broke in, "Now, don't answer yet. Take some time and think about it. I know I ain't got a home right now, but I got lots of prospects. I'm doing fine at the sawmill, and so I'd be steady...reliable. I'd make you happy, too, Annie, if you'd l-let me."

Tears clouded Annie's eyes at Charley's sincerity. She dabbed away the wetness with her handkerchief before she spoke. "Charley, you're the nicest boy I've ever met, and I truly wish I could accept your proposal. But it wouldn't be fair to you. I just don't love you, and you deserve a girl who could give her whole heart and soul to you.

"No one has been a better friend to me than you. You have probably been the main person who kept me alive since I moved into this cabin, and I'll always love you for that. But not in the way you *want* me to love you. You deserve a girl who can love you back." She placed the necklace back into his hands and closed them around it.

Charley Burn rose slowly and put on his hat. He started for the door then turned slowly, "Is it because of Mack James? Is it because you love *him*?"

"No, Charley, I don't love Mack. He's just a friend," Annie replied gently. "You know who it is I'll always love, Charley. I wish I could stop, but I don't think I ever will be able to forget him."

"But Redmond's *dead*. When are you going to accept that? I'm not giving up, Annie, you just need more time." Then Charley left.

To Charley's chagrin, Mack James began to monopolize Annie's evenings, stopping by every night around supper time. She felt obligated to invite Mack to eat supper, and it soon became a habit. Desperately lonely, Annie began to look forward to the company Mack provided. She found Mack was a most determined man, and it was easier to acquiesce than to try and find an excuse to decline his many offers.

So she reluctantly found herself accompanying him to a party at the Ledman's ranch on New Year's Eve, achingly aware of the memory of last year's celebration she'd attended with Will by her side.

"I wish you'd quit wearing that damned awful black," complained Mack as he danced Annie around the crowded room. "You're so beautiful; you should be wearing bright colors."

"I suppose... in a year," answered Annie vaguely.

"A year?" exclaimed Mack. "A year from *now*? Why in the hell would you want to wait that long?"

Annie pulled away and stared at Mack, tears forming in her lashes. "You *know* why, and if you can't respect how I feel, then you'd better take me home right now."

Mack James knew he'd overstepped his bounds. "I'm sorry, Annie girl. I only want you to hurry up and forget Redmond. He's dead, and I'm alive. You're still a young woman, and what you need is a man."

His arrogance simply amazed her. "Mack James, It's only been four months since... I may never 'get over' Will Redmond. I loved...love him more than my own life. If you're waiting around for me to marry you, then you're going to be waiting an awfully long time."

Mack patted her on the arm in a patronizing manner. "All right, now, sugar, don't get riled. I won't crowd you...yet. Anyway, it's almost midnight, and you know what that means. You're *my* girl now. And as soon as you come to your senses, you *will* marry me."

Furious at his presumption, Annie shrugged off his hand, but Mack grabbed her arm. At that moment, the clock struck midnight and all of the lamps were extinguished. As the crowd welcomed in 1884 and began a rendition of Old Lang Syne, Annie was swept into Mack's arms and kissed soundly.

By the time the candles were relit, Mack had released her. "You can't deny that you didn't kiss me back, can you? You need a man, Annie Mitchell, and I'm that man."

Annie wriggled out of his grasp and turned to escape James, only to see Charley Burn, staring at her through the crowd. She angrily turned back to Mack and spat, "Why won't you men leave me alone? I did *not* give you permission to kiss me, Sheriff James. Don't ever presume on our relationship again." With that, she stomped away.

Charley Burn stepped in front of her. "Miss Annie, may I escort you home?"

Annie turned around to see Mack watching them, a satisfied smile on his face. Furiously, she spat loudly enough for Mack to hear, "Yes, Charley, thank you. I'd be happy to have you take me home."

She said little during the sleigh ride back to Grand Lake. Her anger at Mack James' brazenness was nearly overwhelmed by the guilt she had felt at the thrill of Mack's kiss. She *was* still young, and apparently, her body did indeed need a man.

"Are you all right?" asked Charley tentatively, as he watched innumerable emotions cross her face. "Did Sheriff James hurt you?"

"No, he didn't hurt me. I hate the truth sometimes, Charley, don't you?" was her quiet reply.

The young man was miffed by her answer, but he sat up a little straighter. Mack James had ruined it for himself, and now Charley was fixing to take his place in Annie's life. As he was helping her down from the sleigh in front of her cabin, he asked shyly, "Miss Annie, would you let me escort you to the next dance?"

"No, Charley, I don't think I'll be going out for awhile, though thanks for asking. I realized tonight that I've rushed into something that I'm just not ready for yet. I hope you understand."

Charley Burn did not understand, but he knew he would have to accept her decision...and wait some more. Not so Mack James, who knocked upon Annie's door promptly at six each night for the next month, as if nothing had happened. She bolted her door and refused to answer, terrified of the feelings he was able to evoke within her. She cried herself to sleep each night as she hugged her pillow, wishing it were Will Redmond.

The days, weeks, and months of winter passed slowly for Annie. She returned to the Farview to help Lydia. Annie was down on her knees scrubbing the errant bloodstain on the floor of the parlor. No amount of scrubbing had been able to obliterate the discoloration, but Annie kept trying.

Lydia entered the parlor and watched as the young girl worked. "You might as well give up, child. I don't think that blood will ever be removed."

Straightening her back, Annie wiped her hand across her forehead. "I think you're right, Lydia. Why don't you tear out these boards and replace them?"

"Some things can be replaced, and some cannot," answered Mrs. Elder cryptically. "Why don't you take a well-deserved break and have a cup of tea with me?"

"Gladly," replied Annie.

Later, the two women were ensconced at the big diningroom table, steaming cups of tea in front of them.

"I don't want to interfere, Annie, you know that, but I'm a bit worried about you," began Lydia Elder.

Annie's eyes grew wide as she stared back at her friend. "Worried about me? Why?"

"Honey, I know how heartbroken and isolated you've been since Will's death, but there comes a time when you need to get back into the world. I know what it's like to lose the man you love. But you have a second chance at happiness, Annie, and you're letting it pass you by. Lordy, girl, you're fighting it tooth and nail."

Annie stared down at her cup. "If you're talking about Mack or Charley, I'm not interested."

"Not Charley, he's just a boy with little to recommend him except sincerity, and you can't live on sincerity. I'm talking about Mack James. He's got a good job, he's reliable, and he'd make you a steady husband. I thought something might have started between you two last fall, but since the first of the year, you seem to be avoiding him. I know it's none of my business, dear, but if you want to talk about it, I'm here."

Tears welled up in Annie's blue eyes. "I miss Will, Lydia. So much sometimes, I think I would rather have died with him than to keep on living."

The older woman touched Annie's hand gently. "I know, honey, I know. But would Will want you to pine away for him? Would he want you to be unhappy forever?"

Annie broke down and began sobbing. "N-no, he told me to get on with my life. H-he told me to be happy. But how can I be happy with anyone else? I don't love Mack. Should I marry a man I don't love?"

"Listen to me, Annie Mitchell. I may not be your blood kin, but I love you like my own daughter. Will is dead. You have to rejoin the land of the living sooner or later. How do you know you won't start loving Mack James after you marry him? A lot of marriages succeed on less. Do yourself a favor and let him start courting you again. Get to know him better before you shut the door on him. Would you do that, Annie?"

The distraught girl wiped her tears away with her apron. "I can't yet, Lydia, I just can't."

In early March, Annie met Laura Miter on the boardwalk in front of the Mercantile. Laura, blond with big brown doe eyes, was a few years younger than Annie, and they had met numerous times because Lydia and Laura's mother were good friends.

"Good day, Miss Mitchell," began the friendly girl. "I wanted to speak with you, if you have time."

"Of course, Laura," replied Annie. "What is it?"

"The Dramatic Society of Grand Lake is going to perform a drama called "No Thoroughfare", and I thought you'd be perfect for the part of 'Marguerite'. Would you be interested?"

"In a play...me? But I don't know if I can even act? Why me, Laura?"

"The woman 'Marguerite' is so fragile, Miss Mitchell. When I read the script, I automatically thought of you, with all the tragedy you've been through." The girl suddenly blushed to the tips of her ears. "Oh, I'm sorry. I shouldn't have said that. My mother would whale me good if she knew how indelicate I've been. Please forgive me, Miss Mitchell."

Annie sighed. "Think nothing of it, Laura, I'm not offended. I think I would very much like to be in the production however. That is, if you'll help me with the lines."

Laura Miter beamed. "Of course, I'll help you. They've put me in charge of the wardrobe, and I know the dress that will be perfect on you."

The play gave Annie a sense of accomplishment again, and she began to slowly reenter the close social circle of Grand Lake. She even allowed Mack James and Charley Burn to occasionally escort her to the various parties and dances, but only with the understanding that she was not ready for anything close to marriage.

When March twenty-seventh arrived, Annie and the other players were anxiously awaiting the rise of the curtain for the first act.

"Oh, Annie, you look so pretty in that outfit," cried Laura. The girl fluffed out the full sleeves of the costume while Annie took some deep breaths, made difficult by the stays which nearly cut off her breathing.

"I hope I don't forget what to say," Annie exclaimed, going over the words in her head.

"While we're alone, Annie, I wanted to ask you a rather personal question," began her newest friend.

"What is it, Laura?"

"Which one are you gonna choose... Mack James or Charley Burn?" asked the younger girl.

Annie stood on the pedestal in front of the full-length mirror and stared back at her own reflection. Who was that pale girl who looked back at her, Annie mused? She was certainly not the same naive girl who had arrived in Grand Lake a year and a half ago.

The hopes and dreams of a normal life with the man she loved had been dashed last summer in a barrage of bullets on the lake path, and the gaping hole left in her heart over Will Redmond's death might never be healed.

"You mean Mack James or Charley Burn? You think I should pick one? I'm not planning on choosing either one," Annie said finally.

"Then why are you dangling them?" asked Laura. "I've got quite a crush on Charley, but he can't see anyone but you. I just thought if you chose the Sheriff, then Charley might start liking me."

Shocked by the girl's admission of affection for Charley Burn, Annie answered, "I've tried to be as honest as I could with both of them, Laura. Neither one will take 'no' for an answer. As far as I'm concerned, you are perfectly welcome to either one of them."

"I didn't mean to be so forward, but everybody in town is speculating over which one you'll marry," Laura said. "I just hope you choose Sheriff James so Charley will finally quit pining over you."

The girl left the room for a moment, and Annie stared at herself in the mirror. Instead of seeing her own face, though, she saw the strong rugged face of Will Redmond.

"I don't want to have to choose, Will. Why did you leave me?" Annie cried out to the empty room, bright tears threatening to fall.

"Who were you talking to?" Laura asked as she returned.

"No one, just practicing my lines," Annie answered dully.

The play was a huge success, and afterward, everyone went to the Grand Lake House for dancing. Annie found herself studying both Mack James and Charley Burn as they bickered about who had the next dance with her. Either one would make some lucky woman a fine husband, she mused.

"But neither of them are Will," Annie concluded to herself. "I'd be better of with Bear Hawk."

While dancing with Mack, Annie was slightly uncomfortable at how closely he held her. "When are you going to say you'll marry me, Annie?"

"I don't want to get married, Mack. I've tried to make you understand that. If you want to be my friend, then we can continue to see each other. But nothing else, do you understand? I'm not ready," replied Annie stiffly.

"All right, missy, you win, I'll be your 'friend'."

Annie grinned at his dejected expression. "You make 'friend' sound like a dirty word."

Mack smiled back at her. "Admit it, Miss Mitchell, you've missed me a little, haven't you?"

Reddening because she *had* missed his entertaining stories, Annie lied, "You are the most impossible man I've ever met. No, I did *not* miss you...even a little."

"Your mouth says no, but your body says something else," whispered Mack in her ear.

Annie firmly pushed him away. "I said nothing more than friendship, Mack James. Take it or leave it."

Soon the snows melted, and Mud Season came and went. At a performance by the Glee Club, Annie was introduced to Robert Shipmarten, a new arrival from Pennsylvania.

"Nice to meet you, Miss Mitchell," the polite young attorney said. His dark curly hair fell over a high forehead in a most pleasant manner, and his leanness reminded Annie of Jules Thermon, the sweet shy County Clerk who had been buried in an avalanche the winter before.

"What brought you to Grand Lake, Mr. Shipmarten?"

"I recently graduated from Harvard Law School, and I wanted to come West to practice. It seems that Grand County is quite shy of lawyers these days."

"Yes," Annie replied wistfully, remembering the horrible day of the massacre which had changed everyone's life forever.

After their first meeting, Robert had made a point of 'running into' Annie several times in town and at the Farview. Annie liked the young man very much but knew Mack James' jealously was a factor to be reckoned with. Already she'd witnessed Mack's anger to Charley's pursuit and any other men who had dared talk to her.

So one evening in early July when Annie knew Mack James was at the other end of the county on business and Charley had been sent to Denver for supplies by his boss at the sawmill, she invited Robert Shipmarten to dinner at her cabin.

As they enjoyed easy conversation after an exquisite dinner, Robert said, "I'd like to take you to the dance next Saturday night, Miss Annie, but Sheriff James said I'd be seeing the inside of his jail or worse if I tried to court you."

Mack's threat against her new friend angered Annie. "Robert, Mack James does not own me. I can see anyone I please. Don't let him intimidate you. Besides, you are a lawyer, file a grievance or something against him. And I would be honored to attend the dance with you."

When Saturday night came, Robert Shipmarten did not show up. Annie waited over an hour for his knock upon her door. Sitting in the rocker, she steamed as she realized Mack James must ultimately be responsible for her escort's absence. She knew Robert Shipmarten was too much of a gentleman to stand her up with no explanation. After saddling Sugar, Annie rode around the lake path into town...and straight to the jail.

Annie burst into the small office only to see Mack James with his feet propped upon his desk, casually perusing arrest warrants.

"All right, what have you done with him?" Annie asked heatedly, the fire in her blue eyes blazing.

"Well, Miss Mitchell, to whom are you referring?" asked Mack smoothly as he removed his feet from the table and set the legs of the chair back upon the floor.

"You know damn well to whom I'm referring, Mack James," she exclaimed loudly.

Annie heard a muffled sound coming from the cell area. She threw open the heavy iron door which led to the individual cells and stalked into the darkened recesses. There she found Robert Shipmarten, bound and gagged on one of the bunks.

Storming back into the lighted office, she slammed her fist down on the desk. "You'd better open that cell and untie him right this minute, Mack James."

"Oh, are you referring to my guest in there?" Mack asked, innocently. "Well, Mr. Shipmarten happens to be under arrest, Miss Mitchell, and he's gagged because I got tired of listening to him bellyache."

"What are the charges, may I ask?"

"For one, impersonating an attorney," retorted Mack casually.

"Are you crazy? He *is* an attorney!" Annie shouted into his face.

"You may be wrong about that. According to my research, the late Ben Daily and his late nemesis, George E. Miller, were both impersonating lawyers. Neither one of them ever finished law school. And it turns out the late 'Colonel' Ronald Baker, friend of your uncle's and wealthy businessman from the Springs, had falsified his own military records.

"These were supposed to be the most upstanding men in our little community, Miss Mitchell. So I'm merely waiting for verification of Shipmarten's credentials. It should arrive around Tuesday next if the mail gets through," replied Mack coolly as he gazed into Annie's livid face.

"God's Teeth, Mack, you don't give a damn about whether Robert is an attorney or not!" she spat angrily. "You're mad because he was taking me to the dance tonight, aren't you?"

"Whatever can you mean?" Mack replied sarcastically. "Me, mad? That's preposterous. Why would I be mad that some other man was escorting *my* girl to a dance? I have already been made to suffer young Burn's interfering presence. I'm certainly not willing to let Shipmarten come between you and me as well. It seems that you will have to either go to the dance alone, or go home. What's it to be?"

Annie collapsed in a chair across from his desk, exhausted and feeling suddenly helpless against this man. "All right, Mack, what do you want to let Robert go?"

Mack bounded around the desk and placed his hands on either side of her chair, his face close to hers. "You know what I want. I want you to marry me. I'm tired of playing your dog and pony show as you shuffle me around with Charley Burn and any other man who catches your fancy. You are *my* girl, Annie Mitchell, and I always get what I want...and I want you."

Annie stared up at Mack, all at once totally defeated. "Oh, all right, I'll marry you. Now let Robert go...right now."

"You aren't just saying that?" Mack asked suspiciously. "You really intend on walking down the aisle with me?"

"Yes, I told you yes, didn't I?" spat Annie irritably. She was tired of the games, too, and it really didn't matter anymore. She'd never love Mack or anybody else; her heart had been ripped out and left in Utah under a cottonwood tree when the bullet had pierced Will's brain.

"Hey Shipmarten, did you hear what she said?" called Mack, a canny smile on his face. "I want a witness. Now kiss me, Annie, and show me you truly mean to marry me."

Annie stared at his lips a moment, realizing that if she married him, she would not only have to kiss him but also give her body to him. Annie remembered the fire Will Redmond could light in her when he had kissed her.

She placed her hands on the sides of his face and pulled his head down to hers, gently brushing her lips over his. Mack immediately pressed her back in the chair, arching her over the wooden slat. He moved his lips over hers passionately as he had on New Year's Eve. But this time, Annie felt nothing...no fire, no thrill.

When he finished the kiss, he gazed down at her, his blue eyes dark with lust.

"I don't love you, Mack, but I'm tired of fighting you. I'll marry you if you still want me," Annie stated honestly.

Mack wrapped his arms around Annie and pulled her to her feet. She looked him in the eyes as he replied huskily, "You'll learn to love me, in time, and you'll never want for another thing in your life."

Annie knew he would take care of her. And maybe she *would* come to love him in time. She wriggled out of his arms and said, "All right then. I'm going home now. Will you let Robert go tonight?"

"Yep," Mack answered, unable to believe his luck. Annie Mitchell had declared in front of a witness that she was going to be his. "Leave your door open, and I'll be over after I get relieved by the deputy."

Annie turned back toward him, alarmed. "No, no, not until after the wedding."

Mack chuckled. "All right, but plan on having the ceremony soon. I've waited long enough."

Annie walked out of the office...feeling numb. She had agreed to marry Mack James. He would kiss her, make love to her, and she would be his dutiful wife, raising his children and keeping his house. Her life would be good, almost enviable to some. So why did she still feel so empty?

Slowly, she walked Sugar around the lake back to the west side. At the log cabin, she unsaddled the pony and gave her a good long rubdown, speaking soft endearments to the animal. Then she led the horse into the shed and dipped out some oats.

Finally Annie dragged herself inside the cabin, not bothering to light the lamp but making absolutely sure she bolted the door. She was totally exhausted and wanted only to crawl into her warm bed. She slowly doffed her dress, laying it gently across the bed rail. Then she untied the ribbon of her pantalets, letting them flutter to the floor at her feet.

Standing in her chemise and stockings, Annie reached for her nightgown on the back of the rocking chair in the corner and touched something else.

She jerked her hand back as she opened her mouth to scream, but nothing came out. *Someone* was sitting in the rocker in the dark, and Annie could hear the faint squeak as it moved back and forth over the wooden floor.

"W-who's there?" squeaked Annie hesitantly when she could find her voice.

The chair scraped as the occupant stood.

Annie held her breath, too terrified to move. A hand suddenly snaked inside the chemise and cupped her bare breast. She gasped at the touch, fearing she was about be to raped. The shadows changed, though, as the person stepped closer. Though the darkness obliterated sight, she sensed rather than saw.

"Will..." she breathed.

"I told you I was a hard character to kill, darlin'."

She leaped into his arms, kissing him and crying all at once. He lifted her easily off the floor and held her to him, with both strong arms, she realized happily. "But they said you were dead; they found your body out in the desert," Annie sobbed as she clung to him.

"That feller was already dead when I happened upon him. He'd killed himself, so I figured we'd just change identities. I wrote my name in the sand and made sure my things were found on him. I figured if I was dead, then the law would quit looking for me."

"After Sheriff Tom committed suicide, I was terrified that you might, too. And when the news came that your body had been found... I wanted desperately to die, Will, and they wouldn't let me. But I... I did lose our baby," Annie cried, terrified that her mind had snapped and she was being held by a phantom.

Will sat down on the bed, with Annie upon his lap. "Oh God, you mean Tom's dead? And you were pregnant with our baby? Why didn't you tell me?"

"I knew you wouldn't leave me if I told you about the baby, and I couldn't let you take the chance of getting caught. I'm so sorry about your baby, Will." Annie sobbed, burying her face into his shirtfront.

"Oh, darlin', if only I'd known. I *would* have taken you with me. I can't stand to think that you had to go through all that without me!" Will's voice was thick with emotion. He had pulled her tightly against him, and she felt his tears mixing with her own.

"It doesn't matter now, Will, you're here and that's all that matters. I won't let you go this time, no matter what you say!" she cried fiercely.

"I have to leave Colorado for good, Annie, but I couldn't stand to think of living anywhere in this world without you. It won't be easy; we'll probably have to change our names and go far away. W-Will you come with me?" Will asked hesitantly, afraid she still might say no.

"Do you even have to ask?" was her answer as she pulled him down into the soft feather mattress.

Mack James stopped by the cabin the next day after gloating around town about his engagement, but Annie Mitchell was gone. There was no sign of forced entry or foul play; she had just completely disappeared without a trace. All of her clothes and possessions were still in the cabin; nothing was missing but her horse and a pair of old field glasses in a buckskin case. An intense search was organized by James and the citizens of Grand County, but no sign of the girl ever turned up.

Some folks around Grand Lake speculated that the renegade Ute, Bear Hawk, had returned in the night and kidnapped Annie Mitchell again. And several years later, old-timer Squeaky Bob Wheeler swore he'd seen her with Will Redmond up in Saratoga, Wyoming, but no one really believed him.

THE END

About the Author

Katie Gailey enjoys living in Grand Lake, Colorado with her husband, Terry. She has taught reading for thirty-one years and is on the Board of the Grand Lake Historical Society. In her spare time, she volunteers at the Kauffman House Museum as a docent and tutors.

LaVergne, TN USA
28 December 2010
210235LV00003B/1/P